Lunar Flash

Midlife in Aura Cove Book 3

Blair Bryan

To Cece H.

You make me cackle like a witch when you pull out your erotic playing cards for a rousing game of Garbage. Laughter is the key to aging well, and you discovered it long ago. You are an absolute gem.

ONE

Zoya paced at the Castanova compound on the edge of the sea right up until the last second, rage seething from every pore in her body. She raked a brush through her long, white hair, roughly scraping the bristles of it into her scalp just short of drawing blood. Cursing under her breath, she gathered her hair, sweeping the brush upward in rhythmic strokes until all of it was gathered on top of her head into a high ponytail. In the pit of her stomach, a knot twisted. She'd come home empty-handed, and she knew Lilith would not react to this turn of events favorably. But most of all, she'd failed to free Sally's soul, and the defeat ate at her. When you're always a winner, you forget what it feels like to lose.

At her feet, Terrance, her chocolate Labrador Retriever, barked once. She'd promoted him to the head of the pack when she'd freed Magnum from his dog body after years of servitude. It was a jarring sound that snapped her out of her self-destructive spiral.

"What is it?" she snarled at him.

He lowered his head and focused on a spot on the ground, delivering the update she forgot she'd requested. "I've prepared the altar for you, and the dog is waiting inside."

"Very good," Zoya said. "You're dismissed." He jumped to his feet and the metal choke chain around his throat jingled like a bell as he departed. Not able to delay the meeting any longer, she exhaled and opened the door to her meditation chamber. Inside, Rocco yipped and snarled at her when she entered. Seeing the mafioso reduced to a teacup Yorkshire Terrier briefly slid a smug smile across her lips. It never got old, reducing a man drunk on his own power into a helpless creature trained to serve her every whim. Rocco growled and barked again and she rolled her eyes. This one would never learn his lesson.

With a scowl, she snapped her fingers, sending a sharp electric jolt through him like a shock collar. His resulting squeal was satisfying, and it briefly placated her ever-present lust for revenge.

"Use your words," she demanded when he circled the room, yipping non-stop for a solid minute after the shock.

"Free me now or I will end you!" Rocco's speech distorted into a high-pitched Munchkin-style voice, like he'd deeply inhaled helium from a balloon. Zoya found it amusing and roared with laughter. "What in the hell is happening to me?" His voice was even more ridiculous the more frustrated the tiny dog became.

"Do you hear how pathetic you sound?" Zoya mocked him. "With that intonation, your intimidation techniques have lost their usual fervor, darling. I can't take you seriously at all when you sound like a chipmunk."

Rocco growled and then emitted two high-pitched whines.

"I suggest you calm down because we've got a deal to make with the devil." Zoya appraised the tiny Yorkie, hoping Lilith would accept this paltry sacrifice. "Or should I say she-devil?" She mused, "As much fun as we have had together, and it *has* been a raucous good time, you're a necessary sacrifice I'll need to make to get back in Lilith's good graces."

"Lilith?" Rocco's head cocked like she'd asked him if he wanted to go for a ride.

"Oh! She's a hot one. You'll see."

Zoya struck a match on slate and watched the flame light up the room's darkness. One by one, she lit the bank of black candles and sticks of incense in the black obsidian dish. She waved the smoke toward her body and hummed one long note, circling her hands in front of her torso as she kneeled in front of the altar. Zoya chanted and the tines of a tuning fork created a soundwave that rippled through the air.

"What the hell is that noise?" Rocco cried and raced to Zoya's thigh, where he lay down next to her and covered his ears with his paws while his body trembled.

A burst of warm light illuminated Zoya's face, and she chanted louder as the flames grew and transformed into a wall of light. Through the portal, a vision of Lilith's nude form emerged. She was seated on a golden throne where Sally knelt at her feet, massaging them with oil. Zoya's eyes alighted on him, and she felt a tingle of jealousy. Feeling her eyes on his back, Sally turned and his forlorn gaze tangled with hers, sending daggers to her heart. Her personal failure to set his soul free made it difficult to maintain eye contact.

"What is this?" Lilith spat with contempt. "You were to bring me a child, not a worthless dog." She stood to her full six-foot height and leaned forward, crossing her arms across her naked breasts.

"Who the hell do you think you are?" Rocco stood up on his haunches, his distorted voice taking all the power out of his words. "*You* are the one responsible for the death of my child?" He attempted ferocious barks at the wall of flames that only sounded weak and pitiful.

Zoya huffed in outrage, reached out to grab the annoying dog by the scruff of his neck, and placed him on his back in a submissive position. "Shut up! Where is your personal accountability? Your violence is as much to blame as mine for the loss of your child." She returned her focus to the vision, ignoring any further interaction attempts with him. "The child is gone, My Dark Queen." Zoya waved one hand at the cowering dog. "I was hoping to make a deal and offer the father of the child in his place."

Lilith leaned further out of the portal and, with one

fiery hand, grabbed the tiny dog by the scruff of his neck, inspecting him with a scowl. After a brief hesitation, she decided to accept the offering and attempted to pull him through. But as she did, he struck an invisible barrier and fell back to the floor with a pained yelp. Undeterred, she reached through the portal again and again, but each attempt was a failure.

"All dogs go to heaven," Lilith explained. "I guess we've proven the old adage true."

"There is a simple solution to this problem, mistress," Zoya offered. "I will return him to his human form."

Rocco tried to scamper away, but Lilith's hand came through the portal and clasped his neck. Zoya reached out one palm and concentrated all her energy on him. The wall of flames leaped from Lilith's hand, passed through the dog who howled on contact, and then over to Zoya's wrist. The searing pain and scent of burning flesh and singed hair infiltrated her nostrils. Acrid smoke made Zoya's eyes water and sparks flew from her hand. In one surge of strength, Rocco burst into flames. Then he crossed over completely, sprawling out naked on the granite rocks next to Sally, who was still seated at the foot of Lilith's throne.

Rocco stood up. Roaring and enraged, he charged at Lilith, clawing at her with his fingers. An amused expression slid across Lilith's features as he ricocheted off her body and fell to the ground with a loud grunt. When he mustered enough energy to stand, Lilith fastened a thick metal collar around his muscular neck, causing his rigid veins to bulge with fury. In an instant, he dropped to his knees in front of her. "I'm sorry, My Queen, if I have not pleased you." The words came out of his mouth against his will. Confused by the apology he'd just made, he shook his head to clear it. Rocco yanked at the collar in desperation as his eyes darted around the cave of the hellish rocky landscape he was now imprisioned in, searching for an exit.

"Shut up," Lilith chastised him. "From now on, you will only speak when you have been spoken to." A blue vein in his neck bulged, and anger colored every feature of his face. He opened his mouth to defy her, and a metal ball gag shot from her hand to clamp down on his mouth. "Did you think I was playing games?" She rolled her violet eyes and shook her head. "Stupid creatures, the entire lot. Men never learn."

"I couldn't agree more, mistress," Zoya said, eager to prove to Lilith they were similarly minded.

Lilith stood and spread her legs wide, resting her hands on her hips. Obediently, Sally scrambled to his feet and stood behind the glowing woman. His fingers encircled her tiny waist and made their way up her torso. Seeing the sensual display, Zoya shifted uncomfortably on the balls of her feet and averted her gaze. She couldn't bear to see what came next. "Zoya, my child, you must fix your gaze on me." Lilith grinned like a lioness on the hunt and tipped her head down as black horns emerged from the top of her head. Salvatore's shaking fingers dexterously wandered up to her breasts, and he cupped one in each hand. He closed his eyes, and Zoya saw tears break free from the corners of them and cascade down his face. Lilith moaned in delight as the tips of her peach-colored nipples hardened with arousal. "This is your penance. To watch in bitter agony as the green monster of jealousy takes root in your soul." Zoya rankled and bit back her usual harsh retort. "Sally is a very skilled lover, but you already know this." Lilith closed her eyes as her pleasure intensified, and Zoya felt it like a sucker punch. Zoya watched in horror, her heart breaking as Sally's fingers walked down Lilith's hip and tangled into her mound. She bit her lip to prevent a wounded cry from escaping. She would not show weakness. Breathing in through her flared nostrils and out her mouth, tears blurred her vision until she couldn't see it at all. Lilith's breaths came faster, and she cried out as an orgasm crashed over her. Afterward, the dark queen was glowing, her skin dewy and resplendent.

"You have served me well, Salvatore." Lilith detached the chain that was connected to Rocco from her wrist and clipped it to a metal handcuff already on Salvatore's wrist. "This is your reward for pleasing your mistress."

Salvatore's eyes darkened into black holes of hatred. He tugged on the chain and yanked Rocco to his feet, and then quickly disappeared into the blackness. Zoya swiped her eyes with her hands, grateful for the end of Lilith's sexual gratification and Sally's participation in it.

When Lilith's eyes bored into hers, she curtsied and averted her gaze.

"Although I accept your sacrifice, it does not fulfill the terms of our agreement. I know it was difficult to witness my pleasure with your beloved, dark daughter, but that is why it is considered a punishment. It's the only way to convey the seriousness of your infraction."

Zoya compartmentalized the betrayal and tucked it away into the recesses of her mind. Intellectually, she understood what transpired, but in her heart, the jealousy burned. The only way to avoid repeating the act was to make a new deal. She bowed. "The infant died in utero. It could not be avoided. There must be another way I can garner your favor and earn the release of Sally's soul."

A fireball burst into view and obliterated the entire vision. A cunning smile stretched across Lilith's features as her attention focused elsewhere for a few seconds. "Looks like the Gabriano and Lombardo reunion is hitting a few bumps, and I must intervene." She stood. "Testosterone is the downfall of mankind, but at least it always proves to be entertaining." Lilith's eyes leveled on Zoya's as she contemplated her plea. "Bring me another worthy sacrifice, and I will consider your request."

The flames shrank then sputtered out, and Zoya was alone in the meditation chamber again. Her skin was flushed, and she felt desperation sear through her soul. Her thoughts circled back to Lilith, writhing her hips against Salvatore's hand. "No!" She shook her head to clear it, but the image returned over and over in her one-track mind. Stuck in a spiral of jealousy and rage, one truth emerged. She had to find a way to free him because she could not bear the thought of his sexual servitude to Lilith for an eternity.

Two

Katie drove her green Volkswagen beetle with the top down to her grandmother's chocolate shop, Kandied Karma. Sitting in the passenger seat, her dog, Arlo, luxuriated in the buffet of tantalizing scents surrounding him in downtown Aura Cove. His fur rippled in the wind, and he chomped on air with his fleshy jowls flapping, a sight that made Katie grin.

"What?" Arlo asked self-consciously.

"Nothing," Katie answered and reached over to stroke the top of his fluffy head.

She parked and unlocked the back door of the shop, and they slipped into the kitchen where Yuli was already busy at the stove, stirring a simmering cauldron of dark chocolate. Arlo barked once, then circled and plopped down near Yuli's feet.

"Good morning!" Katie called out as she walked over to where Yuli was peering into the stainless steel pot on the stovetop, supervising the chunks of chocolate slowly melting in the double boiler. Katie reached out to give her grandmother a half-hug and a huge smile. Kandied Karma was her second home, and there was no place like it.

"You're here early," Yuli remarked as she pulled the mixture off the heat and added several tablespoons of bourbon and vanilla to the mixture. She stirred it continually until it was incorporated and then covered the pot with a lid and put it into the chiller. The scent of rich, dark chocolate mingled with the heady aroma of freshly roasted coffee beans, Madagascar vanilla pods, and tangy citrus zest.

Back at the stove, she infused a ganache with a splash of Grand Marnier and crystalized ginger. While that cooled on the stove, she returned to Katia and, sensing she had something on her mind, pulled out a stool. She hoisted her body onto it and patted the one next to her.

"I'm assuming this is about our visitors yesterday? Liz and Lorelei?"

Katie nodded sheepishly. "I learned my lesson going solo last time. Instead of going half-cocked into another Karma rebalance, I figured it would be better for us to work together and I'd love your advice."

"That was a tough lesson to learn," Yuli agreed and reached out to squeeze her hand. "Someday, you'll be powerful enough to carry out her plans on your own."

"Her?"

Yuli explained, "In Hindu, Karma is a feminine

name that means action or fate." Then she leaned closer, her sharp eyes missing nothing. "You were good to come to me. Your new abilities are a tremendous responsibility and can be difficult to interpret. I know when I first started receiving messages, I didn't have a mentor and was easily overwhelmed. "

"I'm lucky to have you show me the ropes," Katie said gratefully.

"Ultimately, you will be the one to decide how to best carry out your mission. I will simply share information, guide the flow of ideas, and help you brainstorm solutions."

Katie winced. "That's a lot of pressure."

Yuli reached out and squeezed her hand. "You can handle it. Always trust your instincts. It's what kept you and Marisa alive. Take stock of how far you've come and believe in the powerful woman you are becoming."

Katie considered her grandmother's words for a long moment. "I do believe in myself, now more than ever. After decades of tuning out, it feels so natural and wonderful to tune in. It's almost like I'm secure in my own skin now in a way I never was."

"Of course you are." Yuli smiled. "It's a beautiful transformation I see taking place and strengthening every day. Asking for guidance is not a sign of weakness. It's tapping into decades of knowledge. The witch who thinks she has it all figured out and refuses to rely on anyone can't fully step into the fullness of her abilities."

"Like Zoya?"

"Exactly," Yuli confirmed.

"I don't think I'll get used to the jarring sensation when I receive the flashes. It's a major jolt to the system every time," Katie admitted with a shudder.

"That's to be expected. I've been on the receiving end almost as long as you have been alive. You'll grow more accustomed to the ability over time. Over the years, the shock wears off, so it's more like a zap from built-up static electricity." Yuli added, "Conspiring with Karma is a sacred calling. I hope it never becomes commonplace for either of us. Now, let's focus on Liz and Lorelei. What did you see?"

Katie nodded solemnly before she explained, "When my skin came in contact with Liz's, I saw an exam room at a doctor's practice. I think it was a gynecologist's office. There were stirrups and a speculum," she offered, then with a shiver added, "and then I saw a white coffin draped in pink roses being lowered to the ground."

An audible gasp escaped from Yuli, startling Katie. "Precognition. It's the ability to see probable future outcomes." Yuli's expression was filled with awe as she regarded her granddaughter. "Katia, your powers are being activated with exceptional speed. It took me close to five years after my awakening to harness the power of precognition."

"Maybe it was a fluke, seeing the coffin," Katie said hopefully as sadness welled in her chest. "Losing a child must be the most cataclysmic event in any parent's life. I hope the vision was wrong."

Yuli nodded sadly, looking down at the table. "Notice I said *probable* future outcomes. Ultimately, it is impacted by many things, free will being the most influential force of all," Yuli gently reminded her. "Are these the only messages you received?"

"Yeah," Katie admitted, feeling as if she'd failed.

Yuli mulled over the two visions Katie presented. "We need to gather more information to see where we are needed. Karma always reveals the path we must take. Our job is to allow it to flow through us, not force an outcome based on our own fears and agenda."

"That makes sense." Katie nodded. "Looks like I need to do some detective work and see if we can track Liz and Lorelei down. Maybe I can invite them to the house for dinner."

"That's a great idea."

"What's a great idea?" Frankie asked as she sailed through the back door into the kitchen and sidled over in a drowsy daze to the coffee pot to pour herself a to-go cup.

"Nothing," Yuli said, trying to change the subject, and a distracted Frankie let it go in hot pursuit of caffeine. As she sipped on the piping hot coffee, she absentmindedly scrolled her phone. Then her eyes bugged out. "Oh my God! You have to see this!" She held the cell phone out to Katie, where a YouTube video of the flash mob played, and there were already almost two hundred and fifty thousand views. "Kandied Karma is trending on TikTok and Instagram!" Unable to contain her excitement, she jumped up and down.

"What? No way! Let me see!" Katie pulled the phone from her friend's jumpy hand and watched the four-minute video. "Yuli, can you believe this?" She held it out for her grandmother to watch.

"I will never understand social media as long as I live," Yuli muttered, reaching behind her back and tightening her apron strings. "Young people these days think every moment of their existence needs to be recorded! For who? It's absurd!" Yuli turned on her chef's clog and walked away, not impressed by the video at all. She returned with a kettle of chilled amaretto creams from the chiller and dragged a melon baller through the velvety smooth white chocolate, depositing the orbs in perfect rows on parchment paper.

Still engrossed, Katie's elbows rested on the marble work surface. She leaned closer and scrolled through the hundreds of comments already on the video and found one user handle that caught her eye.

therealgilmoregirl31: @KandiedKarma helped me cross an item off my bucket list today. #bestdayever #PKDsucks

Tucking that morsel of timely information away, she handed the phone back to Frankie. The serendipity of the universe always filled her with awe, and the speed with which answers from Karma appeared made a grin spread across her features.

"Want to hang out tonight after work?" Katie asked.

"I can't. I have a date." Frankie pressed her lips

together to conceal a grin, and her eyes glittered with excitement over the rim of her coffee cup.

"What? With whom?"

"Officer Willey." She pinked up. "Officer *Harry* Willey, that is," she repeated with a snicker. "God, that will never not be funny to me."

Katie rolled her eyes and chuckled. "This is the first date you've been on in ages. He must be pretty special, even if his name is Harry Willey."

"Well, I don't want to jinx it, but he might be *the* guy." Frankie grinned.

"Whoa! That's a bold statement coming from you!" Katie beamed at her best friend, whose cheeks were reddening. "Wait, are you *blushing*?" Katie razzed her with glee. "I didn't think you were capable of feeling embarrassment."

"I know, right?" Frankie laughed at herself. "He's giving me butterflies!" She waved a hand in front of her face to cool herself down. "I'm a goner!"

"I've never seen this version of you," Katie said, thoroughly enjoying the sight of a deeply swooning Frankie. "Now I need to ask the most important question." Katie winked. "Is he shaving-the-legs worthy?"

Frankie winced. "Not the legs. That's far too much real estate to cover. And I don't want to set a dangerous precedent and have him thinking I'm the kind of woman who maintains smooth gams at all times."

"Of course, that would be disastrous." Katie went

along with Frankie's reasoning as she picked up her coffee cup to take a long sip.

"I've found when it comes to men, it's best to keep their expectations low."

"Good point."

"But maybe some light pruning in my lady garden is in order."

Coffee shot out of Katie's nose. "Frank, you're killing me. Lady garden?"

"You know, va-gine, my itty bitty kitty, the foof, my lady bits."

At the other end of the counter, Yuli chuckled, then held up one hand, desperate to stop Frankie's laundry list of nicknames for female genitalia. "I'm going to open the store while you two finish this riveting conversation." She walked away from them, shaking her head, but her lips quirked up in a smile she fought to contain. With one hip, she shoved the swinging door open and walked through, holding two stainless steel sheets of truffles to stock the glass case, leaving Frankie and Katie alone to chat.

"How's Marisa doing?"

"As well as expected when you lose a child," Katie shared. "I think she just needs time. She's tough and was a champ coping with the physical pain, but now, it's the psychological part that can really linger. I need to stay close and keep an eye on her."

"Poor kid," Frankie remarked. "How about I get a rain check with Harry and come over to provide some comic relief?"

"No way! You are not going to reschedule the first date you've had in eons!" Katie protested. "Especially with the man that made Francesca Stapleton retire her NTM philosophy."

"For the record, it's on hiatus. The jury is still out on whether he can permanently send it into retirement." Frankie grinned, then glanced down at her watch. "Shoot! I gotta get to work."

"Have fun tonight." Katie waggled her eyebrows. "I'll expect the full play-by-play at Thanksgiving!"

"Of course. Thanks for the brew!" She raised the cup and left the shop.

"Alright! Let's get this party started!" Katie said to herself. She smoothed down the flowy black skirt she'd paired that morning with a branded magenta t-shirt with the Kandied Karma logo scrawled across it in gold lettering. Her hair was pulled back in a ponytail that was nearly fifty percent white now. Every morning when she looked in the mirror, the white had claimed more hairs on her head. She knew, eventually, her entire head would be as brilliantly white as Yuli and Zoya's, and she found she didn't mind at all.

Until then, she'd decided to rock her bi-colored locks and enjoy every stage in between. She pushed through the swinging door, and one glance through the plate-glass windows revealed a much-larger crowd gathered than usual. The long line of people wrapped around the block and ran down the street.

"Holy cow, Yuli! Frankie was right. Kandied Karma went viral!" Katie walked over to the case where Yuli was stocking the truffles in tidy rows behind handwritten flavor signs. "This is a bigger crowd than Aura Cove Cellular drew during the last iPhone release!"

Yuli clapped her hands together, filling with pride, her excitement twinkling in her eyes. "We might set a new sales record today, thanks to the TikTok."

"So, *now* you're a fan? Weren't you the one who was disgusted to learn that seventy percent of Millennials take photos of their food before they eat it?"

"That was until they started taking photos of our truffles, Katia!" She grinned. Ever the astute businesswoman, she unloaded the trays faster. Katie rushed back to the chiller to bring out double their normal stock for a Monday morning. The crowd already gathered outside the door began to pulsate and hum like a hive of bees. Katie glanced down at her watch and tucked a loose curl behind her ear, then walked to the front door and unlocked the deadbolt. Throngs of people streamed into the shop, some taking selfies, and in their bits of excited conversations, Katie deduced most of the unfamiliar faces were brought in by the viral video. Overnight, Kandied Karma had become a hot spot for the Instagram crowd and had introduced her grandmother's truffles to a new generation.

Over the next four hours, Katie's feet ached, and she fought off exhaustion as she served customers as fast as possible. The line never slowed, and they had to turn away over a hundred disappointed patrons when they sold out at noon and had to close the store early.

"Come back!" Katie begged with a smile and hastily scribbled her initials on the back of business cards to hand out to the poor souls who stood in line but left empty-handed. "Bring this card back to the store and we'll give you fifteen percent off your order."

When she finally locked the door behind the last customer, she fell into a chair at the table closest to the checkout. Yuli stood at the cash register, struggling to yank the drawer open, its contents jammed tight with cash. The tip jar was also overflowing, and she handed it over to Katie with a huge smile. "Great idea handing out our cards," Yuli said. "Maybe social media isn't the devil I thought it was!"

"Does that mean you'd entertain the idea of owning a cell phone?" Katie asked, already knowing the answer. Yuli did not disappoint.

"Let's not get too hasty."

"Can I ask you something?"

"Of course." The older woman walked around the counter and sat down in the chair next to her. "Let me guess. It's about Zoya," she said. It wasn't a question, just a statement of facts.

"What do you think her next move is?" Katie asked.

"It's hard to tell." Yuli was quiet for a moment before speaking. "She put herself and our entire bloodline at risk by practicing black magic and making a deal with Lilith." Yuli thought it over. "She's a wild card. I don't understand her at all. I never have."

"How could you, when she was so cruel to you as a child?"

"She was," Yuli mumbled. "And it's why I cut her out of my life. Wherever Zoya goes, death and destruction follow."

"But now you can't cut her out," Katie deduced, "because she's coming after me."

"Correct." Yuli leaned forward on her elbows, laced her fingers together, and used them to prop up her plump chin. "Katia, look at me."

Her tone was so direct it was alarming. Katie's eyes locked on Yuli's, and then she continued. "We must stay united. A single strand can be cut easily. When two are woven together, they cannot be broken." She stopped for a moment and then added, "We need to communicate. If you see something out of the ordinary or you have a vision or a dream, do not discount it. Your intuition is one of your most powerful gifts. If you feel something is not right, or you get a tingle of fear or apprehension, you must tell me immediately."

"I understand," Katie agreed. "I won't make the same mistake again."

It was true, Katia wouldn't make the same mistake, but Yuli knew there would be others, and that's what frightened her most.

THREE

The ballroom of the Tampa Bay Events Center was aglow in soft candlelight. It reflected in the crystal candlesticks on the elaborately decorated round tables, which were draped with black tablecloths and dripping with lush floral displays. The crowd of medical professionals who had ditched their scrubs and white coats for the evening in favor of cocktail attire began to pour through the doors in search of their place cards. It was the evening of the 53rd Annual Society of American Reproductive Health Awards, and the who's who of the West Coast medical community were dressed to the nines in tuxedos and ball gowns, sipping martinis and champagne near the cash bar.

Upstairs in his penthouse suite at the adjoining hotel, dressed head to toe in Armani, Dr. Damian Blackwell still cut an impressive figure, even at sixty years old. He was tall, with a barrel chest that was only marginally thicker than it had been during his days at Johns Hopkins getting his medical degree in reproductive health.

He sipped on a tumbler of Jameson as his wife, Gloria, swept into the room and stopped in front of him to adjust his bowtie. She was covered in a sparkling black-sequined formal gown that modestly covered every inch of her skin from neck to ankle. Gloria offered him a wide smile, keeping her eyes slightly averted. It made her plain face only marginally more attractive, and her long hair that reached her bottom was braided tightly into a coiled gray circle at the base of her neck.

"Are you nervous?" she asked as she met his discerning gaze. Gloria was an anxious flitter who had a hard time sitting still, often darting from worthless task to worthless task like a hummingbird who'd sipped too much sugar water.

"Why would I be nervous?" he asked, confused by her question. At Hopkins, he learned when you are a trailblazer, you need to harness all your energy to forge a groundbreaking path. There wasn't time to twist in the wind with worry or second-guess yourself. It was a waste of precious resources.

"A Lifetime Achievement Award from the Society of American Reproductive Health is no minor accomplishment."

"Thank you, dear," he said gratefully when she'd finished fussing at him and brushed a dry kiss across his cheek. "It is the pinnacle of my success thus far, but there is still so much more to do."

"You are relentless in the pursuit of your goals. I have been fortunate enough to have had a front-row seat watching you bring them all to fruition, and I couldn't be more proud of you. But would it be too much to ask for you to take a second to enjoy the view instead of finding your next mountain to climb?"

"You should know by now, I'm not built to rest." He took another sip, considered her question, and felt the pleasant warmth of the whisky softening his sharp edges. He never permitted himself more than a single glass of a decent triple malt scotch on rare celebrations, and professionally, this was the biggest night of his career. Damian lived his entire life believing his body was a temple, and he'd gathered a lifetime of data on his physical wellbeing. All his health markers were monitored and measured on a weekly basis for changes and then meticulously documented in his journals. He'd developed the habit of keeping detailed food and exercise logs in med school when they'd been tasked to track their BMI, intake and output, and then form hypotheses around their findings. It had opened his eyes to the clarity data provided and became a daily practice he never ceased.

"Are all the children in attendance?" he asked.

"Yes. I've been told the staff reserved the front four tables in the ballroom for us. We've been blessed, haven't we, darling?" she asked.

"Yes, we have," he answered, bored with her need for reassurance, but giving the simple woman the answer she craved. Gloria filled an important role in his life, freeing his time and energy to focus on his career. She handled the children and the household, while he was the sole provider. She was reliable and even-tempered, knowing her place in his life, submitting to his requests, and never demanding more. It was an arrangement that had worked for almost forty years.

She quickly made the sign of the cross. "I need a few minutes to pray before we head to the ballroom."

He was grateful when she left. On this night, he desired quiet, a solitary moment where he could wallow in his triumph. Savoring the last sip of the whisky, he took a moment to take stock of his life. Every decision he'd made had navigated a path to this night.

Under his constant care and guidance, Blackwell Reproductive Health had become a national institution. Over the years, he'd grown the practice into a vibrant network of seven clinics in the most exclusive areas in the country, with the highest success rates of any fertility practice in the United States.

The achievement filled him with pride and power, knowing that the hopeless women who came to see him with tears in their eyes left feeling restored and whole. They were vessels for his greatness and he had risen to the challenge, taking God's castoffs and giving them their miracle babies.

His greatest successes came from a special protocol he designed in the last twenty years, called the Integrated Blackwell Fertility Method. It was a revolutionary exclusive program that treated the entire woman—body, soul, and mind. After rigorous screening, ideal candidates were treated with a multi-pronged approach that was steeped in religious ideals and married traditional medicine with a strict naturopath diet and rigorous mental health treatments. To be accepted as a candidate was every barren woman's dream. The process was selective by design, and the success rate was unparalleled among his colleagues.

Ten minutes later, Damian escorted his wife to the elevator. She chatted all the way down, a sound he'd long learned to tune out and offer well-timed head nods to make her feel heard. When the doors opened, he pasted on a dazzling smile and offered Gloria his arm. He followed the crowd entering the ballroom and was stopped to shake hands with medical professionals of lower pedigree as he guided his wife of forty-two years to the front of the room. Grinning from ear to ear, it filled him with pride seeing the crowd gather to celebrate his achievements. Sure, there were several other awards being given that night, but he was the actual star of the show.

The emcee at the podium broke through the chatter. "If everyone could take their seats, we would like to serve dinner."

Damian pulled out a chair for Gloria and pushed it back in, taking the empty seat next to her. He beamed at his children and grandchildren seated at the surrounding tables, sneaking in little waves to the youngest members of his clan. His brood was large, now approaching forty, and he was proud of each and every one of them. Thanks to Gloria's wide hips and accommodating demeanor, they'd been graced with healthy pregnancies since the time she was twenty, through her thirties, and even well into her forties. A father of sixteen, he'd worked hard to provide an incredible life for his children for the glory of God. Damian never stooped low enough to require government assistance to take care of his family. He believed providing for them was his sole responsibility and God would provide, and he had.

Half-listening to the small talk around him, he cut uniform rectangles through his prime rib and swiped it through the horseradish sauce. It was a decent offering, but nothing compared to the black-tie fundraising event he was planning next week. Gloria reached under the table and squeezed his hand when the emcee once again appeared on the podium, and the hum of conversation silenced. During the next thirty minutes, several lesser deserving healthcare professionals picked up their paltry awards, and he clapped politely and listened to their acceptance speeches with a smile on his face, but his mind was elsewhere.

He was busy calculating the viability and low motility of the sperm from one of his most high-profile clients. Powerful men never loved to learn of their weaknesses, especially when it came to their seed. It was the reason he was so sought-after. He had helped infertile couples who had exhausted every option of traditional medicine. His colleagues had taken to calling him Sky Daddy, a god-like reference, behind his back.

When he overheard it the first time, he was offended, but now he wore it proudly as a badge of honor.

His most faithful nurse, Diandra Miller, called him the nickname when they were in bed together. The sultry way her full lips spoke the words made his loins drip with desire. After forty, Gloria was too tired to attend to his sexual desires, and so he'd brought in a relief pitcher of sorts. The kind that would fully submit to him and help him get the release he deserved so he could focus on his mission.

Dr. Blackwell simply practiced what the Old Testament preached. While he couldn't afford to keep up with Solomon's seven hundred wives and three hundred concubines, he approached the lifestyle on a smaller scale. Gloria understood the role she played in his life and, even when his special conferences with Diandra came to light, she didn't waver. Instead, she threw herself into her role as the matriarch with even more vigor. As his gaze drifted around the tables that held his loved ones, he was filled with satisfaction. He returned Gloria's squeeze under the table, appreciating her contributions over the years. He cleared his throat, mentally preparing for the speech he would make in seconds.

"Now we have arrived at the most prestigious award a specialist in reproductive health can hope to achieve. This great man has been a pioneer in reproductive technology for over thirty-five years. A graduate of Johns Hopkins with impressive fellowships all over the United States and Europe, he has made it his mission to give every couple the ability to bring a child into the world.

Over the last two decades, Blackwell Reproductive Health has been credited with helping its patients deliver over one hundred thousand miracles. He is the most celebrated fertility specialist in the United States. It's my greatest pleasure to give The Lifetime Achievement Award from the Society of American Reproductive Health to my friend and mentor, Dr. Damian Blackwell."

The ballroom erupted in applause, and Damian stood and made his way to the podium. Around him, the crowd leaped to their feet, giving him the standing ovation he'd secretly hoped to receive. He rode on the wave of their adoration, savoring the feeling of it. The swell of love from the crowd made him tingle with purpose. With a practiced smile, he stood at the podium as he waited for the applause to die down.

The emcee handed him a faceted crystal orb with an engraved plaque on the base. Dr. Blackwell gripped the cool glass in his hands and beamed as he looked out into the ballroom. His gaze landed on Gloria, who swiped tears away from her cheeks with the cloth napkin their oldest daughter handed her. His eyes lingered on the four tables that surrounded the stage, filled with his children and grandchildren. The satisfaction of seeing his legacy seated in front of him took his breath away. Standing in the spotlight's glow and looking out into the sea of faces, acknowledging his greatness, was the culmination of every dream he'd ever had. All the roads he'd traveled and the sacrifices he'd made had led to where he stood now, relishing his moment in the sun.

He opened his mouth to speak. "Thank you to the committee for bestowing this honor on me. I've devoted my life to the creation of humanity, and it has been an incredibly rewarding and fulfilling journey. I don't have any plans to slow down. In fact, I am energized by the leaps and bounds of technology and the tools it gives us to create life." He swept one hand through his shock of wavy silver hair. "I want to thank my wife, Gloria, for excelling at the task of raising our family so I could focus on helping my patients create their own. She has been a partner in every sense of the word and is the reason my children are my greatest contribution to the world. Far above the accolades you fine people have given me tonight, they are my true purpose and give me the drive for the work I do. Thank you." He made his way off the stage to thunderous applause. The emcee drew the evening to a close, and Damian sat at the table with a beaming Gloria, as many of his colleagues filed by to offer their congratulations.

"Are you going to retire now that you've gotten the Lifetime Achievement Award?" his son, Luke, asked.

"Retire? I wouldn't know what to do with myself, and neither would your mother!" The group gathered around him tittered with laughter, and he added, "They are going to have to carry me out of the clinic in a pine box."

"That's too graphic, dear." Gloria patted his arm,

pointing to their youngest granddaughter, whose eyes were now the size of dinner plates. "Little ears."

He pulled her hand to his lips and kissed it. "You're right, sweetheart." The gesture accomplished what he'd intended. Gloria practically burst with joy. He sat with his family in the ballroom until it emptied, his thoughts always his constant companion.

Dr. Blackwell was at the top of his game and at the apex of his career. He was doing God's work, helping the faithful be fruitful and multiply, and it was full speed ahead because Sky Daddy was just getting started.

FOUR

The next day, Dr. Blackwell arrived at the clinic at his usual four a.m. morning hour. His early start afforded him two luxuries. One was an escape from Gloria, who had a proven track record of hovering and smothering with her constant fretting over him. Two was the peaceful silence he believed was essential for his biggest medical breakthroughs to surface. In the quietude of those early mornings, his medical genius glimmered brightly before the burning Florida sun rose and his practice was filled with patients and staff who provided endless distractions. Exiting his vehicle, carrying his insulated lunch box and thermos, he swiped his card at the employee entrance and walked to his impressive office. It was decorated with mid-century modern furniture, sporting clean lines and the bright pops of color his mostly female patients preferred.

Humming to himself, just being in the presence of

the greatness he'd nurtured and built for the last forty years made his skin electric with purpose. Every day, he popped right out of bed, eager to make significant progress on his life's mission.

The moment of conception always inspired him. Implanting young mothers with the seeds of life was as thrilling today as it was when he first started practicing. In fact, it had only grown more exciting as fertility technology grew in leaps and bounds. Thirty years ago, the tools and methods were clunky and unsophisticated —just barely more than a turkey baster. Significant breakthroughs in recent years only increased his success rates and helped even more women plagued by infertility.

Though the tools of the trade improved, the basic components had not. Semen was a finicky substance with a brief shelf life. He believed the penis was an archaic delivery system, but could not argue its efficacy as the world's population swelled to nearly eight billion. Natural ovulation was unpredictable at best, and when left to their own devices, the fallopian tubes released eggs in a haphazard and inconsistent manner. Most women lost a thousand of them each month. If you really wanted to strike the fear of God in a patient, you would share that statistic with them in a grave voice, then pause for a long moment before adding ominously that this number skyrockets higher as you age. It was the one that often sealed the deal, and Dr. Blackwell found it especially valuable during egg-banking consultations. He learned quickly that fear is the most powerful motivator of all, and his practice thrived from the leverage it gave him.

In a laboratory environment, where the egg and semen are separated and exist outside the warm cocoon of the body, there are a million ways a sample can be compromised before it gets used for its intended purpose. Motility could be destroyed if it were too hot or too cold, or if it were too long since ejaculation. It could be tainted with saliva, lube, or improper hand washing. No matter how many preparatory instructions were shared with red-faced fathers and desperate mothers, many samples had to be discarded as medical waste. It was the most frustrating factor in Dr. Damian Blackwell's practice. In the late eighties, knowing fertility clinics lived and died by their reported rates of conception and live births, he made a couple of key tweaks in his collection protocols and his success rates skyrocketed.

That morning, Dr. Blackwell swiped his key card to enter the cryogenics lab. His forward motion turned on the lights automatically as he walked further into the lab, then donned a white coat and washed his hands meticulously for several long minutes. He stood over a carefully organized workstation stocked with Petri dishes and vials for samples, microscopes, and an array of specialized medical equipment. The early morning sounds of a sterile laboratory created a delicate symphony of medical instruments. There were the soft clinks of pipettes chiming against the Petri dishes and the gentle whir of centrifuges. It was a calming lullaby he enjoyed.

He walked to his workstation, pulled open a drawer, and removed the Holy Bible he'd been given as a child. Its brown leather cover was cracked, and he took pride in its well-worn appearance. It was a bible that had been read countless times over and had provided numerous moments of solace and clarity. He turned to it when he first started his practice almost forty years ago, and his pious ways never failed him.

In the heart of the laboratory, a series of waist-high cryogenic storage tanks concealed a collection of meticulously cataloged frozen sperm samples floating in a sea of liquid nitrogen. Each vial housed a semen sample that had been washed and then mixed with a cryoprotectant to prevent damage and then stored under precise temperature conditions. Dr. Blackwell approached the cryo-storage unit with reverence. His gloved hands trembled slightly when he released the vacuum seal, and a puff of white condensation dispersed through the air. Opening the canister, he withdrew several vials from the several hundred entombed inside the tank.

"Dammit!" he muttered under his breath, noticing the automatic system for filling the liquid nitrogen had malfunctioned again. His calls to the manufacturer had been a futile task where they gave him the runaround, requiring him to manually refill the tanks while their technicians helped troubleshoot the underlying issue. The repair fees were already costing him thousands of dollars, and his frugal nature had won out. As a precaution, he had temperature alarms installed that sent readings directly to his phone twenty-four hours a day. Dr. Blackwell preferred to top the tanks himself. It was the only way he could be absolutely assured it was handled correctly. When he traveled, he supervised the tanks remotely, and Diandra was the only person he trusted to carry out the task.

Running out of options with the manufacturer, he decided he would limp by until the next stage of his mission was brought to fruition. It required securing funding for a brand new state-of-the-art laboratory with the latest technology in cryogenic storage. The blueprints for the facility were on his desk, as well as an architectural 3-D model. He was certain full funding would materialize during his upcoming fundraiser.

With careful precision, he returned to the vials and transferred the contents of each into a specialized centrifuge, initiating a high-speed spinning process. It would separate the most viable sperm from the rest of the sample, purifying the semen into a concentrated volume to facilitate fertilization. Then he would conduct a thorough post-thaw evaluation before he could use the sperm to inseminate the eggs.

As the spinning machine came to a full stop, Dr. Blackwell peered into the centrifuge, and a satisfied smile crept across his lips as he relished in the power of creation that pulsed through his veins. It heightened the pleasure he derived from his work, filling him with a sense of supremacy.

One by one, he delicately retrieved the patient's eggs and placed them into a sterilized petri dish. With practiced precision, he injected twenty thousand of the purified sperm into the dish containing the eggs that, over the course of the next twenty-four hours, would allow natural fertilization to occur. Once combined, he made copious notes, then moved the dishes to the incubator that simulated the conditions of the human body, an environment that would promote fertilization and development of the embryos. The final step was preimplantation genetic testing.

Although he had several competent embryologists on staff, he preferred to personally fertilize all the eggs and test all the embryos for his Integrated Blackwell Fertility Method patients. It was a great selling point during his consultations with prospective mothers and fathers who appreciated his fine attention to detail and personal care.

With all the eggs now being fertilized, he pulled off his rubber gloves, placed them in the trash, and then washed his hands at the sink. Only then did he allow himself to go into the break room and make a cup of coffee. He carried it to his office and put on his headset to dictate his notes for patient files. An hour and a half later, his first employees were staggering into work as the sun rose in the sky.

There was a soft knock at the door.

"Come in," he called out as he completed his dictation and sent the file to his medical transcription service.

Diandra sauntered into his office with a wide smile. He quickly crossed over to the door to lock it and pulled the blinds shut. Seconds later, he pulled her onto his lap, seated in his office chair, and laced his fingers through her hair, pulling her in for a deep, wet kiss.

"Congratulations, Sky Daddy." Her plump lips lingering on the last two syllables filled him with desire. He swiped his fingers between her legs outside her clothing, relishing the dampness he felt gathering there.

"I'll bend you over this desk later tonight to properly celebrate," he whispered, feeling the blood rushing through his body at the mere thought of it.

She stood and fanned her flushed cheeks with a file from his desk. "Look what you've done to me." Diandra was an expert at stoking his desire. She was a capable nurse *and* a tigress in the bedroom, and he was perfectly content with their arrangement in both arenas.

"The Newtons are in the waiting room."

"Show them in." He stood and arranged his aching balls, then tugged his white coat on and swiped his fingers through his hair. He sat back down and pulled up their file, looking over the hCG test results. A few minutes later, Diandra settled the nervous couple into the two chairs in front of his desk as Dr. Blackwell gave them a reassuring smile. "I have fantastic news. Your third beta hGG test was outstanding, and your level is five hundred and seventy-one. Any level higher than three-ninety statistically gives you a ninety-one percent chance of a live birth."

Jocelyn burst into tears. "It's a miracle." Craig was

stunned in the chair, unable to put words together, so Jocelyn spoke for him. "You promised we'd conceive, and we did. You prayed with us and it made all the difference. God finally blessed us with the healthy pregnancy we've been wanting for so long."

Dr. Blackwell nodded in agreement, swimming in the warmth of their praise. "God is good."

"All the time," Jocelyn finished with a broad smile.

"Your job now is to eat well, get plenty of rest, and enjoy every stage of this pregnancy." He stood and walked to the edge of his desk and sat down on the corner of it. "In about seven weeks, you'll have your first ultrasound, but all indications are stellar for you to have a healthy pregnancy, as if you'd conceived naturally."

They stood, and Craig thrust a hand out to him. "I don't know how we'll ever be able to thank you," he finally croaked out, pumping the doctor's hand up and down.

"No need. I'm just helping God deliver his miracles to deserving couples." A few minutes later, after receiving instructions and a referral to an OB-GYN, they left buoyant and lighter than when they'd walked in. He watched them walk down the hall, Craig protecting his wife and the unborn child nestled in her womb as if his life depended on it. It was an amazing rush to answer their prayers and make their dreams come true.

FIVE

Jittery and tense after her meeting with Lilith, Zoya escaped to her ensuite bathroom, donned a silk robe, and perched on the edge of the freestanding tub. The light was dim, cast from the crystal chandelier hanging above. She slipped off the robe and into the scalding water, letting out an enormous sigh as she sank into it.

She plucked two sliced cucumbers from the tray her maid prepared and placed them over her eyes. Zoya had finally relaxed when she heard Terrance's claws scraping on the marble floor tiles. Instantly annoyed, she plucked the cucumbers from her eyes and threw them on the ground for him. He paused for a moment. The lure of the treat was tempting, but he pushed past his food lust and waited until the maid set the iPad up on the bamboo tray in front of Zoya. Huffing her displeasure, she sat up, creating a wave in the milk bath that sent gardenia petals skittering across the surface of the water.

"What is it?"

"You said you wanted to be kept abreast of any developments at Kandied Karma."

"Yes."

The maid pressed play on the YouTube video, and Zoya watched the crudely filmed flash mob dancing with the woman in the wheelchair. Kandied Karma's gold leaf sign and shots of Yuli and Katie smiling next to a weeping older woman filled the screen.

"What the hell is this?' She wrinkled her nose in displeasure.

"It's a flash mob, Your Highness. Apparently, it was on the bucket list of a very sick young woman, and the video has gone viral."

"Pathetic." Zoya roughly snapped her fingers and held out her hand to the maid, who rushed to place two more chilled green slices of cucumber in her hand. "Why do they toil away, squandering their energy to make the ordin puppets happy? Don't they know that's a fool's errand?" She settled back into the tub, letting the hot water work its magic on her sore muscles. "Yuli is wasting her time in that stupid candy shop meting out justice for the ordins when we have much bigger fish to fry!"

"I have no clue, My Queen."

"Yuli was always a bleeding heart," Zoya muttered. "Standing on principles with her cankles and thunder thighs."

Terrance barked with laughter. "She never was the ravishing beauty you are, My Queen. No one holds a candle to you, not even the Dark Goddess."

His compliment warmed the cockles of Zoya's stunted heart, which was still filled with jealousy from her interaction with Lilith. "Your loyalty is admirable." She settled back into the tub and placed the circles of cucumber back over her eyes before letting out an anguished groan of frustration.

"If I bring Lilith a worthy sacrifice, she will consider releasing Sally's soul," she explained to Terrance. "But, who...how...?" she mused, before dismissing the dog. "Go now. You're destroying my me time." Terrance trotted out of the room, leaving Zoya to wrestle with the silence. She had been wracking her brain since her interaction with Lilith and kept coming up blank. It had to be a substantial offering. She drummed her fingers on the porcelain as the water in the tub cooled. Instead of getting out, she wiggled her fingers in the water, and the temperature rose to a comfortable one hundred degrees.

With a heavy sigh, Zoya realized she was just as stuck as Sally. The only way out of the pain of their past was through it. While Yuli and Katia wasted their time on insignificant Make-a-Wish fantasies for dying women, she would direct her attention to what mattered —freeing Sally's soul once and for all.

Internally, she was divided. If Sally's soul was set free, she was afraid she would lose her tie to him forever. She wasn't sure who she would be if she found closure and the trauma didn't fuel her thirst for revenge anymore. The grief had been a constant companion she'd grown accustomed to, and part of her was afraid to give it up and embrace the unknown.

"Do you stick with the devil you know, or the one you don't?" she muttered into the air, waffling and unable to make a decision. The water cooled again, and she stepped out of the tub and into a thick terry-cloth robe.

At her closet, she whirred through decades of fashion, on the hunt for a vintage Alexander McQueen gown she wanted to wear to an upcoming fundraiser. She needed a physical distraction and was certain there would be plenty of sexy, powerful men in attendance who would jump at the chance to be with her.

There was something so delicious about commanding a titan of industry to debase himself to do her bidding. It was a snack she would indulge in while she mulled over her next steps. She always got her best ideas after the mind-clearing that resulted from multiple orgasms.

Six

A few days later, Katie pulled up to the front entrance of The Grand Palm Hotel for a special truffle delivery. Unsure where to unload the candy, she walked into the opulent lobby and over to the front desk where a statuesque blonde was attending to guests.

"I've got a delivery for Damian Blackwell from Kandied Karma."

Overhearing her words, a sturdy, plain woman with her hair pulled into a long ponytail turned toward her and said, "That's fantastic news! I'm Gloria Blackwell. I can meet you in the ballroom and show you where to set up. Would you mind pulling your car around back to the door that's marked for deliveries?"

"You got it." Katie smiled and returned to her Beetle and drove to the back of the hotel. She borrowed a rolling cart from catering, loaded it with boxes of truffles, and entered through the kitchen.

Gloria was already in the ballroom supervising the florist and decorator, who were transforming the space into a lush display with exotic florals. In the center of the room, lit by a spotlight, was a white 3D model of a huge medical facility. The lighting technician was making last-minute adjustments to the projected logo for Blackwell Reproductive Health on the wooden parquet dance floor. On the stage, a DJ was setting up and testing his equipment, and music cut in and out as he verified the speakers were in good working order. Seeing her pushing the cart, Gloria made her way over. "Damian insisted we serve Kandied Karma for dessert. He wanted only the very best for our important guests." She offered Katie an agreeable smile and lead her to a table where two waitstaff were busy assembling gold-plated tiered stands.

"We appreciate your business," Katie praised as she started to unload the gold boxes onto the table. She glanced around the room that was brimming with crystal, candlelight, and magnificent floral displays. "It's beautiful."

"Thank you." Gloria grinned the authentic smile of a woman who wasn't used to having her efforts acknowledged. "Tonight is a very special night. Dr. Blackwell is shooting for the stars to secure funding for the new Integrated Blackwell Method East Coast Reproductive Center. I'm sure you've heard of him. He's a legend."

She hadn't, but Katie didn't want to hurt her

feelings. Instead, she said, "You've done an amazing job. I don't know how donors will be able to resist."

Across the room, an elegant man in a navy suit with a thick shock of silver hair entered the room, and Gloria lit up with pride. "Excuse me for one moment." She quickly crossed to him, and they started to walk back to where Katie was setting up. He stopped to examine the decorations, taking one second to move a vase two inches to perfect center, an act that made Gloria's jaw tighten. Katie watched his attention to even the smallest detail emerge as he stopped two more times to correct minor oversights on his way to her. Each time, Gloria's eyes dropped to the floor, and Katie noticed her cheeks had flushed pink when they'd finally made it to the dessert table.

"This is my husband, and the star of the evening, Dr. Damian Blackwell." Gloria was laying it on thick. The doctor turned his discerning gaze over to Katie with a calculated smile. She offered her hand and, when it connected with the doctor's, was surprised to feel a jolt. She heard a chorus of children's voices laughing in her head and saw a visual flash of a group of tow-headed toddlers running on the beach and laughing as the surf tickled their ankles when the tide came in. It was a sweet moment swimming in saccharine, not the dramatic flash of painful events that she'd received with Rocco and Marisa, and the interaction made her wobble in confusion.

She pulled her hand back and saw concern register on the doctor's features. "Are you okay?" he asked.

"I'm sorry," she said. "Low blood sugar."

"You're in luck. You brought the cure with you! How fortuitous!" he joked, pointing at the truffles. He beamed a practiced smile that never quite reached his eyes, and left Katie feeling like she was watching an actor on a Broadway stage.

She was glad when the catering manager pulled him away. Katie shook off the strange energy that weighed on her since she shook his hand and took her time organizing the truffles while she observed Dr. Blackwell. He was being walked around the room by the hotel staff and the event lighting engineers who were running through the final set up, while Gloria flitted around making final tweaks to the decorations and ran through a list on her clipboard.

Dr. Blackwell was a performer. She couldn't escape the feeling the man she met was a carefully curated version he trotted out in public. The vision flashed through her mind again as she monitored him and rummaged for clues.

"He's a fertility specialist. You saw children. Big deal," she muttered to herself under her breath. She was puzzled and couldn't figure it out. Why was Karma being so obtuse? He was a bit of a control freak, but most uber-successful people were. It was probably nothing. She'd put a pin in it for now and make sure to discuss it with Yuli.

———

Hours later, the red carpet was packed with paparazzi. Flashbulbs blinded Zoya on the step and repeat at the entrance to the ballroom. She was poured into a nude, lace Alexander McQueen gown with a dramatic plunging neckline that nearly reached her waist. Her creamy cleavage was exactly the honey she would use to lure her next playmate.

Around her, there was a collective hum of conversation and smacks of air kisses on cheeks as women greeted each other. Zoya detested the whole charade and instead made her way to the bar and ordered a Vodka Gimlet. Sipping on it, she meandered her way through the crowd, waving away spineless little nymphs who whispered to each other, "That's Ana Castanova! I must get the name of her plastic surgeon! The woman is positively aging backward." Hearing her alias, she felt their envious ordin eyes like daggers in her back and feasted on their jealousy. It filled her with power.

She stood in front of the 3D model, built to scale with such attention to detail the sidewalk was even lined with palm trees and impeccably lush landscaping. Bending down to be eye level with the proposed glass front of the enormous medical complex, she heard a deep voice behind her.

"It will be the first of its kind." She rose to see an elegant silver-haired man reaching out his hand. "Ms. Castanova, I'm Dr. Damian Blackwell. Thank you for coming tonight."

She placed her gloved hand in his and leveled her

green eyes on his blue ones as he pulled her hand to his lips and kissed it. Forced to suppress her annoyance at his gesture, her nostrils flared.

"Please, call me Ana. It's a beautiful building," she offered, pulling her hand from his and tucking it away to ward off other advances.

"It will be the East Coast Integrated Blackwell Method Reproductive Center," he gushed, eager to explain.

"That's quite a mouthful." She said, pleased with herself when the dig poked a leak in his puffery.

Quickly regrouping, he continued, "We were blessed with an incredibly talented architect who created this stunning replica. It's one of the many miracles God has in store for us at Blackwell Reproductive Health."

"God is a crutch for the weak," Zoya said, relishing the flash of anger as it washed across his features and disappeared just as quickly. She'd struck a nerve, and the pleasure made her lips quirk up. He sized her up as she tuned in to his thoughts.

Keep your eye on the prize, Sky Daddy.

Zoya couldn't help herself. The nickname was so ridiculously outrageous, she had to use it as ammunition. "God is an omnipotent Sky Daddy who passes judgment on his followers. You give him too much power over your life." Zoya tingled with delight, seeing him visibly tremble in his attempt to keep his anger under control. She peeled off one of her gloves. "This isn't the way to my heart, darling. Keep your eye on the prize."

Taken aback, she watched the confusion flood over him. She leaned in and took his hand.

"I'll give you a hint." She leaned closer to whisper, and his eyes darted to her cleavage, then back again as she waved one hand to the crowd gathering behind her. "Appeal to our greed and our desire for immortality, and you'll have us eating out of your hand. I'm always looking for sound investments."

He licked his thin lips.

Donations are great, but an investment from Ana Castanova will fast-track my plan. We could break ground just after the New Year!

His eyes darkened with greed. The money captivated him like she knew it would.

"I'd like to invite you to Blackwell Reproductive Health for a personal tour of the facilities where I can walk you through the IVF process and my groundbreaking Integrated Blackwell Fertility Method."

Zoya sighed dramatically. "Don't be so desperate, darling." she tipped her chin to the side as she assessed him. "Your eagerness is off-putting."

His lips pursed. This was not a man used to being disparaged. It took everything in Zoya to prevent the glee that welled up from her barbs from spreading over her features.

What a condescending shrew. I refuse to pander to her or anyone else. I am a vessel of God. He alone acknowledges my greatness!

"Send my office the clinics' profit-and-loss statements, balance sheets, and cash flow statements, as well as your projections for the next two to three years," Zoya told him, pulling a business card from her sequined handbag and handing it to him. "Then we'll talk."

Finally, the respect I deserve. That's better.

He smiled. "I'll have my accountant prepare the necessary documents and messenger them over. It was wonderful to meet you, Ana." He tucked the card into his jacket pocket and moved along to the next circle of wealthy socialites, and Zoya walked over to the table where a dazzling display of fine chocolates filled several tiers. She plucked a caramel amaretto cream from the display and pulled the liner off to eat it. When she bit into the creamy center, her taste buds recognized the family recipe instantly, and she moaned with ecstasy. It was obvious, the truffle was from Kandied Karma. She ate two more while surveying the room, looking for her next scintillating distraction. Say what you want about frumpy old Yuli, but her candy-making skills were absolute perfection.

SEVEN

A couple of days before Thanksgiving, a breathless Frankie surveyed the results of her beatification efforts as a flutter of nervous butterflies tickled her insides. In the closet, she craned over her shoulder, checking out her backside in the mirror. She hadn't had an occasion to dress up for in almost a year. When Harry called and invited her on an *actual date*, requesting she wear an *actual dress*, she'd had to make an emergency trip to Seconds, the vintage store in Aura Cove, where she'd discovered a canary yellow lace dress and a pair of strappy sandals. She'd even tried something called curling crème, finally surrendering in the battle to tame her natural curls. To her surprise, the stylist at Supercuts had been right—it actually worked. The result was smooth ringlets that cascaded to her shoulders without the chaos of her normal red frizz.

"Now all you need to do, is never touch your hair

again," Frankie muttered at her reflection with a snort, delivering an impromptu pep talk. "Seriously, stop fussing. It's as good as it's gonna get." She shut off the light and ducked out of the bathroom when she heard a spirited knock at her side door and opened it to see Harry wearing jeans and a sports coat holding a bouquet of wildflowers.

"Awe!" The unexpected romantic gesture delighted Frankie, and she felt her stomach flip. "No one ever brings me flowers!" She swept them into her arms and inhaled their heady lavender scent. "Thank you." She glanced up into his warm brown eyes, suddenly feeling nervous energy surging through her. Her past dating history had taught her it was easier not to care and feign an air of detachment, but she found she couldn't help herself when it came to Harry. She reached out, wrapped her hand around his wrist, and tugged him inside. "Come in while I find a vase."

He shut the door behind him and followed her into the kitchen. Glancing around for any kind of vessel she could put water in, she dumped the glass jar full of change onto the counter and rinsed it out before arranging the flowers inside. Then she picked up a penny from the pile of loose change and plunked it into the water.

"Are you making a wish?"

"No, silly, I read somewhere it extends the life of fresh flowers."

"I thought all you read was smut."

"There's a lot you don't know about me yet, Willey.

Stay tuned." She offered him a lopsided grin, forcing her hands to ball at her sides instead of where they usually ended up—running through her hair. "Where are we headed tonight?" she asked.

"It's a surprise." Harry gave her a boyish grin that melted her into a puddle.

"Really?" She tipped her chin to study him, biting the inside of her bottom lip.

"Uh, yeah?" His chin jutted backward, confused by her question. "Isn't it customary for the inviter to plan a romantic event to sweep the invitee off their feet on a first date?"

She grinned at his natural state of comfort with his intentions. It was refreshing compared to the commitment-phobic men who usually plagued her. "The last few 'dates' I subjected myself to were more of the Netflix and chill variety." She used finger quotes around the word date to emphasize its ridiculousness. "It's a weak sauce, transparent way to get into a woman's pants."

He took a step closer. "I assure you, I plan on getting into your pants, but we're taking the scenic route. Is that okay?"

"Very much okay," she admitted shyly. Her brashness was gone, swept away by the earnestness in his expression.

Twenty minutes later, they parked Harry's El Camino, and he reached over to her side of the car and pulled down the visor. Two tickets fluttered out and landed on Frankie's lap. She reached out to pick them up, but he was faster and tucked them away in the pocket of his blazer. "Nice try. Gotta be faster on the draw to beat me." She shook her head, enjoying his competitive nature, and reached to open the car door when he said, "Wait, I'm supposed to get the door for you." He rushed from his side and over to hers to open her door.

Amused, Frankie couldn't stop herself from smiling. "Dude, I love the effort you're putting in, but you don't need to open doors for me. I know you're being chivalrous and all, but this girl has two fully capable hands. Besides, I want you to save your energy for other, more *important* tasks." She delivered the last two words with a well-timed wink and took pleasure in seeing the tips of his ears pink up.

"Yes, ma'am!" He grabbed her hand and pulled her to a sidewalk that led to a stone and iron building. Once inside, he gave their tickets to the usher and they were led into a concert hall. Banks of flameless luminaries covered every horizontal surface and ran down the aisles that encircled the elevated stage in the center of the room. Completely shrouded in darkness, the house lights were off, but hundreds of candles placed close together and spanning most of the stage illuminated where a grand piano and three stands holding various stringed instruments awaited their musicians. The warm yellow glow from the collection of candles cast soft light across an intimate room with seating for only forty guests.

"Wow," Frankie uttered, frozen in front of the

breathtaking sight. It was the only word her astounded mind could form. She was having an out-of-body experience, taking in that much visual beauty in one glance. The candlelight softly traced the details of the intricately carved concert hall. It kissed the plaster and softened every straight line.

"Frankie Stapleton rendered speechless on our first date," Harry noted, pleased with himself. "I believe that is one for the win column." His competitive jab gently pulled her back into her body. She shoved him playfully away with her hand, but he grabbed it and held it tighter. He navigated to their seats, and they sat down as more guests filled the aisles and the surrounding chairs.

Her hand was still tucked into the warmth of his. "You look so beautiful tonight," he whispered, bringing her hand up to press against his lips.

"Anyone looks great in candlelight. Memorize this view and lock it in your memory bank, because this is the best I will ever look. It's all downhill from here," she joked.

"I highly doubt that," he countered.

Their gazes were redirected as a flutter of movement on the stage made a hush fall over the crowd. Musicians in formal wear walked elegantly to their seats and pulled their instruments close. Unsure what to expect, Frankie gasped when the first few notes of "Bohemian Rhapsody" spooled from a violin and then intensified when the tuxedoed man at the piano joined in. A wide smile spread across her face, and she met Harry's shining gaze as the song continued. Over the next hour, smash hits from the band Queen tickled the ivories and mesmerized the strings. "Fat Bottomed Girls," "Another One Bites the Dust," and "We Are the Champions" were lovingly performed by talented musicians aglow in candlelight. It was unlike anything Frankie had ever experienced before. The golden light bathed the room in a romantic glow that imprinted on Frankie's soul. She squeezed Harry's hand, who kept stealing glances at her, enjoying her reaction to the music almost as much as the captivating sight and sound of the musicians themselves. When the concert was over, they were both still under its spell, oblivious to the crowd dispersing around them, transformed by the experience.

"We better clear out before the cleaning crew comes in," Harry said, and then they navigated back to his parked car.

"That was a religious experience," Frankie gushed. "I have to admit I was a little apprehensive when I saw the cello because the orchestra is not usually my jam, but that was amazing!" She leaned back in the seat and sighed with pleasure. "I'll never forget this night!"

"That was the plan." Harry grinned. The smile took years off his face, and Frankie memorized the way his skin crinkled at the corners of his warm brown eyes.

Her stomach growled, and she laughed. "Feed me, Seymour!"

"How about shrimp tacos?" he asked. "There's this truck near the beach that makes an unforgettable mango jalapeño slaw."

"Buy me tacos and tell me I'm pretty. That's the way to my heart," she quipped.

"You're pretty," Harry said so quickly it made Frankie laugh and flush with warmth. She stole glances at his profile as he drove, never wanting this night to end. He reached out to squeeze her hand.

"Why are you still single?" she asked suspiciously. "Dating at our age is like sorting through the pile to find the pair of least-stained pants at the thrift store."

He winced. "Was that supposed to be a compliment?"

"It was." She smiled and then asked, "Have you ever been married?"

"No. Never married, no kids."

"What is wrong with you?" She narrowed her eyes on him, wary of her good fortune. "You obviously know how to treat a woman. As someone who has been drowning in the dating pool for hundreds of years, you're a freaking unicorn."

He parked the car in front of a food truck that was working through a long line. A small group of picnic tables sat in front of it and, above the tables, a string of lights crisscrossed from pole to pole to illuminate the area. He turned toward Frankie. "To be honest, I always wanted to wait until we found Jessica." He looked down and his voice lowered. "It didn't seem right to do it without her." Frankie reached out to squeeze his forearm to offer support when he whispered, "I didn't think it would take me this long to find her."

"I'm sorry, Harry."

"Me too," he admitted then added. "I also never met anyone who I could see myself being happy with for the rest of my life."

"You know, with half our lives already in the rearview mirror, it's not as daunting a task. You only need to find someone you can tolerate for the next twenty to thirty years," Frankie quipped, ever the realist.

He laughed. "Yep, my criteria has changed dramatically. Now I'm looking for a woman who can identify the signs of a stroke and is strong enough to load me in the back of the car."

Frankie flexed one of her wiry biceps tight, and he reached out to squeeze the sinewy muscle.

"Not bad."

"I'm stronger than I look," she offered.

"Does that mean you're applying for the job?"

"TBD," Frankie said, and she opened her own door, making her way to the taco truck. A dumbfounded Harry joined her a few minutes later. She studied the menu once they were at the front of the line and began to place her order.

"Can we get the shrimp nachos? And a fire-breather quesadilla?" she asked, pulling out her credit card. "And whatever this gorgeous man cake desires besides me." She turned to Harry with a cheesy smile.

He chuckled and added, "And four avocado and scallop tacos with the chimichurri? And a side of chimichurri?" He pulled out his credit card, but Frankie was faster on the draw.

"Hey! I was supposed to buy you tacos. Remember?"

"Well, this way, I don't have to put out on the first date," Frankie said. "It evens the playing field."

They took their boats filled with a Mexican seafood feast and settled into a picnic table. Frankie took a bite of the nachos and sighed deeply. The cilantro and the creamy cheese sauce combined in a tangle of delicious flavors in her mouth. Crunchy tortilla chips studded with chunks of grilled shrimp and the spicy mango and jalapeño slaw made her swoon and close her eyes in delight. "I could die a happy woman right now!"

"Not yet. I have other plans," Harry replied as he pulled off the lid of his bright green chimichurri and poured it between the edges of the soft tortilla. He hoisted it to his mouth and took a bite, chewing with a huge grin on his face.

"Here." He slid the boat with his tacos over. "In my opinion, this is the best item on the menu. You have to try it."

Frankie dug in and took a huge bite. The succulent scallops had been seared to buttery perfection, and with the creamy avocado and tangerine pepper relish, it was elevated to an almost out-of-body experience. "I'm going to need a moment to collect myself." She held up her hand and closed her eyes, savoring the perfect explosion of flavors.

"You weren't lying about tacos being your love language." Harry enjoyed her reaction. "This is the best taco truck in the Tampa Bay area. When you're a beat cop, you get to know all the best places in town, especially the authentic mom-and-pop joints where the food is made with love."

"I can't believe I've lived here all my life and have never heard of this place."

"Stick with me, Stapleton. I'll make your toes curl and your taste buds do a striptease."

She grinned. *It would be so easy to fall in love with this man*, Frankie thought, and she just might let herself.

EIGHT

Early Thanksgiving morning, Katie pulled her turkey out of the cooler she'd been brining it in, patted it dry, and placed it on the roasting rack with a thud, grinning at the nineteen-pound bird. Katie loved Thanksgiving. Of all the holidays, it was her absolute favorite because it embodied her favorite things. It was a day to gather her family and friends around the table, eating delicious food created from scratch. The timing of a holiday meal was a perfectly choreographed dance, with each dish given the attention it needed to create a magnificent whole.

She pinched her fingers and ran them down several sprigs of rosemary and into a Pyrex dish of melted butter. Then she added salt, freshly cracked pepper, and julienned sage to the mixture. Using her hands, she slathered the herbed butter liberally on the skin of the turkey. She stuffed a bundle of carrots, celery, two

Meyer lemons, and two heads of garlic into the cavity and slid it into the oven, humming to herself.

Four hours later, she was pulling the golden brown turkey out for its final baste. The clock on the front of the oven read 11:11. "Make a wish, boy," she told Arlo, who hovered at her feet, licking his chops, hoping a stray morsel from the countertop would land in his open mouth.

"I don't need wishes, because they all came true when you escaped the warehouse and came home safely to me."

"Aww, you big softie!" She stooped down to scratch the patch of soft fur under his chin, and he blissed out, enjoying the sensation, his left leg thumping against the travertine. "It's true. We all have a reason to be extra thankful this year."

"Do you need any help?" Katie whirled around to see a freshly showered Marisa padding into the kitchen on bare feet.

"Only if you feel up to it," Katie said. "Our guests should arrive in an hour, and it's just the sides we need to wrap up and get into the oven."

"I'd love to feel useful," Marisa answered. "The morning sickness is finally gone. I guess that is kind of a silver lining," she offered with a sad shrug.

"I'm glad to hear you're at least feeling better physically." Katie rushed to her side and gave her a half-hug. "Happy Thanksgiving."

Happy? So far, my happiest Thanksgiving was when we had to run through a drive-thru because there was no food in the house after Dad left. The worst was when Rocco called me a dim-witted idiot for not knowing the turkey needed to defrost for four days before it could go in the oven.

"That's so sad." Katie answered Marisa's thought train without thinking as she chopped the sausage for her stuffing.

"What is?" Marisa asked, her bright eyes locked on Katie's. The color was returning to her cheeks and, without makeup, she appeared much younger and made Katie's overprotective heart clutch in her chest.

"Nothing," Katie said, catching herself. She would have to be more careful. Needing to change the subject, she wiped her hands on a dishtowel and asked, "Would you mind cutting up the loaf of sourdough over there into cubes for me?"

"Sure." Marisa pulled out the loaf and accepted the cutting board Katie handed her.

I know I should be out looking for a job, contacting Davina about the next hearing, and moving forward with my life, but I can barely get out of bed. I know I can't rely on Katie's kindness forever, but I'm exhausted.

Katie studied Marisa from across the island. Picking up on the despair and anxiety that coated every thought, she offered, "I'm so glad you're here. I never was a fan of the empty nest." She added a sweet smile, hoping to put the weary woman at ease. Katie turned back to rinsing the haricot vert in a colander in the sink when Frankie walked through the door carrying a box of Chardonnay.

"Happy Turkey Day!" Frankie hollered as she slipped off her shoes at the door and walked to Katie's fridge to chill the wine. She offered Katie a hug, then took an awkward step toward Marisa, who self-consciously did the same. Both women giggled when they nearly head-butted each other trying to execute a polite hug.

"So?" Katie asked from across the countertop, pointing the chef's knife toward Frankie. "Give us the deets. How was your first official date with Officer Willey?"

Frankie's eyes twinkled. She was swooning, already awash in butterfly flutters.

"Whoa! Someone is a smitten kitten already," Katie observed.

More than smitten. God, the things I plan on doing to that man would make a sailor blush. I am gonna need to bathe in holy water.

Katie had to fight back the urge to chuckle at Frankie's thoughts. "What did you do on your date?"

"He got tickets for the Queen candlelight concert, and then he took me to this taco truck out on Corey Avenue. They were some of the best tacos I've ever tasted in my entire life."

"That's a bold statement," Katie said, watching Frankie's whole body quiver with delight as she recounted the events of the night.

"Right?" Frankie clasped her hands to her chest and shimmied her hips. "I might already love this man."

"Be careful, babe. You have a tendency to dive in head-first and then stub your noggin."

"Nope." Frankie laughed at herself. "I can't. I'm already in too deep."

I can't wait until he's balls deep…

Katie choked on the wine she was sipping, and it shot out of her nose. She winced and pinched her burning nostrils together.

"What happened?" Frankie asked.

"Just went down the wrong pipe," Katie lied. The doorbell rang, and she crossed the room to the front door and opened it to see the smiling faces of her children.

"Happy Thanksgiving, Mama Bear." Beckett smiled and wrapped his mother in his arms, depositing a kiss on her cheek.

"Come here, my lovelies," she urged Callie and Lauren, opening her arms to squeeze them tight. Callie nestled her chin into the crook of her mother's shoulder, taking in the fully extended table that was dressed with pumpkin-colored linens and long, tapered candles in crystal holders.

"You've set the table for a larger group than we usually have for Thanksgiving. Who's coming?"

"I invited Liz, her husband Charlie, and Lorelei," Katie explained. "They didn't have any plans, and I couldn't bear the thought of them sitting at home like it was just another day."

"Yeah." Lauren laughed knowingly. "We couldn't have that!"

Good. The more the merrier. That way I'll be able to slip out undetected and meet Tom for a drink instead of being dragged into Mom and Frankie's annual Black Friday madness.

Katie's eyes locked on Lauren. *Tom? Who was Tom?* She studied Lauren, who offered her a wide smile and then started trimming the tips of the green beans. Unable to help herself, she asked, "Are you seeing anyone special, honey? You know I've been waiting for the day when I get to add another chair around the table."

Lauren chuckled and rolled her eyes. "I'm a focused career woman. I don't have time for such frivolities." She shrugged the question off. "Besides, I don't really have the bandwidth right now. My caseload is heavy, and the hours are not really conducive to dating."

"Don't work yourself to death, sweetheart. Leave room for love."

Maybe. I just don't want to lose myself in a man like Mom did for all those years.

"Ouch," Katie said under her breath and shook her head, hoping to clear it. The onslaught of thoughts from people around her was a superhighway of information, some of it she didn't even want to receive. The new ability was invasive, and she forced an even expression onto her face. How did Yuli deal with the constant barrage of random thoughts from those around her and keep her sanity?

"A partner makes life a blessing or a curse," Katie

added, pulling out a kitchen towel and draping it over her shoulder.

"The only partner I want to be right now comes with my name on the letterhead." Lauren grinned.

"Your ambition is admirable," Katie praised. "But promise me you'll keep the door open a crack."

Oh, it's open much more than a crack.

Katie's gaze on Lauren, who offered a secretive smile, before turning to set the potatoes on the cutting board adjacent to the stove. Her curiosity was piqued but would have to wait.

The front door opened again, and Yuli, Kristina, and David appeared. Behind them was Liz, holding a pie. At the bottom of the steps, Lorelei waited with a man who had to be her father. Charlie was medium height with a softness in the belly. He was balding, sporting a dome of shiny pink skin surrounded by salt and pepper hair, and was dressed in khakis and a polo shirt. The everyday dad uniform.

Katie waved them in and took the pie from Liz's outstretched hands before addressing Lorelei. "I'll go get the brawn, Lorelei, and we'll give you the full Cleopatra experience."

Katie walked over to the patio slider where Beckett was seated next to Marisa and asked, "Hey, buddy, can you help lift Lorelei up the stairs? I didn't even think about the house not being wheelchair accessible."

"Of course!" He hopped up and, a few moments later, with the help of Liz's husband, they wheeled Lorelei into the foyer.

Katie extended her hand to the man. "I'm thrilled to have you here. I'm Katie."

"Charlie," he said with a warm smile. A flash made her stiffen, and she fought for a moment to gather her wits. A much younger version of him was rocking a baby in a rocking chair, humming a lullaby. Then another flash. Charlie's body wracked with sobs as he cradled his face in his hands in a darkened nursery. The baby was gone.

Confused, she led the small family into the great room and offered them a seat. "Help yourselves to the beverage station." She waved her hand over to a sideboard that had a glass decanter of lemonade and a silver tray of whiskey and spirits. "And if you're a little peckish, there's charcuterie."

Overwhelmed with sensation, she went to the bathroom to clear her mind for a minute. After splashing cold water on her face, she looked at herself in the mirror and placed her palms on the countertop to steady her racing thoughts.

"You're okay," Katie reassured herself, stepping into the hallway, where the chatter grew louder and bursts of laughter echoed through the air. She lingered for a moment, her gaze sweeping over the scene, taking in every familiar face gathered in her home. A wave of gratitude washed over her as she stood there, soaking in the warmth of the moment. She was blessed. Tears prickled at her eyes as Beckett caught her gaze and made his way over to her.

"You're going to subject perfect strangers to the

water works already? That's got to be some kind of record," he razzed his mother. "Come here, you freak." He pulled her shoulders in closer to him, and she wrapped her arm around his warm waist.

"You always seem to gravitate to the most beautiful woman in the room." She pointed through the glass at Marisa, who was lounging on the chair by the pool.

"That's true." He offered a smirk. "Can't help myself."

"She's going through a lot right now. It might not be the best time to get involved," Katie warned. "Give her a chance to catch her breath and heal. Trauma changes a person."

"It's not like that," he lied, blushing.

It's exactly like that. I want to hold her and kiss away every tear she's ever cried. She's beautiful with a body sculpted by the gods, but it's more than that. I just want to see her happy again. Because when she smiles at me, I feel like I can do anything.

Katie had to fight the urge to respond to his thoughts directly. "You've been known to fall in love too quickly, and she's very beautiful, so I can understand why you would be tempted." He nodded in agreement. "What she really needs right now is a friend."

Friend zone! What the hell, Mom? No freaking way.

Katie had to stifle a chuckle. It was clear her advice was going in one ear and out the other.

"Just be careful and take it slow," she cautioned as Beckett walked away. Leaving her words of advice in his wake, he quickly returned to Marisa's side.

"What can I do to help?" Liz asked as she and Charlie walked over. "I can't believe how kind you've been to our family. To open up your beautiful beachfront home to us for Thanksgiving! What a treat!"

"I think we're in really great shape. As you can see, there are lots of cooks in the kitchen," she said with a smile, watching Yuli take charge and get the serving platters out. She had Lauren cutting the pies into slices, and Kristina stood at the stove with a ladle, scooping drippings into a pan to make the gravy.

"Can I grab you a beverage?" she asked Liz, whose elbow brushed against her wrist. The contact gave Katie an unexpected flash. A calendar showing the month of June being torn in half.

"Sorry." Liz smiled and took a step back. "Stiff knees."

"Are you okay?" Charlie asked, his voice concerned.

"Yes, dear," Liz answered with a weary smile. She patted his arm.

Yuli was carving the turkey into slices with an electric knife, while Kristina called everyone into the house to help carry platters of food to the table. Frankie had popped the corks on three bottles of wine and circled the table, filling glasses. Gleaming white platters with slices of perfectly roasted turkey were placed on either end of the long table, then came the bowls of fluffy mashed potatoes and boats of gravy. Perched in the center, a leaning tower of freshly baked rolls and rosettes of butter defied gravity. On the island, Kristina staged a full dessert bar with five different pies: pumpkin, apple, French silk, lemon curd, and blueberry.

"Everyone, grab a seat and your glass. It's time for the toast," Katie announced as the crowd scrambled to find their name card at the long table that stretched out over fifteen feet. "This is the one day of the year my family allows me to be sentimental and sappy without sarcasm, and I plan on taking full advantage of it this year!" She grinned as Beckett, Callie, and Lauren audibly groaned.

She raised her glass, saying, "I am so deeply grateful to each one of you seated here at our table. This Thanksgiving is extra special because there was a time not too long ago when I didn't know if I'd get the chance to gather all the people I love in one place." She choked up for a moment and looked down at her lap, and then felt Beckett's hand reach out and squeeze hers. She offered him a quick smile and continued. "I'm sure you've all heard the phrase, 'Blood is thicker than water.' But the actual complete quote is 'The blood of the covenant is thicker than the water of the womb.' Which roughly translated means the relationships you choose are far more important than the ones you don't. I am truly blessed because I have it both ways—the blood and the water. So, cheers to all of my chosen ones gathered around this table with me on my favorite day of the year, Thanksgiving Day. I am truly thankful for you all."

"Hear! Hear!" David hollered out, and they clinked their glasses together as Katie found her seat at the head of the table. They passed platters of turkey and mashed potatoes, all the while the sound of their voices chatting together sweetened the air. Katie relished in it, soaking it up like a sponge, feeling thankful and blessed that she was exactly where she was supposed to be and surrounded by the people she loved.

After dinner, the group made quick work of washing the dishes and packing up the leftovers into Tupperware. To entertain himself, Beckett snapped Callie and Lauren with a dish towel while they washed dishes at the sink and Lorelei was busy scraping plates into the trash can.

"Faster!" he cried, taking on a drill sergeant persona and snapping the towel harder.

"I'm going as fast as I can, B!" Lauren said. "You got the easy part!"

"Excuses, excuses!" He grinned.

Marisa watched the exchange from a distance, amused by it, but unwilling to join in.

Seizing an opportunity, Yuli pulled Katie out of sight from the rest of the group and handed her a small box. Inside, nestled in the golden tissue paper from Kandied Karma, was a lavender truffle. It was a perfect circle; the lavender coating was drizzled with white chocolate and violet sprinkles. She fished it out of the tissue paper nest, and it vibrated in her palm.

"This may help with your next assignment."

"Should I eat it now?"

Yuli nodded, so Katie quickly pulled off the crinkled liner and popped it into her mouth, chewing quickly. It was so sweet her teeth tingled as she chewed and swallowed hard. She felt a warmth in her belly trace up her spine, and when she looked down at her fingers, tiny jolts of golden sparks crackled from her fingertips. She waved her fingers in front of her face in awe of it.

"What am I supposed to do? Sit on my hands to hide them?"

"No. You need to harness the energy and slow it down so ordins can't detect it. Take three deep breaths," Yuli instructed.

After she'd exhaled the last breath, she looked down again, and the sparks were gone.

"I'll keep the kids busy. Why don't you walk Charlie and Liz out to the patio and see if you can gather more information?" Yuli suggested. Katie agreed and headed over to Liz and Charlie, who were seated on the sofa in the great room. She tapped Liz on the shoulder and asked, "Want to sit on the lanai while these knuckleheads do all the dirty work?"

"That's a great idea," she said, and Charlie stood to help her to her feet. They followed Katie out to the patio, and Arlo tagged along, eager to get out of the line of fire at the kitchen sink. There were so many pairs of feet to dodge. Even the lure of accidental scraps falling to the floor lost their attraction.

"This has been a wonderful Thanksgiving," Liz remarked after they were seated near the fountain.

"Thank you for opening up your home to us," Charlie added.

"I'm just grateful you could come!" Katie gushed.

"By the looks of things, you've been walking down a tough road."

Tears gathered at Liz's lash line, and she swiped at them with one hand. "We got some tough news this week. We'd been holding out hope that one of us would be able to donate."

"With all the stress we've been under, my blood pressure is all over the place and I'm ineligible," Charlie admitted, getting choked up. "God, I would do anything for our little girl, but I… I've failed her." His voice was jagged with anguish.

"My tissue results have ruled me out, too," Liz revealed, her voice low. "Even though Lorelei has a pretty common HLA type, I'm not a match."

"I'm sure that was disappointing news," Katie empathized.

"They put us on the transplant list, and she's scheduled for dialysis several times a week until they find a donor," Liz explained. "Mentally, it's exhausting because you are basically waiting to benefit from the misery of another family. It's not something I would wish on my worst enemy."

Katie braced and then reached out a hand to squeeze Liz's forearm. "I'm so sorry you have to go through this right now." Her vision blurred completely, then cleared. Dazed, it took several moments for her sight to return. Needing more information, Katie studied Charlie's features and reached out to brush against him with her fingertips. In the flash, she saw Charlie running with a limp Lorelei cradled in a fireman's carry in his arms.

Her eyes widened, and she gulped against the knot forming in her throat.

"We wanted to have an entire house full of kids when we got married," Charlie revealed. "But we struggled with infertility." He reached out to squeeze Liz's hand.

"It took six rounds of IVF to conceive," Liz recounted. "And a hundred thousand dollars."

"But it was worth every penny," Charlie interjected.

"It was." Liz nodded. "We waited for two years to get an appointment at Blackwell Reproductive Health. When we met Dr. Blackwell, I just knew our dreams of having a family would finally come true."

"Dr. Blackwell? I met him last week," Katie recounted, remembering the controlling man who was very different from the one Liz had just described. "Kandied Karma catered the dessert bar for his fundraising event."

"He's an absolute legend in fertility endocrinology. We struggled to conceive for years. I was thirty-seven when we finally got pregnant with Lorelei. That man is a miracle worker."

"Even now, seeing the fate she was handed," Charlie explained, "We wouldn't change a thing. Being Lorelei's father is a gift. Getting to watch her grow up every day has been the greatest joy of my life." Charlie swiped at his teary eyes with a heavy sigh. "I'm sorry to be so emotional." He apologized, "It's not natural to outlive your children."

"Honey, don't do this to yourself." Liz offered him a

smile and reached out to stroke his cheek, then turned to Katie. "Charlie was so certain he was going to qualify as a live donor. We're both crushed."

He looked down to hide the tears welling in his eyes. "But being here is a welcome respite," Liz said and pointed to the kitchen through the patio door where Beckett had pulled the sprayer from the sink and was shooting water at Lauren while Lorelei shrieked with laughter. "I love seeing a smile on her face."

"It's hard to have a bad day around Beckett," Katie answered, watching the interaction. Distracted by the flashes of truth that circled her brain relentlessly, she was now more confused than ever.

"I used to think the most difficult part of parenting was when they became adults and didn't need you anymore, but watching her lose her mobility and having to rely on us again is the most helpless I've ever felt as a parent."

"I can't imagine," Katie empathized.

"If we don't find a donor, this might be her last Christmas," Charlie said.

"Don't say that," Liz interjected.

"It's the truth, and we've been hiding from it for too long," he said, as his tone grew more somber. "We need a miracle, and we need it now."

Nine

At the Castanova Compound, Thanksgiving was barely a blip on the radar. Zoya sat at the head of the expansive wood table alone. A private chef walked through the doors carrying a tray with a silver cloche. He was bare-chested as she'd requested, and she suppressed a grin as he set the plate in front of her. Her fingers were bare, and she walked them down his torso, dip by delicious dip of his washboard abs.

"Dessert, perhaps?" she asked.

"As you wish," he agreed with a wicked grin.

He was young, barely twenty, and the highway in his head was blissfully simple. She pressed her fingers against his abs again and got a five-figure number. He was simple, but he would have a long life. She intended on making their evening romp so memorable he'd be reminiscing about it in the nursing home one day.

He pulled the cover from the dish, and the scents of sage and golden brown turkey wafted up to her nostrils.

Zoya briefly considered asking him to prepare a plate for himself and join her, but quickly cast off the idea when he knelt beside her and nibbled on the soft curve of her neck. She closed her eyes, savoring the sensation. Her two greatest pleasures—men and food being delivered at the same time. It should have made her ecstatic with joy, but it was a confusing letdown. She pushed the plate away in favor of the more titillating feast of pleasure next to her.

He was a gorgeous Nordic blond. His skin was deeply tanned, which only made his teeth contrast more brightly. She tugged on the string behind her back to loosen the tie that held her cleavage hostage and beckoned him closer. Her skin was dewy and youthful and he made quick work, brushing kisses on her flesh and burying his head in her chest. He delivered a network of feather-soft kisses across her skin, then pulled back with a salacious grin. Standing back up, he pulled a chair from the table and set it next to her. Picking up her fork, he cut a small bite of turkey and scooped up some sage and sausage stuffing, then held it up for her.

"Can you dip it in the gravy?"

He nodded eagerly and followed her directions. It was divine. The salty skin of the turkey and the sweeter notes from the caramelized onions and celery from the stuffing melded together in her mouth. She chewed, then swallowed. Playfully, she dipped her finger in gravy and offered it to him. He licked it off slowly, sucking and savoring every drip as a welcome fullness gathered between her legs. Sex always had the ability to idle her bustling brain, and she craved the quiet. Her thoughts had been whirling since her meeting with Lilith. Since her awakening, she didn't have the luxury of sleep anymore, nor the unconscious respite it offered. Instead, over the years, she'd learned to calm her racing mind in carnal ways.

He stood and removed his apron. Her eyes lingered below his hips to where his formidable package was gathering strength, length, and girth. He reached toward her and pulled her to her feet, and then she led him to her bedroom chamber, where he made her legs quiver for the next two hours. Before he could develop an attachment, she put him on her plane with promises to see him again, a promise she never planned on keeping.

With her mind quiet and clear, she showered and dressed in a flowing silver robe. She sat cross-legged in her meditation space and, feeling melancholy, hummed the notes of an ancient Ukrainian lullaby. It was the one she'd sang so long ago to Nadia when she was an infant nursing at her bosom.

Holidays had become masochistic. They were days Zoya felt her skin was paper thin and her memories burned then blistered. When the ache of missing her daughter was especially poignant, and the slightest reminder would fill her with unbearable agony. She punished herself with the pain anyway and connected with the energy of her ancestors as she visualized Nadia's face in her mind. Tears gathered at the corners of her eyes, and Zoya's skin began to glow and emit light. She floated up, levitated, first an inch off the ground, then two more. Her white hair flowed down her shoulders and out from her head in waves as she gently floated in a sea of stars surrounded by a wave of lavender light.

"Mother." The word she'd longed to hear for decades startled Zoya from her meditation, and she fell hard to the ground as she dropped from the astral plane back to the physical one. Her curiosity was piqued as it sounded just like her daughter's voice. She concentrated harder, stilling the heartbeat thrumming in her chest.

"Mother."

Glancing around the space, Zoya searched for the source, her adrenaline rising.

"I don't think she can hear me." It was Nadia's voice explaining, but as if she was speaking to someone else just out of Zoya's earshot. Before she could shout "I can!" another raspier voice that was craggy from too many drags on the pipe she favored cut in, "Zoya!" It was accompanied by two sharp clapping noises. "It's Olena. I'm here with Nadia, and we have an important message for you."

"Olena?" Zoya was in shock.

"Still your breathing and concentrate. Conjure Nadia in your mind's eye."

Stunned, Zoya followed Olena's directions and envisioned a picture of her daughter in her mind. Her long, flowing, ebony hair and her quick laugh, which was a melody she longed to hear again. She'd tried for decades to connect with Nadia on the other side. To hear her beloved daughter's voice for the first time since she'd passed made her heart drum in her chest. She squeezed her eyes tightly shut and visualized Nadia as she remembered her, radiant and alive, her abdomen swelling with life.

"Nadia? Is it really you?" She dared to dream, hyperaware of the lyrical way the syllables floated in a wave, mesmerizing her. "If this is a delusion, I pray I never awaken from it."

"It's me, Mother." Nadia's voice wavered as Zoya faltered in her concentration.

"We've only got a few minutes!" Olena said, snapping her fingers at Zoya. "Pay attention, child! We have important matters to discuss."

Zoya squeezed her eyes shut again and, with total focus and concentration, brought the image of her daughter to the forefront. When she opened her eyes, Nadia floated in the ether, a rippling mirage close enough to touch. Standing beside her was the diminutive Olena, looking impatient as usual.

A cry escaped Zoya's lips, and she reached out to Nadia. There was sadness that traced the lines of Nadia's striking features, and Zoya felt her daughter's hand slip into her own as the connection began to radiate heat. Instant tears sprung up in her eyes as she cradled the warm hand between her palms, unable to speak for several long minutes. She brought their hands to her cheek and closed her eyes, savoring the sensation. She'd yearned to hold her daughter's hand again, and to feel it cradled between her own took her breath away.

"Oh, my sweet girl, how I have missed you!" Zoya cried. "I have never forgiven myself for failing you."

"It wasn't your fault. The body has weaknesses, but the spirit doesn't." Nadia shook her head sadly.

"If only I'd been able to take you to a hospital. You wouldn't believe the medical breakthroughs that are available today."

"The if onlys will kill you, Zoya," Olena interjected.

"They nearly did," she admitted, remembering the dark days afterward. On the timeline of her life, the period after Nadia's death was stoney and black. Relentless despair had consumed her so completely that simple tasks like breathing were all she could accomplish for days.

"How I have begged for your forgiveness for letting you down. For not being able to save you. It was the greatest failure of my life."

"You didn't fail *me*, but you failed my daughter."

The truth spilling from her daughter's lips was a dagger to Zoya's heart. Nadia pulled her hand away, and Zoya covered her face with her hands to prevent an emotion she hadn't felt for decades from spreading across it. Shame. With great effort, she slid her eyes up from the floor to meet Nadia's glowing form.

"Darling, I tried."

"You didn't try hard enough." Olena's words were resolute, leaving no room for interpretation. "There is no replacement for a mother's love, but you could have done better. The child deserved more." The truth stung.

"Is that what you think as well, my love?"

Nadia's lips pressed together and, after a long moment, she gently nodded as her voice lowered. "My sweet Yuli was taken from me and entrusted to your care."

"I did my best."

"No, you let bitterness and anger consume you," Olena reprimanded her. "Yuli was a helpless baby who had no one else in the world. You should have stepped up for her."

"It wasn't my fault," Zoya argued, backpedaling, ignoring Olena, and beseeching Nadia with every fiber of her being. "My heart was broken. The pain of losing you consumed me, and every time I laid eyes on her, it reminded me of all I'd lost."

"All *you* lost?" Nadia asked, "What about me, Mother? I lost everything that day."

Zoya couldn't argue her point. She hung her head in contrition. "I fought my way through those days, consumed by grief and fear. You do not know the lengths I was forced to go to keep us both alive."

"That's not true. Through the veil, I watched the events unfold in real-time." Nadia looked away. "I have so many unanswered questions."

Zoya shivered at the memory. "I can't go back there. To that time in my life when fear was my constant companion."

"What a disgusting display of weakness from a woman I thought was the epitome of strength!" Olena accused, and Zoya felt herself wilting in anguish.

"After you awakened, you were bequeathed every

financial tool and luxury a mortal would ever want, and yet you still could not open your heart to my daughter. How could you?" Nadia cried.

"You know about the awakening?"

"Of course I do. We're all here, all the women in our bloodline who have since passed. There are no secrets when your soul is set free. We are gathered together, and the veil between the living and the dead allows us to see, but we cannot conspire to affect the outcomes."

"You've seen *everything*?"

"Everything." Nadia nodded as her voice caught.

"Turns out the Life and Times of Zoya Castanova is the most binge-able must-see-TV on the other side," Olena said with a harsh cackle. "Some of those moments should come with a XXX rating. They were so filthy, but I just couldn't tear my eyes away."

Nadia winced. "I didn't have any trouble." Even in the presence of Olena's injection of levity, the weight of the past hung heavy on their hearts. Nadia scrubbed her face with her hands and let out an anguished sigh. Hearing the sadness and frustration in her daughter's voice further silenced Zoya. "The mother who raised me was warm and nurturing. Yuli never knew that woman."

"She died the moment you did, and I buried her with you," Zoya revealed bitterly as tears broke free and raced down her face. She brushed them away angrily. "I will not apologize for the woman I had to become in order to survive."

Nadia pressed her lips together in an attempt to hold criticism in, so Olena spoke up in her stead. "We were willing to forgive your transgressions when you had few resources, but after you awakened, you were freed from survival mode thanks to the shrewd investments I made."

Zoya's forehead knotted up in confusion.

"Who do you think scooped up the compound for pennies on the dollar after the crash of 1929? We might have met each other in a brothel, but I had bigger dreams for our legacy. You were given luxuries the women in our bloodline have only dreamed of!"

Nadia found her voice and scolded, "But instead of building a bridge to Yuli, you pushed her away."

"It was all I knew," Zoya admitted. "After decades of struggle, I didn't know how to live any other way. What was left of my heart died the day Sally died. After a lifetime of loss, it dwindled into a pit of nothingness and I didn't know how to reverse it! I was stuck!"

"It was Yuli who was stuck! With you!" Nadia shouted. "She was sixteen years old the day you sent her inside her birthday box! You had to know the truth would destroy her." She locked eyes with Zoya again. "Your cruelty knows no bounds. You drove my daughter away when she was still a child!"

"That's not how it happened," Zoya cried. "She hid away in the cargo hold."

"So many excuses." Olena spat on the ground.

"You didn't even look for her."

Zoya's gaze shifted away. "What do you want me to say? That I'm sorry? I started my life over in a new *country* where I didn't even speak the language when *I* was sixteen."

Nadia barked out a wry laugh. "And look how well you turned out." Zoya waved her hand away as if swatting away an annoying fly.

"If you've come to beat me up, darling, let me save you the effort. What's done is done."

"You're selfish," Nadia stated. "Instead of turning toward Yuli, you turned away and then spent decades trying to fill your life with the idle pursuit of pleasure. How did that feel, Mother? Did it fill the pit of despair that took up residence inside you? Did your lust for revenge and justice keep you warm at night?"

"It was empty, but safe," Zoya admitted in a small voice.

"Are you safe *now*?"

"No," she whispered.

Nadia stood and turned away from Zoya, placing her hands on her hips. Olena took a step closer and crossed her arms across her chest.

"The division between you and Yuli must end. It is not healthy for our bloodline or for our future legacy."

"There has been too much water under the bridge." Zoya felt embarrassed by the criticism of the much older woman. "How do you rewrite a century of animosity?"

"That will be your question to answer," Nadia said sadly. "We cannot do it for you. We can only provide encouragement and an opportunity. You and Yuli have to do the work."

"But it's too late."

"It's never too late," Nadia offered, and she turned to face her mother again. Zoya's gaze shifted over to Nadia's, and she tried to open her heart.

A heart so stunted by hate she didn't know if it was possible, but she felt compelled to ask, "How?"

"There is a rare celestial event that is happening soon, and it will open a portal between the living and the dead for a short period of time."

"What event?"

"The *Fioletovy Mahiya* happens in early February."

"The what?" Zoya struggled to translate the Ukrainian words that used to be so familiar when she was a child.

"Roughly translated, it means the purple magic. It is a planetary and lunar alignment that has not happened for centuries," Olena shared. "On that night, we can pass from the astral plane to the physical one and back again. But only for the twenty-four hours when the moon is full."

Zoya shifted forward, her interest evident, and asked, "Are you saying I will be able to hold Nadia in my arms again?" Nadia's glowing form flickered.

"Yes, you will share the physical plane together for that solitary day," Olena answered.

Zoya gasped with joy and covered her mouth with her hands as emotions raced through her, and then addressed Nadia, her voice cracking. "I'll have one more day with you?"

"Yes. It is a rare second chance to mend the past and heal the wounds of our family."

"Is it not enough to simply enjoy each other's company? Must we take on the devil's errand of rewriting the past, too?" Zoya dared to ask. "The hate is not one-sided between myself and Yuli. We've been pitted against each other for years."

"It isn't hate. It's fear, it's hurt, and it's distrust. All of these can be rebuilt if you are brave enough to do the work," Olena explained as Nadia shone brighter.

Pride welled up in Zoya, and she argued, "It is not fair for me to shoulder all the blame. Yuli participated in the war, too."

"I suppose that is true, but now we have an opportunity to right the wrongs and we must not squander it. I can see it already coloring your interactions with Katia. It has to stop," Olena demanded.

"Katia's been poisoned against me!" Zoya cried. "Yuli only sees what she wants to see."

"That may be true." Nadia nodded. "But Yuli's motives are always pure. Yours, however, are not."

"I wouldn't even know where to begin," Zoya mumbled, realizing the spirits of her daughter and great-grandmother would not be swayed from their mission.

"Katia needs to see the truth. Go to the archives and send her two music boxes on the eve of the next full moon. The night you buried Nadia and the day we met in Chicago," Olena instructed.

"I highly doubt she'll accept a gift from me."

"Katia's seen your darkness, but she's never known its origin. It's not an excuse, but it will give her great insight. Katia is the best of all of us. Her forgiving heart will discern the truth. Now, we must go." Olena repeated her instructions firmly, "Send the music boxes to Katia."

Nadia stood and said, "The *Fioletovy Mahiya* is coming, and that is when we will all be together again. I love you, but I don't like what you've done to my daughter. Fix it."

Zoya felt her daughter's light pull away, and then she lost the connection. The warmth that radiated from the vision of her had cooled, and Zoya shivered in the chilled air, considering all that had been shared.

Trauma had drilled holes in her brain like Swiss cheese, and she'd lost whole years of her life in the depression that followed Nadia's death. They were a blurry blip on her timeline where she'd tuned out the world around her, keeping herself stuck in survival mode. They couldn't possibly be as bad as Nadia said, could they? She tried to recall them with some semblance of clarity, and there was just a gray fog that enveloped her during that time. There was only one way to find the answers she was seeking. She must go back inside the boxes before she sent them to Katia. Human memories were flawed and colored by the beholder's own prejudices. The boxes were a neutral third party that offered an unbiased glimpse into the past.

She was desperate to see Nadia again. To have one more day with her daughter where she could share the deepest feelings in her heart. One more chance to hold Nadia in her arms and show her she was loved and then say goodbye. A real goodbye that death robbed her of almost a century ago.

Zoya left the meditation chamber, pulled out the skeleton key, and sped to the archives. Inside, she stood frozen in front of the two boxes Olena wanted her to send that were glowing on the shelves. Steeling herself to travel inside, she braced for the pain she would experience anew.

"Rip it open like a band-aid," she muttered under her breath before cranking the delicate silver lever on the side of the purple box, apprehensive about what awaited her inside. With her thumb, she pried it open. Old-timey phonographic music spooled out as she drifted away.

TEN

Zoya tumbled out onto the hard ground, feeling an oppressive sorrow weigh her down. Standing, she dusted off her hands and followed the familiar path that ended at the modest stone cottage she'd purchased with the coins her mother had sewn into her slip before her father sent her away to America. She tiptoed inside the dwelling, following the sound of despair and cries from an infant Yuli.

From a distance, she watched her younger self wipe the blood and tears away from Nadia's still face. She washed her hair clean and braided it, wrapping chains of flowers into her beautiful raven hair. With a cotton cloth, Zoya washed the blood from her legs and cut away the placenta and cord with a sharpened knife. She was carrying out a loving ritual to restore the beauty of Nadia's cold body before burial. Trails of tears obscured her younger self's vision and never stopped spilling down her cheeks, hitting her cotton dress and darkening the fabric where they landed. In the shadows, Zoya remained hidden, swallowing against the lump forming in her throat. She was wracked with grief as all the emotions rushed back in, watching herself tend to her daughter for the last time.

In the shabby cottage, she observed her movements were tender with her daughter but gruff with the infant, letting Yuli scream in the basket she was resting in. Ignoring her cries, Zoya's expression scowled in rage and her eyes darkened. Zoya followed herself as she stepped outside into the hot July afternoon and walked her property, finally settling on the most beautiful location for Nadia's final resting place.

She rummaged around for a shovel and crammed her heel down on it, turning up the earth to dig a shallow grave underneath the dappled shade of the huge oak trees that studded the property. Wildflowers in blue and yellow dotted the fields underneath. With tears coursing down her face, she speared the dirt with the shovel and hoisted it out of the ground, shovel by shovel, like a machine. It took two hours of digging, and when she was finished, she was exhausted and filthy. Drained, she sat on a rock next to the upturned earth. The silence was deafening, and she remembered feeling numb inside. She swiped a dirty forearm across her eyes and then stood and began the journey back to her cottage. As they walked closer, Zoya heard the infant wailing in the distance, but it didn't make her younger self hasten her pace.

"The babe would be better off in the ground with her

mother," the much younger Zoya remarked. Out of eyesight, Zoya had to cover her mouth to stop her gasp of surprise from escaping. It was a shocking revelation she did not remember uttering.

Inside the cottage, the scent of blood still clung to the air, a coppery aroma tinged with smoke from the fire that had long been extinguished. Zoya paused, then walked to the basket near the hearth where the baby screamed for sustenance. She plunged her hands into the basin of cold water and rubbed them together to clean herself before grabbing the metal pail and heading to the barn to milk her cow. Her movements were robotic and dazed, and from the shadows, Zoya watched her carry out basic tasks in a trance. As she completed the chore, the tears on her cheeks had dried completely and were replaced by a chilling calm.

The cottage was too far away from the nearest village to consider a wet nurse, so Zoya remembered she had no choice but to use cow's milk to feed the child by the spoonful. Holding the screaming baby in her arms, she watched herself try to administer the milk. Yuli's face was so red and contorted, her body rigid and bucking back, that Zoya had to force the spoon into her mouth. There was a sucking noise followed by a wet choking sound as the infant struggled to swallow the milk without the aid of a nipple. Her fat cheeks eagerly sucked, then choked on it, then promptly opened her mouth for more. After ten more spoons, she finally calmed. Satiated, the infant's body relaxed. Her eyes looked deep into Zoya's, and she reached out one tiny fist to connect with her. Instead of offering the infant a finger, Zoya glanced over at the bed where her daughter lay motionless.

"This was supposed to be your job," she'd said dully. "What am I to do with a baby at my age?"

She pulled the cotton flour sack tight against Yuli and then tucked her into the basket near the hearth and watched her doze off. She exhaled a heavy sigh, then rose and stretched her arms to the ceiling. Her bones cracked, yet she walked to the bed to gather up her daughter one final time. She drew strength from her rage, lifting her daughter like she was weightless. Zoya stepped from the shadows and walked past the sleeping babe and out of the cottage, her vision softened by tears. She followed behind her younger self, listening to her own voice as she spoke to her daughter one last time.

"It's our full circle moment, sweetheart. You began your life in my arms, and now I have gathered you in my arms once again to lay you to rest. I chose the most beautiful spot for you, my darling. In the spring, the birds will sing you lullabies, and in the summer, the wildflowers will burst forth with vibrant colors for you. But their beauty will always pale in comparison to yours." A sob choked the rest of Zoya's words.

A few minutes later, she was at the site and gently laid her daughter in the ground. She wrapped her arms across her body, straightened her braids, and placed a flower crown on her head. Once she was satisfied, she cut bouquets of wildflowers from the fields and showered petals on her daughter's still body. She sat there until the sun set lower in the sky, and then she blanketed her daughter with the earth. Behind a tree, Zoya's legs were wobbly, and she fell to the ground, clutching at fistfuls of flowers, her mind lost in a sea of despair that was threatening to close in on her. The emotions were as real and raw as if she were experiencing them for the first time.

"I don't want to leave you," younger Zoya cried, and she bent down and lay next to the fresh earth that now covered her daughter's body. "What kind of God takes away the light of my life?"

Darkness fell and Yuli's cries cued up again in the distance. A weary Zoya climbed to her feet to head back to the cottage. After brushing a kiss across her fingers, Zoya lingered at Nadia's grave a moment longer before walking down the path. Inside the cottage, she saw herself go through the motions of feeding Yuli, spooning small spoonsful of milk into the infant's wide mouth until she stilled and became silent and sleepy again. While Yuli slept, the younger woman studied her features in the candlelight, searching for some resemblance to Nadia's. The full mouth with a lush cupid's bow was not familiar. Her plump cheeks were unrecognizable as well. It was going to be hard to love an infant who didn't possess a glimmer of her daughter's striking beauty.

A seed of anger took root in her belly and began to grow. In her mind, she knew it was unfair to take her rage out on a helpless infant, but in her heart, someone had to pay.

In frustration, she yanked her heavy wooden table up on two legs and then let it crash back down to the ground, releasing a scream of frustration that awakened the child.

"Shut up! Stop it! You are driving me mad!" she shouted to the inconsolable infant and picked her up roughly. She fought the urge to shake the child to stop the incessant screaming. She palmed the back of the infant's head, resting Yuli's rigid body in her lap, shaking in fury. Yuli hiccupped and was silent for a long moment. Zoya looked deep into Yuli's eyes and asked, "How can I love the creature responsible for the death of the person I cherished most? I will never love you."

Yuli's cries resumed, and Zoya laid the infant back down, then fell against the wall and slid down, pressing her hands to her ears to stifle the screams. The pressure was building, and she balled her fists that hung like stones at her hips. She wanted to hurt someone, to strike a man and draw blood. Terrified of what she might be capable of, she stumbled out of the cottage, afraid to touch Yuli again.

"I will keep your child alive, Nadia. I don't think I can manage much more than that," Zoya muttered as she walked away to dispel some of the energy that crested in her belly. In the forest, she shrieked to release the pain until her throat was hoarse and she was depleted. Then she crawled back into the cottage, fed the baby, and went to sleep.

When her breathing slowed and became even, Zoya stepped from the shadows and crossed over to the sleeping baby. She leaned down and touched the baby's head as if seeing her for the first time. Her eyes darted over to the straw mattress where her younger self tossed and turned. Then she crept out of the cottage and started down the dirt path when she was whisked away.

Eleven

A week after Thanksgiving, the package Lorelei had been waiting for arrived.

"You got mail!" Liz chimed, her tone a smidge too cheery, as she carried a nondescript cardboard box to Lorelei's room and set it in her lap. "Anything good inside?"

"No, just beads for a bracelet I want to make for Callie."

"That's sweet of you, honey. Here's the box cutter. I've got to run some errands, and then I'll be home to make you some lunch." Liz brushed her lips across her daughter's cheek.

"Thanks, Mom." Lorelei waited until she left the room, then quickly cut through the packing tape and ripped open the box. She pulled the kit from Ancestrify out of it and felt a giddy thrill at the prospect of giving her father a meaningful Christmas gift he would cherish forever. Lorelei clutched the testing kit in her hands, filled with hope the results would unlock hidden chapters of their family's past and give them something positive to focus on.

Her hazel eyes sparkled with determination, though her body carried the weight of her relentless battle against the daily challenges imposed by chronic illness. Her PKD was like a parasitic twin, inescapable and draining, and she couldn't remember a time when she lived what most people called a normal life. The constant doctor visits and increasing pain had made keeping full-time employment impossible, and so Lorelei had been forced to move back into her childhood bedroom that hadn't changed at all since she'd left for college over a decade ago. It was a time capsule, and she felt like a giant back in her childhood bed with the white ruffle coverlet and posters of Ninety-Eight Degrees on the walls.

The isolation and loneliness made her world smaller and smaller until it was narrowed to the one hundred and fifty square feet of her bedroom. One by one, her friends disappeared. At first, they'd been understanding, but chronic pain was an isolating bridge few of them were brave enough to cross. Over the course of a year, the girls' night out invitations slowly dwindled as her friends witnessed the daily struggle Lorelei had to go through to make healthy choices instead of indulging in high-fat, high-sodium appetizers, and boozy cocktails. It wasn't her friends' fault. Being around a chronically ill person forces mortality into the spotlight, and most people don't have the stomach for it. Eventually, it was like she'd been banished to Alcatraz, and the only ones mentally tough enough to make the journey to the island were her parents.

Despite the physical pain and discomfort that came hand in hand with her condition, Lorelei fought a daily battle to keep her mindset positive, especially in front of her parents. They had sacrificed so much to take care of her, and it was the only reciprocation she could offer to face each new setback with a smile on her face.

At her last checkup, Dr. Pamulapti, her hematologist, delivered devastating news. Her father's uncontrolled blood pressure ruled him out as a donor, and her mother didn't have the necessary markers and tissue types to be an ideal candidate for kidney donation. The news had destroyed her father. Seeing his face crumple in the doctor's office while he tried to recover enough to smile at her had broken her heart. Her father, who was always such a hopeful presence, was now an extinguished candle, and she was desperate to rekindle his flame.

Charlie was proud of his ancestry. When she was little, she vividly remembered sitting on his lap as he paged through yellowing photo albums whose acetate pages were tearing from frequent use. Inside, perfectly spaced black and white photographs of his elders filled the pages. He would point to each one and read the neat penmanship identifying each person in the photo, and would regale Lorelei with outlandish stories about what life was like in the year written below it. He was a history buff and was fascinated by the past and learning about his ancestors.

To cheer him up from the devastating news the doctor delivered, Lorelei ordered the DNA kit, planning to surprise him with the results. She would bring his hobby into the twenty-first century by giving him the tools to create a digital family tree. Instead of paging through the faded photo albums, she could show him how to research each relative online and create a fuller picture of who they were and what their life was like.

Lorelei was eager to have a project to focus on that would help her father feel closer to his heritage, knowing her branch on the family tree was withering. With her physical limitations, she could not grow any biological limbs, but at least when she got her results, he could immerse himself in a historical world that held less despair than the present one.

She pulled the tubes out of the packaging and reached over to pump hand sanitizer on her hands, rubbing them together briskly. Then she cracked the seal and swiped her cheek with both swabs, sealed them in the return packaging, and rolled herself out to the front porch to await the mailman's always punctual visit. When she placed the package in his hands, she felt a little secret thrill. She'd lost so much of her autonomy. The illness had reverted her back to a child who needed constant assistance, and this act of independence delighted her.

Back in her room, Lorelei read the instructions, understanding the results would be posted to a secure website in three to four weeks. Then she tucked the paperwork into her childhood desk, hiding it from the watchful eyes of her parents. She loved them, but God they hovered. It was almost like she'd been turned to glass, and they tasked themselves with protecting her from injury day and night. She longed to go back to the days when she'd go an entire week without talking to them, and then on Sunday dinner would eat her mother's pot roast and carrots and make milk shoot out of her father's nose with stories about her blind dates or the chauvinistic men she'd encountered at work who thought they knew more about her job than she did.

After getting her diagnosis, Lorelei had been forced to lower her expectations to the basement in an effort to stay outwardly happy. Carrying the happiness of both of her parents along with her own was exhausting. She had always been the center of their attention, but now it felt suffocating. Like they had been shipwrecked deep in the ocean, forced to tread water, but now she was pulling them down with her. The guilt was overwhelming. She felt responsible for the sadness that now consumed them all as her condition worsened.

She rested her hands on her distended belly. The cysts had tripled in size and grown significantly during the last year. It was becoming torturous, being trapped inside her failing body. The frequent abdominal pain came in dull waves and sometimes lingered for days without relief, and the high blood pressure that accompanied it made her woozy even when she was seated. In her bedroom, away from her parents' watchful eyes, was where she allowed herself to fall apart. Outside it, she fought a daily battle to maintain a positive attitude. She owed that much to her parents. She was determined not to add to their pain.

When she'd entered stage-five, dialysis became a part-time job, requiring them to go to the hospital three times each week for half the day. It was a tiring ritual that was now the cornerstone of her life. Now at the top of the transplant list, they all waited on pins and needles for the phone call and the four words that would change their lives.

We have a match.

She longed to hear the phrase and to be able to see a future where her life was normalized. Lorelei understood PKD was never cured, but with a transplant, the quality of her life would improve drastically. She could cut the cord from the dialysis machines and get some of her independence back. Every day she woke up, the first words she said out loud were an affirmation.

"Today is the day we find a match."

So far, she had been disappointed, but each morning when her eyes opened, she repeated it, knowing one day their dream would come true.

When she asked the nurse how long a person with stage-five kidney disease could live on dialysis while waiting for a transplant, she was shocked to learn it could be as long as five to ten years.

Ten years. It was a dagger to her heart. The thought that she might be required to waste away for an entire decade felt like a prison sentence, and she wasn't sure if she was strong enough to handle it. She pushed the brutal truth away and focused on putting good intentions out into the world, finding ways to keep the bitter reality at bay.

Lorelei couldn't wait to get her results from Ancestrify and to take the focus off herself and see the excitement return to her father's face. A few more weeks and they could spend their evenings researching their ancestors instead of dancing around her illness. Who knew what they would be able to learn? With so many documents and old newspaper clippings available now online, it would be like a treasure hunt for her father, and Lorelei was counting down the days.

TWELVE

Pulling on a pair of dark jeans embedded with spandex that made them comfortable, Katie chose a sunny yellow tank top from her closet and tugged it over her head. She was excited when Lauren called and wanted to spend time with her on her day off, but when Katie pressed for more details, she wouldn't give any. Lauren wasn't the type for hand holding, and afraid she would retract the offer, Katie quickly agreed. She was content to tag along, no matter where they were headed, because it was quality time with Lauren, and quality time with adult children didn't happen often.

Two minutes before Lauren was due to arrive, Katie swiped a mascara wand through her eyelashes and raked her fingers through her hair. Her reflection in the mirror revealed the white had now claimed over seventy percent of her thick hair, with the raven hue only visible around her ears. Soon, she would be as white as Yuli, and she decided that wasn't bad company.

Her Apple watch vibrated on her wrist with a notification from her newly installed security camera—there was a new car parked in her driveway. "She's here!" Katie said aloud, then bent down to pat Arlo on the head, grabbed her purse, and rushed out of the house. With a warm grin, she settled into the passenger seat of Lauren's Lexus. "So, are you going to tell me what this super-secret errand is all about?"

Lauren laughed. "Good to see you, too, Mom."

Katie leaned over to brush a kiss against Lauren's cheek. "Sorry, honey. My curiosity has gotten the better of me."

"I decided to freeze my eggs," Lauren answered, getting right to the point. "Actually, I decided last year, but it's taken this long to get an appointment with Blackwell Reproductive Health." The hairs on Katie's arms stood on end hearing the name Blackwell, but she pushed the feeling away.

"Oh?" Katie was surprised. "Why haven't you mentioned this to me before?"

Because I didn't want to get you on the baby train already.

Katie heard the thought, and even though it was true, she was saddened by the truth Lauren had been compelled to keep her desire for motherhood a secret.

I didn't even tell Tom.

Tom again? Katie thought, looking for a way to draw the truth out of Lauren. "You are glowing, sweetheart," Katie offered. "If I didn't know any better, I'd think you were in love."

Lauren froze and blinked twice. "Nope," she lied after a long pause. "It might be the new eye mask I've been using. I'll send a link for it over to you."

"I'm not really into lotions and potions anymore," Katie admitted. "After the chemical peel, I decided to put an end to the madness and embrace the crow's feet."

"Good for you," Lauren remarked. "I still have to fight the good fight."

Katie stole glances at her daughter as she drove the rest of the way to the office. The serendipity of the universe was astounding. It seemed Dr. Blackwell kept popping up in her life like a bad penny. There had to be some correlation to her rebalance for the Sandersons, but she couldn't figure out what it was.

Lauren pulled into a parking spot in front of the ultra-modern black and glass, angled building that was edged with green shrubbery and immaculately landscaped with large palm trees. The modern glass front doors were a work of art in their own right, with their hand-forged gold pulls. Their impressive height made you feel miniaturized as you walked through them and into a well-lit lobby that was filled with plants and a fountain. It set a lush and fertile ambiance that didn't escape Katie. "Wow." Looking up at the ceiling that was elaborately plastered and covered with gold leaf, she commented, "This lobby is impressive."

Lauren agreed. "He's the best in the business, and Blackwell Reproductive Health has been around for decades. I'm not sure *when* or even *if* I'll need the eggs, but I wanted to be sure they were safe and sound with an organization that has a proven track record."

"It makes sense," Katie offered and followed Lauren into a pleasant waiting room. Within ten minutes, they were shown into an examination room, where Lauren was instructed to put on a satin hospital gown. "Whoa." Lauren's eyes were enormous. "It's so soft." She put it on and then sat on the examination table. "And the table is heated!"

"That's got to be the most flattering hospital gown I've ever seen," Katie remarked. It was a far cry from the ill-fitting cotton sack she remembered from her own gynecologist's office.

"The attention to the comfort of his patients is remarkable. It's one of the reasons Dr. Blackwell is the most sought-after fertility specialist in the Tampa Bay area," Lauren reasoned.

Two minutes after they were settled, there was a soft knock on the door.

"Come in!" Lauren called out, and the door opened to a tall, dignified gentleman with a thick shock of silver hair. Dressed in a white lab coat and navy blue trousers, his warm smile put them at ease instantly. Following behind his confident stride into the room was a nurse who looked to be in her forties. He held out one manicured hand with fingernails trimmed short and buffed to a shine. "Lauren Beaumont? It's nice to meet you. I'm Dr. Blackwell." Then he turned to Katie. "And this is?"

"We've met, actually. I delivered truffles to your fundraising event a few weeks ago. I'm Katie Beaumont."

She reached out to shake his hand and gulped when a tremor passed through her on contact. A vision flashed. Test tubes and petri dishes. A room that went on forever filled with bassinets and babies, with Dr. Blackwell standing in the middle of it. Katie had to force a calm expression on her face. It was a reading, but the jumble of images wasn't anything out of the ordinary. Confused, she sat on the seat he offered her.

"Of course! It's great to see you again. The chocolates were a hit!"

"Did you reach your goal?"

The muscle in his jaw twitched. "Not quite. But we're getting there."

Picking up on his discomfort, her next tactic was to try to butter him up. "Didn't you just receive a Lifetime Achievement Award for reproductive health?"

He visibly squared his shoulders and leaned closer. "That's right! How did you know?"

"We have mutual acquaintances. Liz and Charlie Sanderson? You helped them conceive their daughter, Lorelei?"

Jesus, Mom. Can we circle back to the real reason we're here? I wouldn't have had you tag along if I knew you were going to get chatty and monopolize the doctor's time.

Katie held up her hands. Lauren had a point. "I'm so

sorry. Let's get back to Lauren. I didn't mean to distract you. I know your time is valuable."

A smug smile curled up the corners of his mouth as he agreed with a curt nod and then sat on the rolling stool. He logged in to his computer as Lauren made small talk. "Thank you for seeing me and for actually being punctual. You have to know you're an anomaly in health care."

He laughed, revealing perfectly straightened and whitened teeth. "I figure if you wait almost a year to get in front of me, I owe it to you to respect your time as much as you've respected mine."

Katie listened to his words, but more importantly, kept her eyes focused on his actions. He was practiced and smooth. She got the impression she was watching a performance that had been honed and perfected over decades.

"So, tell me why you're here today," he began, and Lauren's brow crinkled in confusion, so he immediately added, "I like to hear my patients' desires in their own words."

"Oh." She nodded and continued, "I want to freeze my eggs to preserve my fertility."

"How old are you?"

"Twenty-seven."

"This is the perfect time to perform the procedure. It will yield the healthiest eggs with the highest chance for successful implantation." He shot Lauren another winning smile that seemed to put her at ease.

"I'm nowhere near ready to have a baby, but for me,

it's an insurance policy for my future. I don't know when I'll meet the right man and be in a place in my life where starting a family makes sense. Freezing my eggs will give me options." It was obvious Lauren had done her homework.

"That's so true," he said. "I can't tell you how many women I meet each week who wish they could go back in time and have this exact procedure performed at your age. The fact is, women are choosing to start their families later in life, but when a woman gets to forty, there is a drastic reduction in both the number of eggs that are released as well as an increase in birth defects. By the time many of them come to me, it's too late, and we have to bring in a donor egg so the biological component is missing. It's a shame. Having children is one of the greatest gifts God bestows on his followers, and I am grateful to help the faithful bring as many blessings as they can into the fold."

Great, he's a fundamentalist. Keep your mouth shut. He's the best of the best.

Katie eyed Lauren. Hearing her feminist-leaning daughter give herself a pep talk to stomach the doctor's remarks was unsettling.

"Is it customary to bring religion into a conversation about fertility?" Katie couldn't stop herself from asking. His jaw tightened almost imperceptibly as his eyes leveled on hers.

"This is a private practice. We don't have the same separation between church and state," he answered. "Why do you ask?"

"No reason. I was just curious." She tried to backpedal after Lauren shot her a cautionary glare. "Sorry. Please continue."

The nurse stepped closer to the doctor, leaning over him. Their body language was easy to interpret—Katie noticed an intimate familiarity in their proximity, the unnecessary touches, and the way their feet pointed toward each other. She briefly wondered if Gloria was oblivious to the threat. Having experienced the sting of betrayal herself, Katie felt a wave of empathy for her.

"Can you tell me more about the procedure and how the eggs are stored?" Lauren asked, eager to change the subject.

"Of course." He warmed up to the question and pivoted to the procedure. "Today, we will do some tests and get your baseline markers. We'll show you how to administer the injectable medications that will help promote ovarian stimulation and prevent premature ovulation. Typically, you'll need one to two weeks on the medication before your eggs are ready for retrieval. To determine when the eggs are ready for collection, you will have a vaginal ultrasound and an imaging exam of your ovaries to monitor the development of follicles."

Lauren nodded as Katie listened. His delivery was competent and educated. His long fingers laced together and rested on his leg that was crossed at the ankle. He wore a simple wedding band on his ring finger and another ring that looked like a quiver of arrows surrounded his pinky finger.

"Egg retrieval itself is a surgical procedure that is

done under twilight sedation. I'll administer a mild sedative through an IV and then extract your eggs with a long needle. It's non-invasive and the recovery time is minimal."

"Will it hurt?"

"There will be slight pain that can be managed with ibuprofen." He answered, "Now, on the day of the retrieval, you will feel groggy and need a ride home. You'll want to take the day off work and have your mother look after you. Meanwhile, your eggs are flash-frozen and stored at our facility for the moment when you are prepared for motherhood."

Lauren nodded.

"What if she meets someone special and decides to have a child the old-fashioned way?" Katie asked.

"That's the beauty of the procedure. It gives a woman options. In that case, you could donate them to an infertile couple or save them for later. Sometimes, women can struggle to conceive their second or third child. Egg freezing is simply an insurance policy you can utilize to create the family of your dreams. It is all about giving you the most options for your future."

"What about the side effects?" Lauren asked.

"Most women report none at all, but about twenty-five percent report PMS-like symptoms—bloating, cramping, and breast tenderness." He went on, "It takes two cycles to achieve the best specimens, and during the egg stimulation timeline, it is important to abstain from vigorous exercise, alcohol, and caffeine."

"Is there a limit to how long they can remain

frozen?" Katie asked.

"The longest successful thaw came after fourteen years, and many healthy babies have been born from eggs frozen for five to ten years. Is this within the timeframe you would consider motherhood?"

Lauren bit the corner of her lip, an overwhelmed signal Katie picked up on right away. "Can she have some time to think it over?"

Mom, I love you, but this is my decision.

The thought silenced Katie. She knew Lauren was an adult, but it was still hard to navigate her desire to help against Lauren's need to live her own life. "Sorry to butt in," Katie conceded and pressed her lips together to stop any more questions from popping out.

"With your permission, Nurse Miller will draw your blood to establish baseline hormone levels, and I will do a vaginal ultrasound to estimate how many eggs we can safely retrieve. Every month, a healthy woman in the prime of her reproductive years will lose around a thousand eggs. Typically, during an ovulation cycle, one egg from the thousands released makes the cut and is housed inside a follicle, which supports the egg within the ovary. What we are seeking to do with the injections is ramp up production. Would you like to start the process today?"

"Yes," Lauren answered, making a quick decision.

"Lean back on the table and put your feet in the stirrups," he instructed, taking the time to wrap the probe in a condom. "Don't worry, the gel has been warmed up to make you more comfortable."

"Thank you," Lauren said.

What the hell am I doing? Should I tell Tom I'm going to great lengths to preserve my fertility? No. Not a good idea. This relationship is new, and it might scare him off. I'll keep it to myself for now.

From her chair near Lauren's head, Katie heard the panic rising in her daughter's thoughts and had a hard time remaining quiet. She sat on her hands to stop herself from reaching out to squeeze her daughter's hand.

It's just an insurance policy. Relax.

Dr. Blackwell studied the screen. "Very good. I see twenty-seven antral follicles. You're an ideal candidate for the procedure. Once we get the blood work back, I can give you a better estimate of how many eggs we can expect to retrieve."

A few minutes later, Dr. Blackwell removed the probe and deposited his gloves in the trash after handing off the instrument to the nurse to sterilize.

"Do you have any further questions?" His eyes leveled back on Lauren, and he offered her his hand to pull her up to a sitting position.

"I can't think of any. Mom?"

Katie rose and held out her hand. She needed to make contact again. "Thank you for your time." He placed his hand in hers and gently squeezed. Katie recoiled when the flashes came into view.

Dr. Blackwell standing in his office with his pants at his ankles, the nurse on her knees with her hand curled around his erect member. Katie wrinkled her nose and cringed, shaking her head to clear the offensive image from it. Ick. Affair confirmed.

She pulled her hand away and discreetly wiped it on the back of her hip, eager to remove the lingering nausea she felt from intercepting his torrid desires from the skin-to-skin contact. He quickly left the exam room, and Katie turned away to give Lauren privacy to get dressed.

"What did you think?" Lauren asked.

"It seems a little extreme." Katie tried to soften the criticism. "I know you love to have options, but what happens when you meet someone significant? Will he feel the same way about your eggs being frozen in a laboratory?"

"But what if I don't meet the right one?" Lauren reasoned. "I know I want to be a mother someday. This will allow me the best chance to become one."

"Maybe you should wait? Think it over, and if you still want to go through with the procedure, you can find a better time to fit the preparatory regime into your life. It seems very rigorous."

Lauren's jaw tightened.

This was a mistake.

Katie was crushed by the thought and quickly added, "I'm sorry, honey. I don't mean to be a wet blanket." She reached out to squeeze Lauren's hand and saw her shoulders relax.

"I respect your decision, sweetheart, whatever it is. Let me know how I can help."

THIRTEEN

The next afternoon, Katie was massaging her weary lower back with the pads of her fingers in Kandied Karma's kitchen after closing. "Another record-setting day! We might need to hire more people if this keeps up." Even in her cushy sandals made of recycled yoga mats, the arches of her feet ached.

Yuli disagreed. "It's simple supply and demand, Katia. We'll raise the prices a little each week until demand slows. More employees only means more overhead and handicaps our profits. With the holidays coming up, we stand to have our most successful year yet!"

Katie marveled at her grandmother's astute business mind. It had taken moxie to open Kandied Karma in Chicago after her husband passed, his widow-maker heart attack accomplishing its goal. She'd transformed her grief into growth, and Katie was often awed by her resilience.

Humming to herself, Yuli walked to the cooler and pulled out a charcuterie board wrapped in saran wrap she'd made at home. She then took out two glasses and the bottle of Horilka she kept in the freezer. Deftly, she poured two fingers of the Ukrainian liquor into her glass and took a sip before sliding the other to Katia.

Seeing the snacks, Katie's famished stomach growled. "You're a lifesaver!" She pulled up a stool next to Yuli, stifling a yawn. Arlo circled, then settled in a heap of caramel-colored hair at her feet. "I've had a hard time sleeping since I ate the lavender truffle on Thanksgiving. I keep running over the visions I saw and the information the Sandersons shared with me. I'm so confused," Katie admitted.

"Don't fret," Yuli consoled. "Interpretation is often the most difficult part of the assignment. Walk me through it."

"So far, it's nothing conclusive, just scattered bits and pieces. I received flashes from both Charlie and Liz at Thanksgiving, and they confided they used IVF to conceive Lorelei, which explains the gynecologist's office I saw. And Lorelei's illness explains the flashes I saw of Charlie's grief over a missing child, but there are no concrete steps Karma is asking me to take."

"Hmm," Yuli mumbled while she sipped the libation with her pinky up as she mulled the flashes over.

"Lorelei needs a transplant, but as an only child, their

options are limited. Charlie was ruled out due to a blood pressure issue, and Liz isn't a compatible match. The guilt rolling off of him at Thanksgiving was palpable." Katie let out an exasperated sigh. "How do we help them?"

"Patience," Yuli answered. "Karma will reveal the answers in her own time. It is not something that can be rushed."

"How can I have patience when, every day, Lorelei is getting sicker?" Katie asked. She took another sip and nibbled on a caraway seed cracker when inspiration hit and the perfect solution appeared. "You're a healer. Can't you just cast a spell and restore her health?"

Yuli tucked a wayward strand back into her white bun at the base of her neck and shook her head in a sad no. "I can slow the progression and give her more time for traditional medical intervention, but I cannot stop death. If the reaper is coming, he can be delayed, but he can never be denied."

Katie sighed, frustrated by their limitations. She took a bite of peppery prosciutto and sharp white cheddar on a slice of cucumber. Letting go of the Karma puzzle for a moment, she switched gears. "I need your help."

"Of course."

"How do you deal with the barrage of thoughts from the people surrounding you? Thanksgiving was brutal. There was so much chatter inside my mind. Beckett's graphic internal dialogue of Marisa's more attractive physical features was hard enough to stomach. But I also learned Lauren was daydreaming about someone named Tom, and Marisa's anxiety was off the charts. It's draining to be an empath and to process everything in your own head, let alone the private thoughts of everyone around you."

Yuli nodded. "Detachment. You need to still your mind and let your attention drift away from the distractions so you can focus it back on yourself. It's harder for you because you have spent a lifetime catering to others, so your factory setting is to allow their problems to overshadow yours. Instead, you need to set a boundary. Right now, you are bombarded with their thoughts because you are sharing the same space. When you set a boundary, it moves them out of your head and back into their own space where you can decide to participate in the flow of information or not."

"I always thought detachment was selfish, but I must do something. I cannot keep living like this."

"Just calmly recenter and release. With practice, they will quiet to a murmur. Then you can tune in and out like a radio station."

"How come I can't hear your thoughts?"

"You can only hear ordins because they are weaker," Yuli told her. "Supernatural beings have more layers of protection woven into their consciousness."

"Just think, if you could hear Zoya's inner dialogue," Katie mused, equally curious and terrified at the prospect.

Yuli shivered at the thought. "That is one bleak and dark place. I imagine it like Dante's ninth circle of hell —a frozen tundra of emptiness devoid of all emotion."

Katie yawned again, then admitted, "And Lauren threw me for another loop. She's decided to freeze her eggs." Arlo sat up and barked twice, then whined and lay back down. "She invited me to her egg banking consultation at Blackwell Reproductive Health and, oddly, while I was there, I got a reading from the doctor."

"You did?" Yuli's eyes narrowed and darted around the room. Katie studied her face, which was pinched with fresh worry and lost in thought.

"What is it?"

"It's all connected."

Katie dismissed her concern right away. "Dr. Blackwell is the same doctor the Sandersons used to conceive Lorelei, but since it's the oldest practice in the Tampa Bay area, and has the highest success rate, it's probably just a coincidence. Lauren always does her research."

"Doubtful," Yuli mumbled and poured two more fingers of cola-colored liquor into their glasses. "What did you see?"

"Test tubes and petri dishes. A room filled with bassinets, each housing infants, that went on forever with Dr. Blackwell in the middle of it." Katie clamped her lips down and her cheeks pinked up. "There were a couple more obscene visions, too."

"Like what?"

"Dr. Blackwell in his office being pleasured by his nurse."

Yuli was visibly shocked at the admission. "I'm

curious, Katia, why is Lauren consulting a fertility specialist?"

"Sounds like it's just an insurance policy. I think she's starting to hear her biological clock tick now that she's almost thirty. You know Lauren has always been my cautious overthinker."

"A baby would change everything," Yuli said thoughtfully. "Especially a female one."

"How so?"

"Our longevity is only allowed to span three supernatural generations. With the birth of your female grandchild, there will be a passing of the guard. Zoya will weaken, die, and pass into the spirit world to join the eternal coven."

The truth made a tendril of fear wrap around Katie's heart. "Do you think she would be selfish enough to jeopardize her own lineage?"

"We've both learned Zoya is capable of anything." Yuli added, "She is still indebted to Lilith. I doubt she would even pause to reconsider sacrificing your grandchild to the dark goddess if it set Sally's soul free."

Katie shivered. It was a chilling admission, yet she knew Yuli was speaking the truth.

FOURTEEN

The next evening, while Katie was having her weekly dinner with Frankie, getting all the gory details of her new relationship with Harry, Zoya arrived at Katie's house to have her weekly check-in with Arlo.

He ran into the guest room where Marisa was watching television and whined, then raced out and jumped at the patio door.

"Do you need to go outside?" Marisa asked, her voice quirking up at the end as she walked to the kitchen. He answered with two sharp barks. "I think that's a yes." He barked again. "Okay, okay!" She patted him on the head and slid open the patio door to let him out. His tags jingled as he ran down the stairs to the pool patio, where Zoya emerged from the shadows dressed in black. Her white hair was braided and coiled into a bun at the base of her neck, and she pulled a wide-brimmed hat down over it.

"Why are all the lights on?" Zoya asked. "Katia should still be out with Frankie." She glanced down at her watch. "She usually doesn't come home for another several hours."

"Marisa is home," Arlo said, sitting at attention at her feet to deliver his weekly report. "She started looking for an apartment though and will be moving out after the New Year. I know you didn't come here to discuss Marisa's future plans." He glanced over at the door anxiously. He couldn't dawdle in the backyard forever. Marisa would come looking for him soon. "Can we focus? I don't have much time to file my report."

"Out with it then," Zoya urged, circling her hand in annoyance to speed things along.

He glanced around and, confirming they were out of earshot, said, "I'm afraid I have some disturbing news."

"Speak, you imbecile!"

Arlo swallowed a growl at the insult and forced himself to continue. "Lauren is freezing her eggs to preserve her fertility. She took Katie to an appointment at Blackwell Reproductive Health a few days ago."

Zoya's eyes narrowed, and her mouth set in a hard line.

"You said you wanted to be kept informed of developments around potential heirs in the line."

"I did."

"I hope you can appreciate the delicate line I have to walk to stay your informant," he barked at her.

"Careful," she warned. "Remember who you are speaking to."

Irritated, Arlo stood and paced the patio, making distressed yips. "I don't like keeping Katie in the dark. It feels wrong. It's a betrayal of her trust and doesn't sit well with me."

"If you're intent on your freedom, then I will remind you your loyalty is to me, *not* Katia," she spat at him, frustrated with how fickle his allegiance was.

"But I love her," he muttered and lay down in a huff.

"Of course you do. You're a dog. She's imprinted on you. Your unconditional love for your master is built into your canine DNA."

"It's not that simple." He wanted to explain, but she shushed him, eager to move on to more important matters.

"Blackwell Reproductive Health," she repeated to herself, turning it over in her mind. She received the financial documents she'd requested from Dr. Blackwell a few days ago. Now, she had another reason to take a much closer look.

Arlo continued, "It might be a coincidence, but that name also came up at Thanksgiving. Dr. Blackwell was the one who helped Liz and Charlie conceive their daughter."

"Nothing is a coincidence," Zoya muttered to herself. She reached down and patted his head. "Very good. You may go." He bowed into a downward facing dog pose for one long moment, then stretched forward and sprawled his legs out behind him. Finally, he shook his coat vigorously and raced back up the stairs.

Zoya glanced around to make sure she wasn't being

watched before creeping out of her hiding place and hurrying down the street. It had always been a matter of time before the next generation would be conceived. The next supernatural female in their line would unseat Zoya as their mortal ruler, but she never dreamed it would be so clinical. The scientific and technological advancements she'd witnessed over the years were mind-blowing, but she was concerned about the consequences of defying natural selection. A genetically engineered baby would go against centuries of natural laws and, as guardian of the bloodline, she would never let that happen.

FIFTEEN

The first week of December, the immaculate streets of Aura Cove were filled with its residents, all joyfully attending the annual tree lighting ceremony. It was cooler, and it always made Katie laugh when the temperature dropped into the forties and native Floridians were scrambling to wear layers to stop their teeth from chattering. She'd gleefully surrendered her trusty midwestern parka when they'd first moved but regretted it when she found herself just as sensitive to cold snaps in spite of her formative years in the frozen tundra of Chicago.

The square was decked out in twinkling lights, and Christmas carols piped in from outdoor speakers, which were thoughtfully hidden in flower planters in front of downtown shops. Crowds poured through a tunnel of lights draped with sparkling tinsel. It was whimsical holiday décor, erected every November and removed in January, that bathed the surrounding area in a soft glow.

At Kandied Karma, Katie flipped the sign to closed and followed Yuli out onto the sidewalk. Yuli's long, green, velvet dress swept over the cobblestones and hid the black crocs on her feet. In her arms, Yuli carried a basket filled to the brim with individually wrapped truffles. Katie's deep purple skirt swished in the light breeze as she strolled with her grandmother to the town square.

The brilliant, flocked Christmas tree stood twenty-five feet tall, and each branch was adorned with twinkling lights and vibrant ornaments that sparkled and shimmered against the twilight sky. The scent of freshly baked sugar cookies and cinnamon wafted through the air, and Katie closed her eyes and inhaled deeply to drink it in.

"Gosh, I love this time of year," she whispered as a group of children filtered around them and encircled the tree. A few moments later, their teacher hummed on a harmonica, then dramatically swept her hands from side to side, conducting the choir, who began to sing classic Christmas carols. A block away, the soft jingle of sleigh bells added a nostalgic soundtrack and was accompanied by the clip-clop of a horse-drawn carriage. Riding in the carriage was a fully decked-out Santa Claus, complete with a long white beard and wearing white gloves that waved to the scores of children lining both sides of the street. Their hands strained toward him, their excitement swelling with the music and their shouts of joy tumbling together.

"Christmas was so much fun when the kids were

little," Katie mused, lost in sweet memories for a moment.

"It's nothing compared to how wonderful it is through the eyes of your grandchildren," Yuli said with a warm smile. "You'll see."

"Someday," Katie said wistfully.

"It will happen sooner than you think."

Katie's eyebrows arched, and she turned to Yuli with a grin. "Do you know something I don't?"

"Of course not, Katia." Yuli laughed. "Do you think I could keep such a secret from you?" She covered Katia's hand with her own and gave it a squeeze.

As the song finished, the crowd fell into a hushed silence, eagerly awaiting the tree-lighting ceremony. The mayor of Aura Cove, a regal woman with long gray hair, climbed the steps of the podium wearing a red Chanel suit. An assistant handed her an ornamental switch and she leaned toward the microphone and said, "Ladies and gentlemen, distinguished guests, and beloved citizens of Aura Cove, tonight, we gather here in the spirit of unity and joy to celebrate the annual tree lighting ceremony. It is a time-honored tradition that brings us together, reminding us of the warmth and light that radiates from within our vibrant community. Children, please help me count down."

"Five, four, three, two, one!" Mayor Whitely flipped the switch and the jubilant smile on her face wilted when nothing happened. She flipped the switch back and forth two more times in frustration before handing the useless gadget back to her assistant. With forced cheer and a clenched jaw, she beamed at the audience who was murmuring among themselves.

"Ladies and gentlemen, please accept my sincere apologies for this unforeseen technical glitch," she announced, her voice steady, "Don't worry! We will not let this moment dampen our spirits or dim our enthusiasm!" she exclaimed, and the crowd burst into applause.

"Looks like Mayor Whitley could use a little help," Yuli said to Katia with a wink. She reached into her pocket and pulled out a delicate hand-carved ornament. It was an intricately painted wooden female nutcracker dressed in traditional Ukrainian finery. She handed it to Katia, who was surprised when it vibrated in her hand. Katie heard a crackle and was enchanted by the golden sparks shooting out of it.

"It's so beautiful," Katie gushed, looking down at the bauble.

"The nutcracker is a symbol of protection and good luck in Ukrainian folklore," Yuli explained as Katie reluctantly handed it back. "This ornament holds the light of our female ancestors, and tonight, we will share that spirit with everyone."

Yuli stepped closer to the tree as the mayor filled the dead air with apologies. Her voice strained and her frustration increased as each minute of the delay dragged on. Katie saw Yuli reach up and place the ornament on the highest branch of the tree she could touch.

Thinking quickly, the mayor addressed the audience

again through pursed lips, "Citizens of Aura Cove, while we work diligently to rectify this setback, let us remember the true essence of this ceremony. It is not solely about the flickering lights or the radiant tree, but about the light we each carry within."

"Children, please lead us in *O Christmas Tree*. Maybe we can coax her to turn on with flattery!"

The crowd tittered, and the children started to sing. Around them, the celebration goers joined in, their voices swelling in unison with the chorus. Katie watched Yuli at the tree, feeling a tingle spread from her core to her limbs in the presence of Yuli's heightened supernatural energy.

"Let's try this one more time," the mayor announced, clearly ruffled by the persisting delay. She glared at the nervous electrician who was fiddling with an electrical box a few feet away. With a decisive nod, she reached for the switch as Yuli reached up and cradled the nutcracker with both hands before small bolts of electricity surged from her fingertips into the ornament. Finally, a flicker of light raced around the tree, circling higher and higher as the audience erupted into applause. Their cheers echoed throughout the square.

Katie applauded with the crowd as relief washed over the mayor's face. Her tight smile was replaced by a calmer one as she joined in the celebration. Even though the mayor's embarrassment had transformed into a sense of triumph, Katie knew who had performed the real miracle.

Yuli turned away from the tree and walked toward Katia, a wide smile on her face.

"You saved Christmas," Katie whispered into her ear after pulling her grandmother into her arms. Yuli pulled back with a knowing grin as those surrounding them dispersed to gather around tables for hot cocoa or to get in the long line to see Santa.

Katie and Yuli picked their way through the crowd, pausing to hand truffles to everyone they met. It was one of Katie's favorite Christmas traditions in Aura Cove.

"Mama!" Beckett's voice grabbed her attention, but what was even more attention seizing was seeing Marisa's arm threaded through his. Her curious eyes met Marisa's, whose cheeks pinked up as she extracted her hand gently from his forearm. Unaware, Beckett opened his arms wide to pull his mother in for a hug.

"Are you two…?" Katie couldn't help but ask.

"It's not a date or anything," Marisa rushed to add. Hearing her explanation, Katie saw Beckett's face fall like it had when he was a little kid and had his dream crushed by a mega dose of reality.

"It's none of my business," Katie offered. "I'm just happy to see two of my favorite people out enjoying one of my favorite Christmas traditions."

"Mayor Whitley is usually unflappable, but we were close enough to the action to see her sweat!" He laughed. "She was losing her mind up there! I bet heads are going to roll at the electric company tomorrow."

"Saved by the magic of Christmas," Yuli said with a sparkle in her eye.

"It *was* magical, wasn't it?" Katie agreed with a secret grin as she glanced at Yuli, who offered her a sly wink. Seeing the long line forming behind them, she turned to Beckett. "Looks like the crowd is getting restless. We need to hand out the rest of these before there is a mutiny." He brushed a kiss on Katie's cheek, and she offered parting instructions.

"Make sure to give Marisa the full experience."

Oh, I will if she lets me.

Katie stifled the urge to gag at his innuendo. She would never get used to the ick factor of hearing her son's innermost thoughts. "I'm referring to the Christmas at Aura Cove tree-lighting experience," she clarified, and he just grinned. As she watched them walk away, Beckett reached out to hold Marisa's hand. She blocked him by shifting her handbag into it and increasing the distance between them. Katie winced. It was obvious the poor kid was going to get his heart broken again.

"Do you have any good ones left?" Oz interrupted her train of thought, stepping closer, and holding Shasta in his arms. He bent down to set her gently on the ground.

"We only make good ones," Yuli said with a smile. She pulled out a golden orb. "Double caramel dark chocolate ganache with a chili oil center."

His eyebrows raised. "Yum! Challenge accepted. I have no doubt it will be worth the Pepcid."

Yuli nodded and put it in his outstretched palm. "Merry Christmas."

"How did your weekend at The El Conquistador go? Were you able to connect with any spirits?" Katie asked, making conversation. "I've been eagerly awaiting your next podcast."

He frowned. "It was kind of a bust, but we're going to try again. My buddy just made a significant investment in some new ghost hunting equipment—an electromagnetic meter, a digital voice recorder, and a thermal imaging camera." He rattled off the list quickly. "It should capture any voices of spirits attempting to communicate with us." His eyes twinkled with boyish excitement at the prospect. "We figure since the El Conquistador has been in existence for over a century, someone interesting has to come forward."

"We can't wait to hear all about it," Katie told him as Yuli waved him goodbye. She pointed over to where a couple was standing, cuddled up with their arms wrapped around each other. "I think that's Frankie! Let's go say hi."

They took a few steps closer, and when Frankie casually glanced over her shoulder; she flashed them both a bright smile. "Merry Christmas!" she hollered as Katie's eyebrows arched up at the obvious public display of affection. Harry untangled his longer limbs from Frankie's waist, and Katie pulled her in for a hug.

"Merry? That's usually my line."

Frankie grinned as she pulled back. "Can't help but be merry around this one." She was dressed in an ugly sweater with tinsel dangling from stars precisely placed at her nipples. Katie swatted at the dangling tinsel playfully, and Frankie circled her torso and shimmed her shoulders, causing the tinsel to whip around in a circle like a burlesque dancer. Harry was wearing an equally offensive sweater featuring a well-endowed snowman whose carrot nose had been relocated lower and offered her an amiable smile.

Katie reached into the basket and pulled two truffles out. "I present our flagship flavor, caramel macchiato." She placed them in the center of his open palm, and his grin widened as he looked down at them.

A second later Frankie whisked both of them away with a devilish grin.

"Hey!" Harry cried, a wounded look on his face

"Gotta be faster on the draw, Willey! Artisanal chocolate waits for no man!"

"I guess I'll go console myself at the hot chocolate stand. Anyone want one?"

"No, thanks," they answered, and he snaked his way through the crowd and away from them.

"So?" Katie asked, leaning in. "You didn't call me today, no texts, nothing."

"I'm sorry, I was a little busy." She cupped one hand and leaned closer to Katie's ear. "A little busy on my knees, paying homage to Harry's Willey." She snorted at her own joke.

Katie chuckled and winced at the revelation. "I don't need *all* the gory details, but I *am* happy for you, Frank. He seems like a good fit."

"It's a perfect fit!" She gleefully ribbed Katie with her elbow. Frankie leaned in, pinched the corner of her lips together, and spoke out of the other side of her mouth. "That's what she said." Pleased with herself, she dissolved into a fit of giggles.

"You're the worst." Katie laughed, shaking her head.

"He's the male version of me."

Katie grimaced and ribbed her back. "Isn't one Francesca Stapleton in the world enough? God save us all."

"It's just so effortless. I've never been in a relationship that is so easy."

"Wait." Katie took a step back. "You're in a relationship?"

Frankie's cheeks pinked up, and she grinned. "Yeah, we made it official a few minutes ago."

"At a *small town Christmas tree-lighting ceremony*?" Katie teased. "Are you trying to live inside a cheesy Hallmark movie?" Katie dropped her voice to a lower register, infusing it with the dramatics of a movie trailer announcer. "She was a lonely office administrator, and he was a small-town police officer. Will the Christmas spirits conspire to bring them love again late in life?"

Frankie chuckled. "Sweet Jesus. When you put it like that." She stuck a finger down her throat and made a gagging face.

"Stop," Katie said. "Enjoy it. You seem to have found a good one." She pulled her friend in for a hug and noticed a substantial line was forming again behind

Yuli. "We better hand out the rest of the candy. Come by next week for dinner and let's catch up!"

"You got it!"

Katie turned away with a smile and spent the next several minutes passing out truffles. She felt a warm tingle in her fingers, and a golden spark shot from her hand. Letting out a confused yelp, she quickly stuffed her hand in her pocket to hide it from the crowd, and when she glanced up, she saw Yuli had witnessed the bolt of energy. Quickly, she tugged Katie away from the crowd as her smile diminished, sending the first wave of panic through Katie.

"What is happening to me?" Katie asked, immediately picking up on the shift in her grandmother as they quickly darted between the shops and into the darkened alley behind Kandied Karma.

"I'm not sure," Yuli said. "The moon is a power source in our bloodline, and the upcoming *Fioletovy Mahiya* concerns me."

"The what?"

"The *Fioletovy Mahiya*. It's a once-in-a-lifetime lunar event happening in February. Think of it like the fullest moon you've ever witnessed on steroids."

"Oh, dear." Katie felt a shiver pass through her.

"Have you ever heard nurses fear full moons because it brings out all the crazy?"

"I thought it was an old wives' tale."

"The legend is true. Just think, if the crazy comes out on a run-of-the-mill full moon, what kind of insanity do you think will accompany a rare lunar event like the *Fioletovy Mahiya*?"

Katie sighed. "You might have a point."

Yuli held out her own palms where golden sparks lit up the darkness. "It's not just you. Our energy is gathering and is unpredictable. We must be cautious." She pressed her hand to her chest. "Do you feel it?"

Katie nodded. "Honestly, I thought it was my new whole food vitamins. I *do* feel stronger, and my energy levels are rising."

"If we are being impacted this way, just think about how it's affecting Zoya."

Katie's eyes bugged in terror. "What do we do?"

"Nothing. Right now, we watch and we wait," Yuli said. "A powerful event has already been set in motion. Sooner or later, the path will reveal itself to us."

SIXTEEN

The night after the Aura Cove tree-lighting ceremony, Lauren was in her townhouse mixing drinks and humming to herself. She plucked a lemon from the bowl on the table and began to zest it onto a plate. Then she sprinkled in white sugar, cut a slice of lemon, rubbed it on the rim, and dipped the glass into the mixture. In a stainless steel tumbler, she added Ketel One Vodka, simple syrup, and lemon juice to the ice, placed the top on it, and shook the mixture together.

The doorbell rang, and she walked over to the frosted glass front door. Pausing at the mirror, she smoothed her hair and returned to the door to open it with a huge grin. On her front step, Tom stood over six feet tall, dressed in a well-tailored charcoal gray suit. Seeing her, his eyes lit up, and he swept her up into his arms and swung her into a circle, depositing her back on the ground with an endearing grin. He breathed into her hair, and she melted into his chest then tipped her chin up to kiss him. He laced his fingers through her hair and deepened the kiss, leaving them both breathless when they finally pulled away.

"You have no idea how impossible it is to keep my hands off you at the office every day. They should award me a medal for my self-control."

"You better not!" Lauren protested, balling her fists and beating on his chest with them. "We'd have to file a Consensual Relationship Agreement with HR. I don't want everyone at work having insight into my private life."

"You mean ours, don't you, sweetheart?" he teased with a grin, and Lauren felt her cheeks flush red with embarrassment as he pulled her close and pressed his lips to her forehead.

"Fine. Ours," she mumbled in agreement.

"Under threat of perjury, counselor, will you acknowledge you are in a relationship?" She pushed him away, laughing, then gave in to his desire to label it. Smiling, he tugged her back into his muscular arms and laughed into her kiss. "Good. Now that we have that settled, we can move on to more important matters. I've been dying to debrief you all day."

Lauren groaned. "That's the worst legal pun in the history of legal puns." He laughed the criticism off. His easy going good nature was one of the qualities Lauren loved most about him. She had a tendency to be too intense and overthink situations, which was good at work but had never served her well with love.

"Does our confirmed relationship status mean I finally get to meet your family?" he asked, prodding her. "You've already met my mom."

Lauren winced as she pulled back. "My family is a lot. You're an only child. I don't think you're ready for that kind of scrutiny."

"I *am* ready," he declared without pause. "*You're* the one who isn't."

Eager to distract him, Lauren picked up the martini glass and held it up. "Lemon drop?"

"My favorite." He accepted the glass and took a sip. "Delicious. But I see what you're doing here, Beaumont."

"What?" Lauren asked innocently, batting her eyes up at him over the rim of her glass as she took a long sip. Then she playfully and slowly unbuttoned her jacket and pulled it off, draping it over the arm of her sofa, revealing her lacy silk camisole underneath. She winked at him and dropped one strap off her shoulder, savoring the sexy groan that escaped from between his lips. "See something you like, counselor?"

"I *love* everything I see." He tugged Lauren closer, his hands wrapped around her trim waist, and asked, "Are you hiding me? Or embarrassed to be seen with me, or something?"

"What? No. Of course not," Lauren scrambled to answer. "It's just that I am selective about what I share. The last guy I brought home had a harder time saying goodbye to my family than he did to me." She brushed her lips across his. "I'll promise I'll introduce you soon, but I need to do it in my own time."

"Okay," he relented. Bending forward, he brushed his lips over her collarbone and, with one finger, traced down the long elegant line of her neck. It was a seemingly innocent gesture that generated a pool of heat between her legs. She dropped the other strap, and he buried his face between her breasts, rubbing her nipples with his thumbs until they poked against the silk. With a sexy grin, she grabbed his hand and tugged him down the hallway and into her bedroom. A few minutes later, and by the time they were both completely naked, Lauren's doorbell rang. Her long legs were wrapped around Tom's waist, and he was mere inches from entering her when another chime of the bell made them groan in unison.

"Ignore it," Lauren insisted, refusing to let go, and kissed him again. "It's probably a door-to-door salesperson."

The doorbell rang six more times in quick succession.

"Agh!" Lauren groaned and untangled herself from Tom. "Give me two seconds. I'll get rid of them, and we can pick up where we left off."

She wrapped a robe around her body just as there were three more quick, jaunty jabs to the doorbell. "I'm coming!" she shouted.

"Not without me!" Tom hollered and then laughed at his own joke from the bedroom.

"Good one!" Lauren said as she strode down the

hall. Once at the front door, she tightened the belt on the robe and yanked on the doorknob. Her jaw dropped as shock froze her completely still.

"Mom?" Lauren said, surprised. "What are *you* doing here?" After a long pause, knowing she had no other choice, she stepped aside reluctantly to invite her mother into her living room.

"I was in the neighborhood and wanted to see if you could grab a quick dinner. Did you eat yet?"

"I just got out of the shower," Lauren lied.

"But your hair is dry," Katie noticed.

"It was a quick body wash. I only wash my hair every fourth day."

Shit. Shit. Shit.

Katie heard the thought and was instantly confused.

"I wish you would have called first."

Because then I wouldn't have to hide the naked man currently lying in my bed.

Katie's eyes widened at the thought. She had to pinch her lips together to force the surprise from registering on her face.

Lauren kept stealing glances down the hallway. The cut lemons and bottle of vodka resting on the countertop presented the perfect opportunity for Katie to pry information out of her tight-lipped daughter, "Are you entertaining?"

"Just having an after-work bubble bath and martini," Lauren lied.

Katie took a couple of steps down the hallway, her

curiosity getting the better of her. This was getting ridiculous.

"Where are you going?" Lauren asked, panicked, as she chased her mother down the hallway and ducked between Katie and the closed door.

"Honey, it's obvious you are hiding a man in your bedroom. Is it too much to ask for you to introduce him to me?"

Lauren blushed from head to toe, her cheeks searing with heat.

Katie offered Lauren a warm grin and made an X over her heart. "I promise, one little intro and I'll get out of your hair."

Lauren groaned. "I can see this is the only way to turn this bus around. Can you at least give us a minute?"

"Of course," Katie agreed. "I'll wait out in the kitchen."

Lauren disappeared into her bedroom, and a few minutes later, Katie heard heavy footfalls nearing as they walked down the hallway. Lauren had thrown on a t-shirt and a pair of jeans and was followed by an attractive dark-haired man. He flashed her a winning smile and extended his hand. Katie reached out, and when their skin connected, she got a flash of Lauren, her face partially obscured by the cathedral-length bridal veil that floated behind her in a breeze. It was a vision that filled her with joy. She held on to his hand to make the moment last longer.

"I'm Tom," he stated, his smile wavering the longer Katie clutched his hand. She saw a flash of Lauren raising her hand-tied bouquet in triumph before a blissful walk down the aisle where rows of their friends and family were packed into folding chairs draped in fabric and crystals.

"Mom! Let the man go." Lauren pulled her out of her dreamy vision. "You're making it weird."

"Oh, sorry," Katie apologized with an embarrassed smirk. She focused intently on Tom, who met her gaze unflinchingly. "It's so great to meet you," she gushed. "I'd love to have you both over for dinner sometime."

"We'll see," Lauren answered.

"We'd love to come," Tom asserted, seizing his chance while dodging a glare from Lauren, and his response made Katie grin. Her daughter needed a take-charge man who would force her out of her comfort zone. "Would you like a cocktail?" He moved over to the countertop and washed his hands before slicing fresh quarters of lemon.

"Why, yes I would!" Katie beamed and took a seat, settling in now that she'd been officially invited. She watched as Lauren's eyes flashed a fervent warning that Tom ignored, then landed on hers.

So much for leaving after one little intro.

Katie heard the thought and briefly felt guilty, but pressed on, eager to know more about the man who could be Lauren's future husband. "How did you two meet?"

"We work together." Lauren finally gave in, seeing her mother had no intention of leaving, and pulled out the chair next to Katie.

"I'm sure I don't have to tell you this, but your daughter has a brilliant legal mind. She's the best patent lawyer on the East Coast."

Lauren flushed pink from his praise. "Maybe not the East Coast, but certainly in Tampa Bay." Tom placed the lid on the stainless steel shaker and started shaking it playfully, shifting from side to side like it was a tambourine. Then he set it down and rimmed three fresh glasses with the lemon zest and sugar. With tongs, he plucked ice spheres from her freezer and equally dispersed the liquid, then offered glasses to Katie and Lauren. His familiarity with Lauren's kitchen did not go unnoticed.

"Yum," Katie said after her first sip. "You certainly know your way around a bar cart."

"I put myself through law school on tips," he offered. He took a long sip from his glass and then set it down. "Give me the dirt on this one." He pointed at Lauren.

"She's always been my most serious child," Katie confided. "Since she was seven, Lauren set her own goals, and I have watched her achieve each one. She's driven and brilliant."

"Mom." Lauren shifted in her seat, uncomfortable with all the praise.

"Lauren has always been a foodie. When she was five, I remember her asking if we could make creepies for breakfast. Do you remember that?" Katie turned to Lauren and asked.

Lauren nodded her head, chuckling at herself. "Yeah. Crepes. I wanted to make crepes."

Tom reached out and brushed Lauren's cheek with his hand, grinning. Katie loved he was unafraid to show his affection for her daughter, and she melted.

I am going to marry this woman.

Overhearing Tom's thought gave Katie a thrill in her belly. She turned to him with fresh eyes.

"You're an attorney, too?"

"Yes, ma'am," he confirmed. "I was in the Army right out of high school and then went to law school."

"Thank you for your service," Katie said. "Do you have a big family?"

"No." He shook his head. "I wish we did, but it's just Mom and me."

"Does your mother live close?"

"Yep. She's in St. Pete. She moved here when she got out of the service."

"Your mom is a veteran, too?"

"West Point grad even!" He was obviously proud.

"That's incredible! I'd love to meet her!" Katie took the last sip of her lemon drop. She thought for a moment, then snapped her fingers. "I've got it!"

"Oh, no!" Lauren groaned, then face palmed. She knew her mother well enough to know what was coming next.

"Say you'll both join us for Christmas dinner."

"We're in!" Tom answered before Lauren could object. To soften the blow, he sweetly pulled her off the stool and hugged her from behind, wrapping his hands around Lauren's waist and drawing her close. It was a gesture that Katie could already see happening often when her belly was rounded, nine months deep into her first pregnancy. It was hard not to fall in love with Tom.

"That's fantastic news!" Katie took a final sip and stood. "Well, I better get going, Arlo won't walk himself." She opened her arms to hug Lauren, then turned to Tom and offered her hand. He gently pushed it away and pulled her in for a hug. "It was great to meet you." Her fingers brushed against the skin on his neck, and she received a flash of him in a tuxedo dancing with a woman Katie knew was his mother by the way she cupped her hands to his face and gazed up at him with total admiration. Katie forced herself to pull away. She knew she'd already pressed her luck as far as she could with Lauren and didn't want to overstay her welcome.

"I'll send the details for Christmas dinner over to Lauren."

Lauren followed Katie to the door and gave her mother one last hug, leaving Tom in the kitchen.

"Are we still on for tomorrow?" Katie asked, keeping her voice low.

"Yeah." Lauren leaned in closer to whisper, "He doesn't know, and I'd like to keep it that way for now."

"Totally understandable," Katie answered. Lauren shut the door behind her and returned to the kitchen where an amused Tom waited.

"Look who's wrangled an invitation to the family dinner." He gloated as he pulled her into his arms and nuzzled into her neck.

"You don't know what you're in for." Lauren giggled as his breath tickled her collarbone. "I tried to warn you."

He dismissed her fears instantly with a sexy smirk. "Now, where were we?" Tom asked with a mischievous glint in his eye.

Lauren reached down and unzipped his zipper. "Here." She kissed him, relishing the feeling of him hardening. "I think we were here."

SEVENTEEN

The next morning, Lauren sat in the waiting room next to Katie at Blackwell Reproductive Health. Cranky from the hormone injections she'd been secretly administering to herself, she flipped through a *Parents* magazine to pass the time. Its articles on cord blood banking and advertisements for the Gerber Grow Up Plan were incredibly sobering.

"Cord blood banking?" She sighed. "I didn't even consider it. God, there is so much to think about when you bring a child into the world."

"Are you okay?" Katie asked, concerned that her normally stoic daughter was nearing full-blown panic mode. "You don't have to go through with this if you are uncertain."

"I'm sure." She cut her mom off with her razor-thin patience. "I've been stabbing myself with needles for the last ten days. There is no way I'm not seeing this through to the end."

Katie patted her hand and decided to keep her mouth shut. Lauren was the most decisive of her children and had already made up her mind, so to try to convince her otherwise was futile.

Lauren feverishly whipped through another series of pages in the magazine, and when one tore free, Katie gently pried it from her hands. "Relax, sweetheart. He said it's no worse than your run-of-the-mill cramps. I've got the heating pad at the ready and all your favorite snacks stocked at the house. Red Rageous Mike and Ike's, Mallow Magic popcorn, and the shrimp is marinating for those tacos you love."

"You're being so wonderful to me, and I'm a miserable bitch right now. I'm sorry, Mom," Lauren apologized as tears gathered at her lash line. "I'm starving from fasting for this procedure, and the fertility meds are making me irritable. I'm crawling the walls right now and can't wait for this emotional roller coaster to be over." Her voice cracked.

"Oh, honey. Are you going to cry?" Katie asked. It was unnerving to see her usually unshakeable and confident daughter breaking down in public.

"It's these damn hormones. Not to mention I've been on edge, hiding all this from Tom." She exhaled a heavy sigh and continued to explain. "We haven't been together long enough to scare him with the premature notion of fatherhood. He hasn't signed up for his all-access pass yet. Believe me, bringing up the subject of children too early in any new relationship is the kiss of death."

"I like to think I'm pretty great at reading people, and he seems like he has a good heart."

"He does. I just don't want to jinx it. Besides, working in the same office adds another layer of drama to all of this, and I'm not ready for my colleagues to have a front-row seat to the implosion of my personal life," she explained.

"Lauren Beaumont?" the friendly nurse said, standing by the door.

They both got to their feet. "Did you want me to come with you, sweetheart?"

"No, you're strictly here to drive the getaway car."

"Okay." Katie sat back down as Lauren was led away by the nurse, who promised to notify Katie when the procedure was finished. Katie sat in the waiting room filled with anxious women. Their deepest fears and worries were a sad chorus that infiltrated Katie's thoughts.

The last embryo. If this one doesn't implant, I'll never be a mother.

Where are we going to find forty thousand dollars for the next round of IVF?

I am barren, and my uterus is hostile. Fantastic.

I'm not the problem. It's Gary and his lackluster swimmers.

Some women were alone while others sat next to their partners, who despondently focused their attention on their phones to pass the time. A few provided comfort and reassurance, draping their arms across their wives' shoulders for support. Katie closed her eyes and tried to tone down the sadness and fear. Hearing thoughts was obtrusive. It was a loud soundtrack of overlapping fears in her head, making it hard to concentrate on reality. Oddly enough, her new ability gave her new compassion for the schizophrenic. It was exhausting to live in an internal world so heavily trafficked.

One by one, women in the waiting room were called by name and disappeared behind the swinging door, and a new batch of replacements appeared like clockwork as she fought through the process of quieting their thoughts in her head. It was a mind-control boot camp. In the time it took for the procedure to wrap up, she got much better at it, though it was draining and she couldn't wait to leave. When they called her name, she popped up and grabbed her purse, eager for the lesson to be over.

The nurse brought her back to Lauren, who was dressed and sitting in a wheelchair. She had a sleepy innocence to her expression that reminded Katie of the day she'd had her wisdom teeth extracted.

"Hey, Mommy," she said with a goofy, sleepy grin. Katie melted. Lauren hadn't called her Mommy since she was in kindergarten.

She bent down next to the chair. "Hey, sweet girl. Now we get to leave, and you get to have some food."

"Hooray!" She punched one hand in the air. Katie turned to the nurse.

"She might get a little loopy or weepy-eyed, but it's perfectly normal. The best thing to do is head straight home and let her go to sleep." The nurse grabbed the handles of the wheelchair and pushed Lauren down the corridor. "The valet has already pulled your car up."

"Wow, it's a well-oiled machine around here!" Katie had forgotten she'd handed off her keys when they'd arrived a few hours earlier.

"That's why we're the highest-rated fertility clinic on the East Coast," the nurse said, bursting with pride. She stepped behind the chair and disengaged the brake. Katie followed her out into the warm sun of the December day. Lauren slowly got to her feet and climbed into the passenger seat of the Beetle while the nurse handed over her discharge papers then left with the empty chair and a wave.

Katie started the car and eased into traffic, stealing glances at Lauren as she navigated their route home.

"Tom. I want Tom," Lauren cried, teary-eyed from the passenger seat.

"I know, sweetheart."

"He's the one, Mom," Lauren admitted, and Katie smiled. The light sedation made her usually closed-off daughter very chatty, and she wasn't going to miss out on this opportunity.

"How do you know?" Katie asked.

"He feels like warm socks on a cold day fresh from the dryer," she gushed. "Tom is my best friend and there isn't anything I want to hide from him." She looked down at her pelvis. "Oh, no! What if I ruined everything by keeping this secret?"

"If Tom is the one, he won't hold it against you. You can tell him when you're ready and he will understand."

"How did you get so smart about healthy relationships when you and Dad were a toxic mess?"

Katie's cheek ticked, and she sucked in her breath. Lauren made a good point. "Maybe that's exactly how I know a healthy one when I see it. It's the opposite of what we had. When you know what you *don't* want in life, it makes it crystal clear what you *do* want."

"I do," Lauren mumbled as her eyes closed. "I do want to marry that man."

"Someday, you will," Katie confirmed as a satisfied grin tugged at the corners of her mouth. Lauren calmed down and relaxed into the seat, letting fresh air wash over her face from the ride in the convertible. Katie made the final turn onto her street and pressed the garage door opener to park inside.

"We're home." Katie unbelted Lauren's seatbelt and led her inside as she stifled a yawn.

In her own bedroom, she pulled back the comforter and lowered the shades to darken the room. She patted the bed and Lauren climbed into it. Katie tugged the comforter up under her chin, tucking her in like she had after a nightmare when Lauren was a child.

"It smells like you." Lauren closed her eyes and started to drift off peacefully.

Katie brushed her lips across Lauren's forehead and turned out the light.

"Sweet dreams, my beautiful girl."

"I hope when I'm a mom, I'm exactly like you," Lauren mumbled, and the statement made Katie's heart burst with love. Maybe she hadn't made all the right decisions in her life, but they ultimately landed her here. She was loving this new stage of her life and looking forward to the possibility of grandchildren. It was a desire she'd tucked away in her heart, never pressuring the kids to settle down and reproduce. If Beckett, Lauren, or Callie wanted to become parents, she wanted it to happen because *they* chose it, not because they caved to societal norms. But now that she'd gotten a glimmer of hope from Lauren, she had to be honest with herself. She *did* want to be a grandmother.

Eighteen

Dr. Blackwell opened his email in the pre-dawn hours of December seventh.

"Dammit," he swore under his breath as he studied the screen in his darkened office while sipping on a cup of coffee. "Another one."

Quickly, he turned away from the offensive report and made a hushed phone call, even though no one was present to overhear it.

"This is Genesis. We have a broken arrow," he said. "I'll upload the file to the server."

Frustrated, he punched the button to end the call. He pulled a set of keys from his desk drawer and slid open the filing cabinet, then pushed the medical record folders forward to access the false bottom of the drawer. With one hand, he lifted up the metal that formed the bottom, pulled the hidden files out, and set them on the desk. He created a new folder and labeled it, taking several minutes to write copious notes in perfect penmanship on a sheet of paper inside. Then he printed out the report on his screen and tucked it safely away before returning the folders to the cabinet and placing the metal bottom back over it. It incensed him that his most productive hours of the day were being wasted on trivial bullshit.

Needing to clear his head, he stood, stretched, and walked over to where the 3D model of the East Coast Integrated Blackwell Method Reproductive Center rested since the fundraiser. He was still six million short of their funding goal and couldn't break ground until it was secured. It had been radio silence since his accounting firm had sent the requested documents over to Ana Castanova, and he was sick of waiting. How dare that ungodly woman ignore him? His lips twisted up in contempt at the memory of their interaction. Women like her were jezebels, emotional harlots whose control of precious financial resources infuriated him. They had no business at the helm of an organization nearing a net worth of four hundred million dollars. Men were far better decision-makers.

"I know it is not the place of your lowly servant to question your blessings, but why, Lord? Why?"

On his phone, an alert sounded. He picked it up and noticed that the liquid nitrogen was low again. Quickly, he strode back to the lab and put on the protective gear necessary to handle the hazardous liquid. The act only enraged him further. He was stuck in the weeds with irritating problems cropping up almost daily.

Frustration roiled in his belly. He was so close to

realizing the vision of the future God called him to create. Having to slow to a turtle's pace in order to jump through the regulatory and financial hoops on earth made him long for the ease the bible promised him in heaven.

Dr. Blackwell felt anger roar through him, intensifying every second. He was becoming a volcano on the verge of eruption and was desperate for a release. He glanced down at his watch. Diandra would be in early, and he could take his frustration out on her. Maybe afterward, a clearer head would prevail. Maybe he'd invite her to come along with him on his monthly check-in at his other clinics. There was important business to discuss with his closest advisors in light of this morning's discovery. He deserved a treat, and God knows he couldn't make brilliant decisions in such a heightened state of arousal. He yearned for a release and the quietude it would offer.

Diandra was barely in his office for five minutes before he drew the blinds, bent her over his desk, and was deep inside her.

Yes. This is what he needed to carry on his mission. This is what he deserved.

Nineteen

Katie slept fitfully and struggled through a restless early December night, tossing and turning. On the eve of the next full moon, nightmares plagued her, and she woke up with a start, drenched in sweat with her heart pounding. She stripped down to bare skin, depositing the clammy pajamas into a hamper, and splashed some cool water on her face. Sweating from the lingering hot flash, she pulled the remote from her bedside table and turned on the ceiling fan. She flipped the pillow over as her heavy head sank into the cool side, and finally drifted away into a blissful, deep sleep.

On her nightstand, the clock flipped to 3:00 a.m., the witching hour. In Katie's dream, rainbow prisms of color washed by as she crossed the sky like a shooting star. Galaxies of lavender and gold spun around her as she rocketed through the atmosphere, the exhilarating sensation greater than any roller coaster she'd ever ridden. When she reached her destination, she drifted to the ground like she was riding a feather. The grass tickled between her toes, and Katie glanced around to get her bearings. She noticed she was standing in a field of wildflowers and lavender as far as her eyes could see. In the distance, she heard the rush of a waterfall and started toward it as the sun danced through the rippling sea of wildflowers that were as high as her waist. The natural beauty surrounding her was completely immersive, and she felt love filling her heart.

"Katia."

It was a sing-song whisper from an unfamiliar voice, and she searched the field, looking for the woman who'd uttered it. She quickly glanced over both shoulders and laughed at herself when she realized she was alone. Katie breathed in the air, heady with the scent of fresh blossoms as she continued to follow a path snaking through the flowers to get closer to the sound of the water. She rounded the corner and felt the breeze, and then a burst of fine mist hit her face. It was a welcome cooling sensation and she shut her eyes to savor it. She stretched her arms out from her sides and spun in a circle, lost in the soothing mist.

"Katia."

Hearing her name again, her eyes popped open and landed on a beautiful woman with long dark hair standing waist-deep in the middle of the lagoon. A female little person sat on the bank next to her, an odd old woman with stunted limbs puffing on a pipe dressed in a tailored men's suit.

The woman in the water raised one hand and beckoned Katie closer. Drawn to her, Katie tip-toed into the water, relieved when she discovered it was warm. Beneath the surface, schools of brightly colored fish swam together and then flowed back out again, and vibrantly-colored coral studded the ocean floor. The water was so clear she could see all the way to the bottom where sea creatures frolicked in full technicolor, a vision so breathtaking it was hard to tear herself away.

"Katia," the woman whispered again, and Katie pulled her focus reluctantly away and floated closer. The woman was stunningly beautiful, and when Katie got within ten feet, she immediately realized she recognized her.

"Nadia?" she asked, astonished that her great-grandmother was standing in the pool of water in front of her with her arms open wide, wearing a flowing dress and a warm smile. Katie reached for her but fell into the water with a splash when her hands didn't connect with Nadia's body. Seconds later, she regained her footing and rose to stand again, sputtering and embarrassed by the misstep.

The little woman roared with laughter from the shore.

"Sorry about that, sweet girl. I forget we are mere holographs," Nadia explained, tucking her hands behind her back to prevent herself from reaching out again.

"It's nice to finally meet you," Katie said. "What are you doing here?"

"All in good time, my dear." Nadia let her gaze rest on Katie. "No wonder my Yuli thinks the world of you."

"Does she know you're visiting me?"

"No, my darling." Nadia's expression changed. "I'm here because I need your help. The *Fioletovy Mahiya* in February is coming and will lift the veil between the living and the dead. It's a once-in-a-lifetime lunar event that offers the opportunity to convince my mother and my daughter to set aside their feud and reunite for the good of our coven."

Katie winced. "I'm not sure a rare lunar event will undo the damage that has been done between those two."

"We have to try."

Katie exhaled a hot breath between her lips and shook her head.

"We will only have twenty-four hours. It is my hope that, during this time, they can open up their hearts and forgive."

"In theory, that sounds like a grand plan, but Zoya and Yuli have decades of resentment between them that I'm not sure can be overcome in one night." Katie was wary.

"It has been difficult to see the divide and to witness the anger and animosity grow between the two women I love most in the world. I've been unable to help and have felt powerless watching it unfold, but now that we are being given this opportunity to right their wrongs, we must."

Katie hesitated. "I don't think it's possible."

"With enough love, anything is possible," Nadia declared. "Hatred eats your energy and has been a drag on both Yuli and Zoya. It has prevented them from stepping into the fullness of their supernatural abilities. We need to bring unity to the coven before Mother transitions to the next place, or she cannot enter into the eternal coven."

"The eternal coven?"

"That's where all the females in our bloodline gather, supernatural and ordins alike, after their mortal lives are over. Where all the secrets of our descendants are revealed and the playing field is leveled. It's where our souls exist for eternity."

The truth made Katie's head swim. "I have a whole lineage of female descendants gathered together in the afterlife?"

"Yes!" the little woman shouted from the shore. "It's one hell of a humdinger."

"Who is that?" Katie asked.

"Olena, she's Zoya's grandmother. She's famous for playing the men's game of investing in the stock market after the great depression and winning big. It's because of her fortitude that the Castanova Compound even exists."

"Wow." Katie regarded the little woman dressed as a man in a different light.

"Don't worry, her bark is far worse than her bite." Nadia advised, then asked, "Will you help me?"

"But there is so much bad blood between them. I wouldn't even know where to start."

"You leave the how up to us, but can we count on you to be our greatest mortal ally?"

Katie considered her proposal. "I will try, but my loyalty right now is to Yuli."

"I am grateful for your allegiance to my daughter." Nadia smiled. "As for my mother, all I need is for you to keep an open mind."

"I will do my best," Katie offered. "But I've faced Zoya's destructive heart before. She's ruled by revenge and retribution and will not give an inch."

"There's a reason her heart is so hardened," Nadia explained. "Imagine being tossed away like trash and forced to start over, pregnant at sixteen, in a foreign country where you do not speak the language."

Katie's brow furrowed, and she felt her resolve soften after learning this new nugget of information.

"It doesn't justify her actions, but perhaps it can help you understand. Come, there isn't much time," Nadia instructed as she navigated to the shore, stopping near Olena, who patted the area next to her and invited Katie to sit down. The sun instantly dried them both.

"When you wake up, go to your front door. Two music boxes from the family archives have been sent to you," Olena said.

"Are they from Zoya?" Katie was suspicious.

"Do not worry. She sent them at our request," Nadia assured her. "We simply want you to see what occurred, without bias from either of the strong-willed women in our family." Nadia offered Katie a tired smile. "They are more similar than they will ever admit. We are made from the same stock."

"I'm sorry, but I don't see it. Zoya and Yuli are as opposite as oil and vinegar."

"And yet, when they are thoughtfully combined, they bring out the best in each other like dressing fresh lettuce leaves."

"Or as a delicious dip for focaccia bread," Katie offered, trying to inject levity into the conversation.

Olena stood. "You're making me hungry." She tapped the used tobacco out onto the ground and tucked her pipe into the pocket of her suit coat. "It's time."

"I must go, sweetheart. Wake up and go to the front door." Katie closed her eyes and felt a whisper of lips brush across her forehead. She blinked, and she was back in her own bed. Disoriented, it took a long moment to understand the dream was an alternate reality. She'd been in the presence of Yuli's mother, who needed her help. She stood to stretch and threw on some shorts and a tank top. Arlo shook his coat, then jumped off the bed and followed her to the front door.

In the warm light of sunrise, placed in the center of her welcome mat, she found a plain cardboard box. She bent down to pick it up, but it was so heavy she couldn't lift it. Katie went back inside and returned with a box cutter. Slicing through the packing tape, she pulled out black tissue paper that was wrapped around a deep purple box. She reached down to lift it and found it was ice cold, and it left a trail of dirt behind as she walked it into the kitchen. She returned to the front door and pulled out even more tissue paper to reveal a gold art deco box. The sharp edges of it pricked her fingers, and she accidentally dropped it back into the nest of tissue paper. A single drop of blood fell onto the tissue paper and spread into a wide crimson circle. Afraid to touch it again, she hoisted up the entire box that was barely manageable and carried it inside. With both boxes on her island, she stared them down, knowing the answers to some of her questions would be inside and afraid of the truths they would reveal.

TWENTY

I n her sunny kitchen, Katie's chin rested on her forearms as she eyed the music boxes. Unable to make a decision about which to enter first, she winced as she picked up the gold leaf art deco music box, turning it from side to side. She admired the exquisite craftsmanship of the instrument. It was like a rose with thorns, beautiful to look at but difficult to hold. She gingerly set it back down on the granite countertop and stifled a yawn with one balled-up fist. Still drained from her restless night, she was conflicted when she called Yuli at Kandied Karma.

"I don't feel well," she blurted when Yuli answered the phone on the first ring. "I hate to leave you in a lurch, but I think I need a day off to rest."

"Of course," Yuli said. "I'll see you tomorrow. Let me know if I can bring you anything."

Katie didn't like keeping secrets, especially from

Yuli, but she couldn't abandon her responsibility to go inside the boxes.

She decided to fortify herself with a quick omelet before entering the music boxes. Katie was at the gas stove, caramelizing onions and scooping in chunks of honey-baked ham, when Arlo trotted over and sat on her feet. He looked up to flash her his puppy dog eyes, and she laughed.

"You're really working me this morning. Isn't it easier to use your words and ask for a scrambled egg?"

"Why ask when one glance is all it takes?" His wide mouth turned up at the corners.

"Is that a smile?" She grinned. "I didn't think dogs could smile."

"Only the best ones can."

She picked up his dish and scraped a pale yellow egg into his kibble before stirring it around. "There, are you happy now?"

"Ecstatic!" He jumped up and down, following her to the pantry where she set the bowl of food on the splash guard next to his water bowl.

Back at the stove, she was lost in thought as she sprinkled a handful of gruyere cheese over more eggs and waited for it to melt before folding it over and sliding it onto a plate.

Having wolfed down his own food in seconds, Arlo's tags jingled together as he returned to her feet. Katie bent down to give him a long scratch under the chin, and his warm brown eyes studied her worn expression. He jumped up and hugged her with his paws on her shoulders, and she rubbed his furry undercarriage. "I'm concerned. You're pushing yourself too hard, and you're already exhausted. Don't you think you should rest up before you go into the music boxes?"

"Time is of the essence. I have to see this through, and since I'm not really sure what awaits me inside, sooner is better than later." Katie stood, tucked a long white wave of thick hair behind her ear, and pulled out a seat at the island to eat. "I trust Yuli's judgment on everything, but when it comes to Zoya, her past trauma makes her vulnerable and colors all their future interactions. I promised Nadia I would participate during the *Fioletovy Mahiya* with an open mind, and I won't let her down." She stabbed a strawberry and bit into it.

"Your integrity is one of your most attractive qualities."

She blanched, swallowing the overwhelming shame of being a hypocrite for calling in sick. "I feel guilty concealing the real reason I needed time off today from Yuli."

"And your loyalty. It's a refreshing trait to find in a female!"

She chuckled at his odd compliment. "If I didn't know any better, I'd say you have a crush on me." Katie laughed at herself, and Arlo was grateful his pink skin was covered in fur.

"Of course not. That would be silly," he muttered and slunk under the table to hide.

After breakfast, she washed her dishes and then sat

down at the island with the boxes. Tentatively, she reached out to touch the Art Deco box and was startled to realize it was now warm to the touch, like it had been preheated and was awaiting her arrival. Feeling a pull, she cranked the golden triangular knob, then tugged at the corner carefully to open it, avoiding the sharp points, and felt herself float and then drift inside.

A few moments later, Katie landed hard in the field of grasses and wildflowers where Nadia's remains rested in the earth beneath the branches of a century-old oak tree. She walked over to the crudely made cross that was shoved into the ground and took the time to pay her respects. Then she gathered a few daisies to make a daisy chain which she placed on the marker before following the familiar dirt path to the cottage.

A sharp, rancid scent rankled her nostrils that intensified as she stepped further down the path. To stop the offensive assault on her senses, she pulled her shirt up over her nose, inhaling through the fabric. Less than twenty feet from the cottage, the source of the stench was revealed. It was the carcass of Zoya's cow being picked apart by vultures and maggots. Katie stopped by a tree and fought the urge to retch up her breakfast as her mouth watered, when baby Yuli's muffled screams through the heavy wooden door drove her into action. Her cries were hoarse and repetitive like she'd been wailing for hours.

Listening intently, Katie pressed her palm flat on the middle of the door and turned the knob with the other hand, slowly opening the door as Yuli's cries intensified.

Inside the cottage, the scent of excrement lingered. Dirty cloth diapers sat in a pail of dank water. Zoya sat at the table in a daze and didn't even turn her head when Katie entered the room. Her hair was limp, greasy, and disheveled, a far cry from the wealthy and glamorous socialite she now was. It was a revelation so startling Katie froze in place. When Zoya got up and made her way to the fire where a large kettle was simmering, Katie ducked back into the shadows.

"What is the point of eking out an existence anymore?" Zoya wondered aloud as she stirred the pot of vegetables over the low fire that made the cottage oppressively hot. She ladled a scoop of soup out of the kettle into a bowl and used her fingers to create a mash of the softened carrots and potatoes that she thinned with water to form a thin soup she fed to Yuli. The infant choked on the thickened broth, swallowing only small portions of it and making strangled cries in between bites.

"You need a wet nurse." Zoya talked to the baby like she understood. Yuli seemed to calm down over the next twenty minutes as Zoya fed her more and more small spoonfuls of soup. As she worked, Zoya hummed a lullaby and burst into tears as she knotted a cloth diaper on the baby. Yuli's chubby thighs poked out and kicked in the air, and her little hands reached up and balled into fists. Now relatively clean and fed, Zoya swaddled the baby in more flour sack cloths, and Yuli drifted into a peaceful sleep just seconds later.

Katie watched Zoya walk to a corner of the cottage,

kneel, and pry a loose floorboard up. She bent down, reaching deep into the hole, and then pulled out a rusted coffee can. Zoya tugged off the lid and then tipped it upside down, and a few loose coins fell out into the palm of her hand.

"We must go to the city to find you a proper wet nurse," Zoya said out loud. "I can sell the last four coins mother sewed into my petticoats and maybe find some work. Without the cow, we will surely both die if we stay here." She didn't bother to put the empty can back. Instead, while Yuli slept, she tried on the gown she'd worn on the boat when her father had banished her the first time. It now hung on her thinner frame. The fabric had faded and didn't catch her fancy like it had decades ago when her father had purchased it for her like she was a doll he had to dress.

The garment was stiff and musty when she tugged it off. The stitches were ancient and threadbare, and she dipped the material in a pail of water before hanging it out to dry over a chair near the fire.

Decision made, Zoya left the cottage to visit Nadia's grave while Yuli slept. Katie darted from the shadows and followed her, ducking behind trees, ping-ponging down the forest path, and staying out of sight. The wooden cross Zoya had fashioned from cherry branches stood firm in the ground with only a single name carved across it. Confusion darted across her features when she pulled the daisy chain off and held it in her hands, glancing over her shoulders for the person who'd left it behind. Katie glued herself to the tree and stilled her breathing. A few seconds later, Katie peeked around the trunk to see Zoya had gathered the daisy chain to her face as tears coursed down her cheeks.

Delicate lily of the valley emerged from the shaded green grass that surrounded the fresh grave. Zoya sunk to her knees in it. Her hand brushed over the marker as a keening sound drifted into the open air. For several long moments, she gathered her knees to her chest and wailed into the wind as she rocked back and forth. When she finally composed herself, she whispered, and Katie had to take a step closer to hear her.

"We have to leave in the morning, my darling," Zoya cried as she looked down at the ground that embraced her only daughter's body. In the woods, birds were singing without a care in the world, and the last shaft of sunlight illuminated the cross, tracing it and casting light onto the earth below. "I don't know if we'll return. But I vow I will always carry a piece of you in my heart wherever I go. God, I wish you were here. I don't know what to do with this child that hates me. She needs her mother, and the unbearable cruelty of life tearing you away from both of us has shattered my heart."

She swiped at the tears in her eyes. "I am trying, but I miss you terribly, and every time I look into her eyes, instead of love, I feel sadness. I feel loss, and I can't get past the pain. Please, forgive me."

The next morning, she leaned down and picked up the baby; the action made her lightheaded and weak. Zoya dressed in her tattered gown and wrapped Yuli snuggly against her with long strips of cloth, thankful that the baby finally quieted down to a whimper when her movements were restricted. She set out to walk toward town as Yuli slept, being rocked by her jerky movements. As she picked her way through the woods, she found a few berries to eat, but it wasn't enough.

Hours later, her feet blistered and her back weary from carrying the extra weight of the child, she sat down near a stream and unfastened the baby. She stretched for several long moments and drank water from her cupped hands, giving sips of the water to Yuli. Weak with hunger, she was desperate to continue her journey toward Chicago, knowing that darkness was her enemy.

Four hours later, her heart rejoiced when she came upon a farm. It was a humble dwelling with a thatched roof. In a corral, skinny livestock munched on bales of hay. Her pride had diminished on the journey, her growling stomach and Yuli's cries muffled against her chest had drowned out the lion's share of it. She had no choice but to knock on the door and rely on the kindness of strangers. She rocked from side to side to quiet the baby, but it was futile. The only thing that would calm Yuli was food. She was starving.

"Yes?" A woman answered the door. She was plump and unattractive, wary of the beautiful traveler with the baby strapped to her. She wiped her hands on a dirty apron.

"Do you have any milk? My granddaughter is starving, and we are weary from a day of traveling to the city."

The woman narrowed her eyes, sizing her up. "Do you have any money?"

Zoya hesitated to give away the four gold coins hidden in her petticoat, aware that this lowly farm wife wouldn't pay their true value. She bounced up and down, shimmying from side to side, trying to soothe an angry Yuli.

"Please," Zoya begged. She hated feeling hot tears skate down her cheeks. "I am not asking for myself. My granddaughter needs sustenance, or I am afraid she'll die." Katie's heart panged at the obvious desperation in Zoya's voice.

"Come in." The woman moved to the side, and Zoya stepped into the small cottage.

Inside, a fire was going at the hearth, and her eyes locked on a loaf of bread. Just seeing the golden brown loaf made her stomach clench and then growl.

"What do we have here?" A low voice from the corner snapped Zoya's focus from the bread to a man standing just feet from her. He walked out of the shadows, and Zoya stiffened as he advanced. Unshaven and wearing worn and soiled clothing, her nose wrinkled at the ripe smell emanating from his skin. He licked his lips, an action that made her recoil, and reached out a dirty hand to touch her face. Zoya held herself like a statue, and Katie felt tremors of outrage tingle through her as she watched their interaction.

"Do you have any milk or food to spare? We've been traveling all day, headed toward the city in search of a wet nurse."

"Why is that? Has the cow run dry?" He smirked, his teeth yellow with flecks of tobacco stuck in his gums. His hand lowered to Zoya's breast, and she had to fight the urge to slap it away. Katie had to bite back the rage that was a gathering storm within her.

Zoya took a step back and his eyes narrowed. "We're not a charity. I cannot give milk to every weary stranger who shows up at our door." He crossed his arms across his chest, and his eyes slid from hers, moving lower to fixate on her bosom. "But perhaps we could make a trade."

"What did you have in mind?" she asked, although she already knew the answer. Yuli's face was reddening and her body was constricted and tight. Likely reacting to the fear and anxiety peaking in Zoya, Yuli started in with another blood-curdling scream.

"Shut that baby up!"

"I can't until she has something to eat. She's only a few weeks old. You can't reason with an infant."

He pressed his hands to his ears and, for once, Zoya was grateful for Yuli's endless screaming. She heard him mutter under his breath and then he promptly left the cottage, slamming the heavy door behind him. The woman huffed, then placed a small bowl of milk on the table. Then, cursing softly, she tore off a hunk of the fresh bread and put it on a tin plate before she slammed it down in front of Zoya.

"Thank you," Zoya said, averting her eyes from the woman. Feeling her searing hatred washing over her, Zoya took a seat and tried to feed Yuli. She tore off tiny pieces of the bread and dipped them in milk to soften them. Yuli gagged, then swallowed the small bites, followed by more spoons of milk, but eventually, she was satiated and full.

Zoya changed the baby's diaper and then was surprised when the woman appeared at her side.

"I'll hold the little one," she offered.

Grateful for the break, Zoya stretched her arms above her head. Carrying Yuli strained her back, and she rubbed the knots that were gathered at the base of her spine. "There is a pitcher of water on the table if you want to freshen up." Zoya was too exhausted to wonder why the woman was being so kind. She washed the dirt from her face, relishing the feel of the cool water when she heard a heart-stopping scream from the kitchen.

Her body stiffened, and she raced out to see the woman had stripped Yuli down and was holding a knife to the baby's throat.

"A woman like you would never travel alone without resources. Let me see your pack."

Zoya held it out, and the greedy woman grabbed at it, but she clutched it tight. "I will trade it for the baby." The ugly woman weighed her options and, deciding it was amenable, set down the knife and handed the baby back to Zoya.

When Yuli was in her arms, the woman dumped the contents onto the ground. Seeing nothing of value, she charged Zoya with the blade.

"There has to be something." She stared her down. "Take off your dress," she demanded, and Zoya's heart dropped. She hesitated, trying to figure out her next move, taking several long moments to redress Yuli as her eyes darted around the farmhouse, looking for any object she could wield as a weapon. The door was too far away, and with Yuli in her arms, she could never outrun a woman who looked like she hadn't ever missed a meal in her life.

Slowly, she unbuttoned the dress and untied the laces that held it taut against her body. She pulled it over her head and handed it to the greedy shrew. Refusing to back down, Zoya balled her hands and placed them on her hips, standing defiantly in front of the fire, staring down the hateful woman, unaware the firelight made her petticoat practically transparent. Four small shadows at the hem piqued the plump woman's interest.

"I knew it!" The woman lunged at her with the weapon, and Zoya wrapped her arms around Yuli, holding her close to protect her soft skin from the sharp blade. The woman sliced through her petticoat, where her four gold coins remained. Cutting them free from the fabric, she squealed with delight when they fell into her hand, triumphantly grinning from ear to ear at the bounty that had fallen in her lap. Dread filled Zoya, seeing her precious coins between the thumb and forefinger of a woman she now found repugnant. The gold glimmered in the firelight, and a wide, satisfied smile slid across the woman's features.

"This will be payment enough for your ride to Chicago. Jeb is leaving in the morning. We'll make a bed for you in the barn."

Zoya shivered, barely concealing her hatred for the woman. Out of options and exhausted, she reluctantly followed her to the barn with Yuli and slept fitfully.

Hours later, Zoya awoke in a daze with her head pounding. It took several long seconds to get her bearings. The scent of straw and horse droppings made her nose crinkle and, in the dawn light tracing all the edges of the surrounding stalls, she was confused. She pressed a hand to her forehead, and the warmth surprised her. On the straw, in a bundle, Yuli was still fast asleep.

She dragged herself to a standing position and rummaged around the barn, finally finding an old bucket and a stool. She sat down on it and tugged at the udders of an old cow who rewarded her with a stream of milk. Yuli was going to be hungry when she woke up, and she wanted to be prepared. The pounding in her head was excruciating, adding to the strain. Each long tug made her hammering headache increase in intensity. By the time she'd gathered enough, Yuli had awakened, and she spoon-fed the baby until Yuli couldn't drink anymore.

The door creaked as Jeb slowly opened it. "We need to get a move on." Zoya stood with a moan, already exhausted. She gathered Yuli to her, wrapped the infant around her torso, and climbed into the back of the buggy. The ride was rough, and her bottom was sore from the jostling, but eventually, they stopped in front of a saloon. Jeb glanced over his shoulder and said, "I'm going to wet my whistle, but when I come back, I expect to receive your total gratitude." He hopped down from the buggy and disappeared inside. Zoya took the opportunity to jump out of the back of the carriage, desperate to put as much distance as she could between them and Jeb. She stepped out onto the street and glanced around. On one side of the road was a general store and a bakery, and people bustled around her. Her eyes widened, not used to being in a crowd that rushed by her, but quickly she realized their value. She walked by the fruit seller and swiped two small apples, tucking them away into her pocket under a sleeping Yuli. Her mouth watered in anticipation and, exhausted, she darted down an alleyway.

Her vision started to swim, and she felt the world going gray. Unable to stand any longer, Zoya slid down the brick wall onto the ground, clinging to Yuli. Faintly, she could hear the baby crying as if underwater or down a very long hall.

"I just need to rest for a moment," she whispered. "Then I will be able to put more than two thoughts together." Her eyes fluttered shut and her head bobbed back as she lost consciousness in the alley, her arms tightening around Yuli.

————

Katie watched as Zoya woke with a start in a bedroom that she didn't recognize, stripped down to a nightgown that wasn't hers. The scent of jasmine lingered in the air, and she glanced around, looking for the baby.

"Oh, good, you're awake," a tiny old woman said from the doorway before she entered the room, followed by a younger, scantily-clad girl brandishing a tray. She was barely four feet tall, and she walked with a cane. Her white hair was shorn tight to her head with impossible dimples deep in her cheeks and bright, inquisitive green eyes.

"Where am I?" Zoya asked, still drowsy.

The woman snorted. "You might want to ask another question." Zoya heard a piano start playing and boisterous singing from below. Through the doorway, she got a glimpse of creamy breasts as another woman darted past the door with a giggle, being chased by a calloused man unbuckling his belt.

"Is this a brothel?" Zoya asked, putting the clues together.

"Careful with the judgment, dearie." The tiny woman waggled a knobby finger at her in warning.

Zoya let it go and asked the second most pressing question. "Who are you?"

"I am Olena, your grandmother."

"What?" Zoya was confused. "I don't have a grandmother. Father said his mother died in childbirth."

"Ha!" It wasn't a laugh. She uttered one barking, stunted syllable. "He lied to you. That ungrateful son of mine cut his ties as he climbed the social ranks in Ukraine. My dwarfism made me a freak in his eyes and wasn't palatable for his lofty political aspirations, so he cut off all contact. I left for the New World before you were born."

Stunned by the revelation they were related, Zoya curiously eyed the little woman, instinctively knowing Olena was speaking the truth. "Sounds just like Father," she muttered.

"We have a common enemy then," Olena said.

Zoya fought to sit up in the bed as bits and pieces came trickling back. She rubbed her eyes, but then realization hit her and she swung her legs to the ground, readying herself to stand. "Where's the baby?"

"She's with Erina." Olena snapped her fingers, and the young woman who had been standing at the side of the bed awaiting further instructions set the tray in front of Zoya. She pulled out a chair and a stool for Olena before rushing out of the bedroom.

Olena climbed up the stool. Her short legs, forgoing a traditional women's dress, were wrapped in pantaloons, tights, and a pair of men's shoes.

"Eat," she said to Zoya, who refused. "You need to keep your strength up."

"How do I know it's safe?"

Olena threw her head back and roared. "Oh, that's rich. You think your long-lost grandmother would poison you?"

"Considering our lineage, I'd say evil lurks in our veins."

Olena reached over, picked a small piece of roasted chicken from the plate, and popped it into her mouth. "See? It's perfectly safe. Now, Your Highness can eat without fear."

"Yuli is probably hungry."

"She was," Olena admitted. "Erina took care of it. Yuli nursed for ages, had a nice warm bath, and has been sleeping ever since." She studied Zoya for a long moment. "You haven't been taking proper care of your child. Sitting in her own mess for so long gave her a nasty rash. No wonder she wouldn't stop screaming."

Zoya should have rankled under the judgment, but she felt nothing. She was numb. She pulled pieces of meat from the chicken bones and stuffed them into her mouth. Stealing glances at Olena, she wrapped her arms defensively around the plate, propping her elbows outward, and bent her head close to it, fearful the old woman would snatch it away. She continued stuffing large bites into her mouth, chewing quickly before shoveling in more, too ravenous to take the time to chew properly. On the tray, she saw an apple and bit into it. The sweet juice dripped down her chin as she devoured it.

"Tastes better when you swipe it, eh?" the diminutive woman asked. Zoya didn't confirm or deny her accusation. With her hunger finally receding, she used her forearm to wipe off the chicken grease from around her mouth and turned back to Olena. Her eyes leveled on the older woman's, and then several inches lower where a large mole kissed the corner of her mouth. Bored with the once-over, Olena pulled a pipe from inside her tiny jacket. It was styled with remnants of fabric in bright colors and patterns. One gold button held it closed. She struck a match on the side of her chair and held it to the end of the pipe, sucking in as the end glowed brightly.

"I am not running a charity here," she declared. "Every person in my home has a job to do."

"Oh, I'm not staying," Zoya insisted.

"Is that right?" She puffed on the pipe. The scent of it wafted over and transported Zoya to her childhood, when she spent many nights gathered near her father while he smoked his tobacco. The memory lit her fuse and her eyes glittered with rage. Olena detected the shift immediately. "What is it?"

"The pipe. It reminds me of someone."

"Let me guess, your father," Olena stated.

Zoya recoiled like someone had slapped her, ashamed she was so transparent. She couldn't give the older woman the satisfaction of admitting she was right.

"Where did the child come from?" Olena asked. "It's obvious you are not her mother."

"Her mother died in childbirth," Zoya said flatly. "She was my daughter, Nadia, and I couldn't save her," she whispered as her eyes grew watery.

"But you *can* save this baby."

"How?" Zoya finally found her voice. "I am penniless and alone!"

"You don't have to be," Olena implored. "We can offer you a place here as long as you pull your weight."

"What is this place?"

"It's a lot of things. A cathouse, a brothel, a house of ill repute, a massage parlor. It depends who's asking."

Zoya stood, panic rising. "I can't." She felt the

world closing in on her again and fell back down onto the bed.

"There are many ways to contribute, and not all of them will have you on your back and spreading your legs."

Zoya wanted to ask more questions but felt a wave of exhaustion crash over her, and she gave in to it as Katie was pulled away, drifting through space and time. Katie found herself just as drowsy as Zoya had been, and when she opened her eyes, she was seated at her own island. It took several long seconds to still her quivering hands.

"Katie." Marisa's forehead was knotted in concern. "Are you okay? Do I need to call an ambulance?"

"What… no." She smiled at Marisa. "Sorry. I was meditating, using a new relaxation and visualization technique. I didn't think you'd be home yet." Eager to change the subject, she asked, "Didn't you have to appear in court?"

"I have some incredible news," Marisa offered, shimmying her shoulders, her mood buoyant. "Because Rocco didn't show up at our hearing today, the judge is going through all the paperwork, and we should have a final decree in a few weeks."

"That's wonderful! You'll get to start over in the new year." She rushed to hug Marisa, eager to shift the young woman's attention away from her. After a few minutes of idle chit-chat, she stifled a yawn with the crook of her elbow. She excused herself and picked up the music boxes, stashing them in her walk-in closet for safekeeping. Then Katie fell into her bed to sleep for a few hours, to build her reserves to enter the second music box later that evening. She already knew it would be an emotionally draining journey. As she drifted off, she thought about what she'd just witnessed and her heart cracked wide open. It was impossible not to have some compassion for Zoya after witnessing the atrocities she'd endured to survive.

TWENTY-ONE

A day later, Zoya's private plane touched down on the airstrip at the airport. Dressed in aubergine from head to toe, she stepped out of the aircraft, down the stairs, and onto the ground, one eggplant-colored ostrich leather boot at a time. Her lightweight cape flared out at the waist and dark purple gloves covered her fingers, keeping her skin fully covered and out of reach.

After settling into the back seat of the waiting town car, she watched the miles spool out until she breached the wrought-iron gate and crossed into Aura Cove. Higgins pulled to a stop in front of Yuli's house. It was a home Zoya had stalked online but had never actually stepped a foot inside. The photos on Zillow were over ten years old and didn't do it justice. All smoked glass, black, and chrome, it was a far cry from the beachy pastels the Parrotheads preferred. The home was unusual—a floating geodome. The structure was a perfect circle and defied gravity, being held aloft by the pilings underneath it, giving the entire structure an ethereal quality. It almost looked like the house hovered in the air instead of being built on a foundation.

Floor-to-ceiling windows wrapped around the entire circular structure, and the roof was black with a four-foot overhang to block the punishing Florida sun. The circular dwelling was ringed by enormous palm trees that fanned out from the house and over the sugary white sand that led to the sea. Years ago, when Yuli moved with Kristina and David to be closer to Katie, the iconic home was put up for sale, and she outbid every buyer to secure the property.

The floor was a wooden pentagram, and at the tip of every point of the star was an altar for each element. Yuli had a daily practice of calling on the elements each morning and each evening. Twice each day, she stood in the center of the pentagram and began her practice facing east. "Element of Air, I call on you to provide peace and protection." She would repeat the phrase for fire, water, earth, and spirit, and after she acknowledged them, she would cast a circle of protection above, below, and within.

Sensing the same energy shift she'd felt in the warehouse, Yuli peeked out the window noticing a sleek town car parked in the driveway. "Zoya. Great," she mumbled, muttering to herself as she paced the length of the hardwood floor.

Inside the car, Zoya closed her eyes and, like a beacon, she sought out and then connected with Yuli's presence. She was always aware of the energy shift when she was in close proximity to her supernatural ancestors. She tugged on the edge of her glove, waiting for her driver to open the door. A minute later, her thoughts were disrupted by a whoosh of air and bright light.

"I guess we may as well get this party started," she muttered to herself as she stepped out and strode down the sidewalk to the formal entrance. Up a staircase between two gargoyles, Zoya landed on the impressive entry and pressed the doorbell. Inside, she heard it ringing, and through the opaque glass saw a flicker of movement. She crossed her arms over her chest and drummed her fingers against her arms impatiently.

"I know you are in there!" Zoya called out as she pressed the bell four more times, then knocked on the glass of the door. She would not be ignored.

Unable to delay the inevitable any longer, Yuli yanked open the door with her eyes narrowed. Still holding the knob in her hand, she refused to allow Zoya entry and waited for her to speak.

"Is this any way to treat your grandmother and your oldest living blood relative?"

Yuli scoffed at the remark and stuffed her hands in the pockets of her long black dress. She was resigned to get this meeting over with and took a small step back to allow Zoya entry.

"Love what you've done with the place," Zoya remarked as she strode in, feeling her gathering strength as she entered the circle footprint of the dwelling. A tingle of electricity ran its circuit up her arms. "Now I know why you love it here. Living inside a sacred circle is brilliant!" She tapped her finger to her temple. "It's not just a hat rack, is it? Even though you look like a dumpy lump, clearly, your mind is in excellent shape."

Frustrated already, Yuli looked down at the floor. "Stop trying to butter me up with flattery," she deadpanned, her sarcasm thick. "What do you want?"

Zoya held up both of her hands. "I come in peace."

"I don't believe you," Yuli spat back the truth.

"Admittedly, things got a little out of hand during our last visit."

Yuli emitted a *pfft* sound that reflected the absurdity of Zoya's statement. "Admittedly?" Her lips turned into a scowl and she continued, "You never change." Yuli took a step toward the air altar. "Element of air, instill peace and protection." She repeated her invocations under her breath as she circled the edges of the home, stopping briefly at each altar. After completing her pilgrimage of the sacred circle, Yuli felt centered enough to ask, "How did your meeting with Lilith go?" She couldn't resist the jab and rejoiced when Zoya flinched.

"We are still in negotiations," Zoya answered, unwilling to give Yuli any further details.

"Did you even stop to think for one second before involving the Dark Goddess?" Yuli asked. "You put our whole bloodline at risk."

Zoya pursed her lips and squared her shoulders. She

wasn't used to having her decisions questioned. "High risk equals high reward."

"Not always," Yuli mumbled. "But caution and patience were never your strong suits. God knows I learned that lesson when I was younger and stuck under your thumb."

"It was my choice to make."

"It was self-serving, as are most of your decisions."

Zoya shrugged, and Yuli continued her tirade.

"It was the selfish last-ditch effort of a third-generation witch who knows her days are numbered," Yuli accused, then clammed up and tightened her arms across her wide chest.

Rage ignited in Zoya's eyes, and her lips tightened into a scowl.

"Lauren is consulting a fertility specialist," Yuli said with glee. "One of the most successful reproductive endocrinologists in the country. God, I can't wait to say good riddance to you!"

"I already know," Zoya admitted, refusing to take the bait. This conversation was going nowhere fast. Changing tactics, she asked, "Can we set aside this feud for the greater good?"

"Greater good?" Yuli scoffed. "No good ever comes from interactions with you."

"You'll be interested to know I received a message from your mother." Zoya dropped the delicious secret and enjoyed watching Yuli stagger to a seat at the table near the kitchen. They were the only words she could say to capture Yuli's undivided attention. Instantly, her eyes snapped over to Zoya's, and the pinched look her face had adopted softened.

"What was the message?" Her voice was a whisper filled with longing. Yuli pushed away the intense jealousy that reared up discovering her mother had chosen to connect with Zoya instead of her.

"A rare lunar event is happening in February that will allow passage between the realms of the living and the dead. She is requesting our presence and participation."

Yuli took in the information Zoya offered, unwilling to open up and give any in return. "Surely, she knows you aren't much of a team player."

"Team-building is a waste of time. The women bold enough to change the course of their destinies *act*. They don't sit on the sidelines singing "Kumbaya" to foster a sense of unity." Zoya looked down and straightened her cloak. "But I will not miss out on the opportunity to see my daughter again. Even if it means subjecting myself to your hostility."

"You act as if it is unwarranted."

"You've even turned Katia against me."

"Playing the victim card? Hmm. I expected more from the great and powerful Zoya."

Incensed, Zoya rolled her eyes.

"*Your* actions turned Katia against you. I will not accept responsibility for your transgressions."

Refusing to accept blame, Zoya sidestepped Yuli's comments with ease. "Nadia is on a quest to heal our rift."

"Our rift?" Yuli was outraged and couldn't keep her emotions in check any longer. "The only memories I have of you are filled with hatred and anger. You detested that I drew breath and then refused to live in a world where my mother had to give up her life so I could live. Do you have any idea how that kind of anger eats at a child? Of course not. You never see outside yourself."

Zoya was silent for a long moment, letting the criticism go in one ear and out the other. "Looking for a scapegoat will not make you feel any better. It's time to take some responsibility for the trajectory of your own life."

"I have, you hypocrite! And now, dear grandmother, I must ask the same of you!" Yuli stood and walked to the door to show her out.

"I can see there are certain topics on which we will never see eye to eye."

Yuli let out an aggravated huff. "You're right, child neglect will never be acceptable to me."

"Neglect?" Zoya asked. "Come on."

"What would you call it?"

"We were in survival mode, and I was doing the best I could."

"The best you could!?" Yuli's voice was strained and pitchy, and her eyes bugged in astonishment.

"You are obviously committed to holding a grudge," Zoya started in, and Yuli palmed her face in frustration. "Will you participate or not? Say yes and I'll leave."

"Before I answer, I want you to understand my

decision has *nothing* to do with you or wanting to repair or build a relationship with you. We crossed that bridge a million years ago, and I am never going back. But I am choosing to participate because I have the desire to know my mother and to spend time with her. I will jump through whatever fiery hoops of hell I have to in order to see her."

"At least there is one thing we can agree on," Zoya said, then turned on her heel to leave. Yuli closed the door behind her, shaking off the oppressive energy that Zoya's presence had brought with it. She watched Zoya climb into the town car and then speed away. Her anger only began to dissipate when the car had completely disappeared from sight.

Twenty-Two

Later that evening, Yuli sat at her circular table in the kitchen and poured the turmeric milk she'd simmered on the stove into a heavy earthenware mug. She was agitated and restless and knew, even with the help of the milk, she would remain awake tossing and turning. It seemed, the older she aged, the more elusive sleep became, and she got less and less of it every year. She peeled apart a vanilla bean and scooped out the seeds, swirling them into the milk before taking a long sip.

"Hateful, superficial shrew," she muttered under her breath and drained the rest of the milk from the mug, and then she stood to rinse it in the sink before retiring to bed. Dressed in a long nightgown, she pulled the pins out of her hair one by one and pulled a brush through her thick white locks that dropped to the middle of her back. She brushed her teeth and then slipped into the circular bed at the edge of the room. She fluffed up her pillow and fanned her hair out behind her, and after several long calming breaths, she felt herself finally succumb to sleep.

An hour later, as she shifted into REM sleep, a rainbow of brilliant spectral color washed over her. In the distance, she heard a woman's voice singing a lullaby that tugged at her heartstrings, stirring something sweet and innocent from her past. She crept toward it as a gentle breeze swept her hair back from her shoulders. The closer she came to the voice, the more beautiful her view was. She heard the rushing of water and followed the lush path that cut through a crop of tropical plants. Yuli inhaled the scent of fragrant gardenias as she continued closer. Her being filled with lightness, and with each step nearer, she felt joy bubble up in her heart.

Finally, in a clearing, the singing woman was revealed, and the sight made her gasp and quicken her step.

"My Yuli. Oh, sweet girl, how I have longed to see you again." Nadia stood, and Yuli pitched forward, breaking her fall with her arms. She let out a yelp and scrambled to her feet as the vision of her mother flickered, then began to glow more brightly. She heard a snort of laughter and glanced around to find its source, her gaze eventually landing on a small-statured little person smoking a pipe.

"Happens every time!" She slapped her thigh and dissolved into another guffaw.

"Don't mind her," Nadia instructed. "Soon, I'll be able to hold you in my arms."

"Mama?" Yuli whispered. "Is it really you?"

Nadia leaned closer. "Yes, my darling."

"You don't know how many times I've prayed for this to happen," Yuli explained. "It crushed me yesterday when I learned you appeared to Zoya."

"Life has not been easy for you without me," Nadia whispered, "and for that, I am deeply sorry."

"Don't apologize, Mama. You are here now. That is all that matters."

Nadia nodded. "Come. Sit. There are important matters to discuss." She walked to a large bench and patted the spot next to her. Yuli followed and then reached out to grasp her mother's hand in her own, but her hand passed through it. She wanted to cradle it like a precious treasure, to trace the elegant lines of her mother's much smaller hand, but she could not make contact.

"This is a dream come true." Yuli smiled through her tears. Nadia reached up, stopping inches away from Yuli's face, and brushed the air. A burst of breeze tickled Yuli's cheek, and then it dissolved into a bubble that twinkled before floating away.

"You have become an incredible woman, despite all the hardships you have endured, and I am so proud of you," Nadia praised. The sentiment choked Yuli up, and she cleared her throat. "Mother disappointed me, and I promise she will be held accountable. Soon, we will have an opportunity to right all the wrongs of our past."

Confused, Yuli asked, "How? There has been so much trauma and damage, it's unforgivable." Yuli looked down. "She blamed me for your death from the moment I was born. Her hatred is seared into every cell of my being."

"I know, my sweet. But you must try to forgive."

"I cannot," Yuli stated, spiting the words out. "I cannot forgive that woman."

"Then you are drinking poison and waiting for her to die."

Yuli gently slid away from the vision of Nadia, her anger needing to occupy more physical space. "I *am* waiting for Zoya to die. Although wanting might be more accurate."

"I understand why you would feel that way," Nadia empathized and, after a moment, boldly continued, "The *Fioletovy Mahiya* is approaching. On that day and into the night, we have an opportunity to heal the coven."

"I don't need healing," Yuli remarked, and it made Nadia chuckle. "Nor do I want it."

"Sweet babushka," Nadia said. "Do you know why the goddesses bestowed the triumphant power of healing on you?" She waited, then added, "Because you are the only one in our lineage strong enough to heal our brokenness."

"No." Yuli was stubborn. "I cannot heal her. Zoya is too far gone. She's evil, relying on dark magic to carry out her own selfish plans. She's been summoning Lilith."

"I know this already." Nadia sighed. "It's true, I

have been very disappointed by the decisions she has made, but I believe in the deepest part of my heart that every woman is redeemable. There is still love inside her heart, but she's built a fortress around it to survive. It was the reason she could never give you the love you needed and deserved."

"She did so much damage. I am not sure I can find it in my heart to forgive her."

Nadia's lips pressed together, and she nodded. "I only have one thing to ask of you."

"What is it?" Yuli was skeptical.

"Can you use some of your true ability to heal your heart enough so that on the night of the *Fioletovy Mahiya* you can come with an open heart and open mind?"

Yuli felt the sting of tears in her eyes, and when Nadia slid closer to her, she felt a burst of warmth. Yuli longed to rest her head on her mother's shoulder, and a choked sob hastened the flow of tears down her cheeks. "I've missed you so much."

"I've been with you, my darling," Nadia consoled. "I am in awe of the woman you became. I watched you create a thriving business and start your family, and recently take on the task of guiding our newest Yaya, Katia. There is so much love in your heart." She was silent, then continued, "The lunar event gives us an opportunity we will never have again. I will get to live with you, side by side, for a single day."

"Why would we want to waste one minute of that one precious day trying to repair the impossible?"

"It's important for our family lineage. To keep it thriving and protected and intact. We must unite and heal the past in order for us to create a vibrant future legacy for our family."

"I don't know." Yuli was hesitant.

"Do you trust that I only have your best interests at heart?" Nadia asked. "From the moment I knew of your existence, I loved you. I have always loved you." She started to glow, and the light seeped into Yuli. It filled her with a reverent peace and contentment that made her entire body hum with delight. For several long moments, she felt the sweetness of it fill her.

"I trust you, Mama," Yuli whispered, her resolve strengthening. "I will do my best to do as you ask."

"Thank you, my love."

They grew quiet, sitting on the bench together. Nadia began to sing again, a lullaby that Yuli now had placed. It was a song that Zoya had sung only a handful of times when she was washing dishes or was consumed by the sadness of missing her daughter. Yuli let the song wash over her as Nadia's beautiful voice carried her higher and higher.

When she woke up in her bed, her pillow was soaked with tears. Her stomach flipped when she realized it was only a dream and her mother had faded away into the warm light of day. She closed her eyes, willing herself to go back to sleep. Desperate to return to the beautiful bench she'd been sitting on. She tried for an hour to conjure it back up but was unsuccessful.

Finally giving up, she rose and got to her feet to start the day.

The *Fioletovy Mahiya* was only sixty days away. To get to spend an entire twenty-four hours with the woman she missed most was a gift. Even if she had to endure interacting with Zoya, it would be worth it.

TWENTY-THREE

The next morning, Katie was anxious on the drive to Kandied Karma. "I'm hesitant to talk to Yuli," she confided in Arlo, who was belted into the seat next to her. The top was down and she was driving down Main Street enjoying the comfortable mid-December temperatures.

"Yuli always appreciates the truth," Arlo offered, squinting his eyes in the warm rays of the morning sun as they zinged past palm tree-lined streets of downtown Aura Cove.

"There are old scars between her and Zoya, and I don't want to reopen them."

"You're the most empathetic creature I know," Arlo said. "Just follow your heart. It will never fail you."

"Aww! How did you get to be so smart?" Katie patted him on the head, and he circled and lay down on the seat next to her. She exhaled a heavy breath to let the tension escape, then pulled into her reserved spot behind

Kandied Karma and said, "Might as well get it over with first thing." It was a weak pep talk she muttered under her breath as Arlo followed her into the darkened chocolate shop. Katie started the opening routine and, eventually, an exhausted Yuli walked through the back door and right to the espresso maker. "Why don't you go have a seat, and I'll bring it over," Katie offered.

"Thanks, dear." Yuli covered her mouth and yawned into her palm. "Are you feeling better today?"

"Much," Katie replied, feeling the sting of guilt that fortified her resolve to tell Yuli the truth.

The only sounds were the whirr and sputter of the machine as Katie mentally walked through potential opening lines of the sensitive conversation she was determined to have.

"I need to tell you something," Katie said, finally breaking the silence and setting the cup in front of her grandmother. She pulled up a stool and sat down, crossing her legs in her long khaki skirt. She hooked her sandals on the bottom rung of the stool and propped her elbows up on the countertop, waiting for Yuli to respond.

After a long sip of the espresso that seemed to bring her back to life, Yuli finally asked, "What is it?" Her intelligent eyes narrowed. She was already wary.

"Your mother came to me in a dream several nights ago," Katie confided, and Yuli gasped.

"What did she say?"

"A lunar event is going to open a portal, and she wants me to help her reconnect the generations of our family." Katie watched Yuli wrap one shaking hand around the handle of the tiny espresso cup and bring it to her lips. She closed her eyes, and Katie was afraid to go on but knew she had to. "And there were two music boxes delivered to me from the archives."

Yuli's eyes shot open. "Did you go inside them?"

"I did." She nodded. "I promised Nadia I would." She wrapped her hands around her own cup of coffee that was cooling. "They revealed the overpowering hardships Zoya endured when Nadia died and the very early days of your life. It was difficult to watch."

"What's done is done," Yuli muttered. She was uncharacteristically closed off, and the distance concerned Katie.

She reached out a hand to squeeze Yuli's. Trying to connect and open the flow of communication, she asked, "What is your earliest memory from your childhood?"

Yuli took another sip, considering the question. "I'm afraid my actual memories are rather fuzzy, just bits and pieces cobbled together, but I was subjected to the cruelty contained in my birthday box when I turned sixteen."

"Zoya… she struggled." Katie was searching for the words to soften the blow that she knew her compassion for Zoya would wield on her grandmother.

"We *all* struggled," Yuli admitted bitterly. "It's not a valid excuse."

"Agreed," Katie said quickly, "but survival mode changes a woman. It reduces her to basic instincts and fight or flight. Neither of those realities are conducive to creating a loving environment where an infant can be nurtured and loved."

"There is always a choice," Yuli demanded.

"But Yuli, she saved your life. You would have died in that cottage after you were born if it wasn't for Zoya. You at least have to acknowledge that."

"Perhaps." Yuli took another sip. The cup rattled when it connected with the saucer.

"She walked for miles with you strapped to her back to find a wet nurse."

"Am I to be grateful?" Yuli asked.

"Losing her daughter had to have been the most devastating loss of her life, and yet she pushed through the pain."

"So you say," Yuli muttered. "If that is true, it was the last act of compassion she ever endowed to me. Her heart hardened, and she became selfish. Olena and her crew did all the heavy lifting when I was a child."

"I met Olena, too," Katie remarked. "She's a feisty one. What a character!"

Yuli smiled her first genuine smile of the morning as her tone softened. "Yes, she was one of a kind. They broke the mold when they made her. She's the reason the Castanova compound is in our family."

"Really? How so?"

"She took the money the brothel made, invested in the stock market, and pulled all of it out the week before Black Monday. She picked up the property for a song when the previous owner hadn't made as wise investments after the market crashed and had to sell it for pennies on the dollar."

"Wow." Katie was stunned. "When did she pass?"

"1973. On your birthday," Yuli said.

The admission sobered Katie up instantly as Yuli continued, "I never learned the truth until I had my awakening, but Olena was pulling the strings behind the scenes. She's the one who deeded the keys to the compound to Zoya. She's the anonymous benefactor who helped me escape the island when I was sixteen." Yuli looked into her cup. "She's been secretly looking after me since I was an infant."

"Olena doesn't seem like the maternal type."

Yuli guffawed at the statement and slapped her hand on her thigh. "Olena would roll over in her grave if she heard you make another declaration as ludicrous as that one!" She dissolved into more peals of laughter at the idea, and it was so infectious, a smile broke out on Katie's face, too. Finally getting herself under control, she said, "I'm not sure what transpired between them, but they had a falling out when Zoya moved us in with Salvatore. Later, when he was killed and Zoya was terrified we'd be next, Olena secretly came to our rescue again." She exhaled, then leaned closer and made her own confession, "Mother came to me, too, last night. She and Olena visited me in a dream together."

"Why didn't you say anything?"

"I've been trying to figure out how I feel about it." Yuli looked deep into the bottom of her cup, lost in thought for a long moment before she uttered, "Zoya was a monster. Nothing has changed, she still is."

Based on their recent interaction, Katie couldn't disagree. "You have every reason in the world to hate her guts, and believe me, I am not making excuses for Zoya." She cocked her head to the side and pressed her lips together in defeat. Seeing the firm set of her grandmother's shoulders, there was still a chip resting there the size of the ocean. "But forgiveness is for *you*. It is not for Zoya." Katie started to explain, "It allows you to set aside the hatred and reclaim the energy you've been funneling into hate for more productive things." Her voice softened. "This animosity has been a heavy rock you've carried around your whole life. Aren't you tired? Don't you want to set it down?"

"I can't," Yuli whispered. "I just can't forgive her." She laced her fingers together in her lap.

"I'm not taking her side, but there *were* extenuating circumstances. I can't imagine the inner strength it takes to survive after losing your daughter and then having all of your meager resources stripped away by opportunists, leaving you starving with an infant to feed."

Yuli's lips were set in a hard line. "I agree. Those circumstances would test the mettle of any woman, and many would lash out. I can forgive those sins, but the ongoing neglect and lack of love, I cannot. To thrive, a baby needs to be held and feel love as much as it needs sustenance, and she chose to withhold those basic needs. That is unforgivable. The few actual memories I have from childhood are a confusing mash-up of events that left me feeling unwanted and like a burden." She wiped a tear from the corner of her eye, then continued, "No one is perfect. I am far from it, but she made her decisions long ago, and now she must live with the consequences of them. This lunar event gives me a chance to connect with my mother and Olena, and I am looking forward to the reunion with great joy. If reconnecting with Zoya is the price I have to pay in order to spend real time with them, I am willing to pay it." Yuli stood, signaling the end of the conversation.

Katie knew her grandmother well enough to leave it alone. She watched her unlock the safe and get the cash register ready for the first orders of the day with a sigh. Katie was torn in two. She smoothed the front of her shirt and continued to stock the truffle case and prepare her orders for delivery.

In the silence, she tried to work out solutions in her mind. She was sandwiched between two of the most formidable and stubborn women she'd ever known. Their mutual hatred made it impossible to see their similarities, but Katie saw them. Both women were a product of their survival modes. Both were holding on to grudges that didn't serve them anymore. Both were opinionated and immovable once they made a decision. Reuniting the family wasn't going to be an easy task, and Katie felt like the monkey in the middle, laboring to create a peace treaty. While her loyalties would always align with Yuli's, inside the boxes she'd witnessed firsthand some of the painful events that shaped Zoya and turned her into the woman she was. It was impossible not to feel compassion for her after being inside them.

At her hip, Katie's phone vibrated with an incoming text message. She pulled it out of her pocket and glanced down.

Frankie: *Call me 911.*

Nervous terror unleashed in her belly as she tapped Frankie's face in her favorites and slid into the walk-in cooler as a hot flash made beads of sweat break out all over her body. The heat seared through every pore as she listened to the phone ring.

"Hello?"

"What's the emergency?" Katie cut in. "Are you okay?"

"No."

"You better start talking."

"Well, I was doing some shaving, getting ready for a steamy night with Harry Willey, and I found something."

"Oh my God." Katie cried. "A lump?" Her mind instantly went from zero to a full-blown cancer diagnosis in the span of two seconds.

"What?" Frankie asked impatiently. "No. I found a white one."

"A white one?"

"Yeah, a white pubic hair in my lady garden."

"Dude." Katie exhaled with a chuckle. "Texting someone nine-one-one is for emergencies only. It's not for when you find an insignificant physical imperfection."

"But it sticks out like a sore thumb. What should I do? Pluck it?"

"I mean, you can, but if you do, legend says two more will grow in its place."

"No!" Frankie cried on the other end as Katie felt her fears wash away. She rolled her eyes and chuckled at the ridiculousness of this conversation. "Besides, what are you going to do when you're salt and pepper down there? You can't pluck every single one."

"Two words. Full Brazilian."

Katie burst out laughing. "Have you ever *had* a Brazilian?"

"No, I mean yes, if you count Renaldo during that vacation in my twenties…"

"Frankie!" Katie cried, exasperated. "I'm referring to the full-on hot wax treatment where all the hairs in your nether region are ripped off in one long, excruciating yank by a ruthless aesthetician."

"YOLO?" Frankie asked, and Katie heard her gulp.

"With a Brazilian, once is enough. God, I remember Jeff bought me a gift certificate for a Brazilian wax a week before our vacation to Hawaii for our fifteenth anniversary. I'm telling you, I was not prepared for the level of torture it would inflict on my tender bits. I swear my soul left my body for a moment." She shuddered in the cooler, remembering.

"Will you come with me?"

"To the *waxing salon*?" Katie asked, chuckling at

her best friend's outrageous request. "How about this? I'll give you a ride and take you out for ice cream afterward, but some things you must experience on your own."

"Now you're speaking my language." Frankie always appreciated a sugary reward.

"I need to warn you. There will be bleeding and stinging pain, and for God's sake, don't put any lotion on the area or touch it for a few days."

"You're making this sound so delightful."

"Just trying to set realistic expectations for you," Katie explained, then asked, "Are you also having them do your bum crack?"

"The what now?"

"You heard me." Katie laughed. "If you're waxing the kitty, doesn't the boom crack-a-lacka deserve the smooth five-star treatment, too? That's included in a Brazilian." She laughed out loud. This conversation was becoming more ridiculous by the second.

"Is this a trick question?" Frankie asked, aghast. "I've never waxed my crack. People actually do that?" The thought of it repulsed her.

"People do *all kinds* of weird things to appear more attractive to the opposite sex."

"Does it work?"

"It really depends on the guy," Katie said. "Maybe you should float this idea past Harry."

"I'm a grown-ass woman. I can make my own decisions where body hair is concerned, and he will have to learn to live with it."

"You're ridiculous." Katie laughed. "I gotta run, but the offer still stands, and no more nine-one-one calls involving your pubic region. Got it?"

"Got it."

Katie ended the call and put the phone back in her pocket. It was time to unlock the front door.

Over the next few hours, time flew by. Katie's fingers were sore from the repeated act of folding boxes and swiftly gift-wrapping them. The line of holiday customers snaked out the front door and didn't slow down until thirty minutes before closing time. She swept and mopped the floors while she chewed on her thoughts. It was a Zen-like task she enjoyed, the physicality of the strokes putting her into an almost meditative state. She only had eight weeks until the *Fioletovy Mahiya,* and she didn't know how she was going to bridge the gap between Zoya and Yuli.

"I need help," she whispered. "Or this family reunion is going to be doomed from the start."

TWENTY-FOUR

In the middle of December, Dr. Blackwell stood at the entrance of Blackwell Reproductive Health. His discerning gaze swept the area, attempting to assess the clinic with fresh eyes as a new visitor would. He was pleased to see the building and grounds were immaculate, indicative of the high standards and attention to detail he provided to his patients. With a flash of irritation, he tugged the sleeve of his white coat up to check the impressive timepiece on his wrist. Yep, she was ten minutes late, and a rush of self-righteous anger tasted metallic in his mouth. He wasn't used to waiting for anyone, let alone a woman. But compelled by his mission, he was forced to set his personal feelings aside for the greater good.

Last week, a representative from the Castanova Foundation finally reached out and requested a facility tour. This was the big break he had been praying for, and Dr. Blackwell understood what a substantial injection of capital for research and development from Ana Castanova would mean for his clinics. He was already spending the lofty endowment he was certain he'd secure today in his mind, thrilled it would bring his greatness to fruition faster.

Frustrated at the lack of respect for his time, he pressed his thin lips together and tapped his foot impatiently. Finally, a sleek town car pulled up to the valet lane at his practice, and he pasted a fake smile on his face. The car eased to a stop, and the driver promptly exited and stood waiting by the door as Zoya had trained him to do.

Studying the doctor through the tinted glass, Zoya sized him up. She loved making men like him wait. Intuitively, she felt the crackle of power resonate through him, but it was mixed with something she couldn't put her finger on. She smoothed her long, flowing lavender dress and tugged the black gloves up under her biceps to avoid any accidental skin-on-skin contact. Ready to engage, she briefly knocked on the window with a loose fist, and it was promptly opened for her.

"Thank you for waiting," Zoya offered, extending a gloved hand to Dr. Blackwell, who wrapped her hand in both of his. It was an off-putting manipulative technique that was more favored among politicians who spent their days pandering for public approval. She fought a wrinkle of disgust from spreading across her features as his touch sent a shiver down her spine.

"Welcome, Ms. Castanova, to Blackwell

Reproductive Health," Dr. Blackwell greeted, sweeping one hand back toward the modern office building behind him. "I'm delighted to have you here today. I hope this visit will shed some light on the possibilities that lie ahead in the work we can do together."

Zoya followed him through tall glass doors and down gleaming white marble corridors, passing framed photos of hundreds of babies alongside written testimonials from grateful parents who had realized their dreams of having a child. In the corners of the waiting room, on closed-circuit televisions, parents gave tearful testimonials enhanced by tender soundtracks whose only purpose was to tug on the heartstrings of the infertile. The manipulation he practiced was almost diabolical, but she had to admit they were an effective marketing tool to use on the ordins. Zoya saw right through the charade, but judging by the chairs in the waiting room they'd just passed that were filled to capacity, ordin women didn't.

"Here, we have our state-of-the-art laboratory," Dr. Blackwell announced, swiping his security card and opening the double doors with a flourish. "Our embryologists work tirelessly to ensure the best possible sterile environment for the fertilization process."

Zoya stepped inside, her eyes widening at the sight of rows of incubators and microscopes. The room hummed with the sound of well-maintained medical machinery, and the air was filled with a sterile, clinical scent.

"This is where we make miracles happen," he

declared proudly. "With groundbreaking techniques and a dedicated team, we strive to fully restore fertility to families who have struggled to conceive. It is our mission to help every faithful woman who wants to conceive a child. We are bringing the kingdom of God into a state of fullness."

Zoya closed her eyes and connected with the energy in the room, and the first of his fundamentalist thoughts invaded her mind.

Glory be to God.

Annoyed by his religious crutch, she was just about ready to tune him out completely when she heard his next thought.

Easy does it. Securing this Jezebel's donation is the crucial next step. We are crippled by our current lack of resources to serve more families and create more soldiers for Christ. One "yes" from her, and we will change the world.

The thought piqued Zoya's curiosity, and her eyes widened as she concentrated on intercepting the flow of his consciousness.

They continued the tour, and she followed closely behind him, grateful he couldn't see her face and judge her reactions. His aura should have been orange, but it was an unsettling brown. Greed. She brushed her concerns aside to continue the tour. Greed she could work with.

As he guided her deeper into the labyrinth of the lab, Zoya marveled at the precision and orderliness that defined each workspace. The laboratory technicians, clad in pristine white lab coats, moved with graceful efficiency, their every movement a testament to their complete dedication to his mission. Glass vials, slides, and Petri dishes lined the shelves, poised and ready to be used for their highest calling—creating life.

In one corner, a technician meticulously prepared a culture medium, carefully measuring and mixing the ingredients with the precision of a chemist. On one long stainless steel countertop, a row of microscopes stood like sentinels, and behind each lens, a highly skilled embryologist inspected fertilized eggs. Their eyes were trained to detect even the subtlest signs of change and growth.

The lab was divided into specialized sections, each serving a specific purpose in the process. In one corner, a warm room was filled with incubators cradling embryos inside. Meticulously monitored and controlled, they provided the optimal conditions for cell division. A few steps further, Zoya arrived at the cryopreservation area, where a maze of storage tanks housed frozen embryos, preserved for future use. Each tank contained a viable embryo suspended in frozen limbo, waiting for the moment they would be chosen and implanted into their mother's womb. Zoya peeked in through the small window and heard the voices of young boys speaking over each other.

Daddy! Sky Daddy! We are soldiers ready to further your mission to create a fully submissive army for the Abundant Quiver Movement. We love you, Daddy.

Confused, Zoya had to shake the creepy high-pitched voices off and quickly rushed away from them to quiet her mind.

The Abundant Quiver Movement? What in the hell was that?

Next, they entered his sun-drenched office, painted a nurturing green, filled with plush armchairs and lush houseplants. On the walls, impressionistic paintings depicting serene landscapes were the backdrop to bible verses. "You knit me together in my mother's womb." Another depicted a verdant green pasture with the verse, "I praise you because I am fearfully and wonderfully made." Dr. Blackwell motioned for Zoya to take a seat while he sat opposite her, his calculating eyes studying her intently.

"I've got something very special to show you," Dr. Blackwell announced proudly, gesturing toward the architectural renderings of an expansive laboratory he rolled out on his desk. "Since you took such an issue with the name at my fundraiser, I'm proposing we call it The *Ana Castanova* Center for Reproductive Miracles. We will capitalize on the same cutting-edge technology that made Blackwell Reproductive Health successful paired with unparalleled success rates. With your support, we can bring joy to countless families."

Surely, this vixen won't be able to resist funding a clinic named after herself.

Zoya's discerning eyes scanned his plans, her mind processing the information with an uncanny clarity. Deep within her, an ancient stirring of intuition chimed in. To the ordins, Blackwell's cunning smile kept his true intentions hidden behind a practiced veneer of charm. But in front of her, Zoya saw his aura become brownish-black. Despite his claim of godliness, wickedness seeped from his soul that he white-washed away with his bible thumping.

Oh, it is going to be delicious to bring this one to his knees.

Dr. Blackwell leaned closer, his voice lowering to a conspiratorial whisper. "Ms. Castanova, I must confess that our methods are somewhat unorthodox. We have developed a unique approach to fertility that involves using donor sperm from a select group of individuals in our very own clinics, carefully chosen for its genetic potential."

A sinister smile tugged at the corners of his mouth, and he licked his lips in anticipation.

Zoya's eyes widened in surprise. "But... I thought your patients could choose their own donor or provide one?"

Dr. Blackwell smiled, a chilling glint in his hooded eyes behind the black frames of his modern glasses. "Of course they can. But when utilizing our select group of donors, success is virtually guaranteed, and many women, when they discover the odds they are facing, choose to exercise every advantage."

"What criteria are used for a donor to be added to the select group? Are they screened for super semen or something?" She laughed, and his eyes narrowed.

"There is a rigorous screening process, and only the

most robust genetic material is selected. It's a very elite group."

She pressed him for information. "I would need my team to be granted full visibility into the selection process before we could move forward."

"I should mention that donors typically prefer to remain anonymous for religious reasons. I'm sure you understand," he said in a dismissive tone, as if she were a foolish woman incapable of grasping the concept. The condescension in his voice ignited a spark of anger in Zoya.

Suppressing her rising fury, Zoya maintained a composed façade. "I appreciate your transparency, Dr. Blackwell. But I must ensure that ethical guidelines are followed and that the donors are properly vetted. I'm sure *you* understand," her eyes flashed, "that in order to attach the Castanova Foundation's name to your clinic, I will need to hire a team of auditors to personally oversee the process from start to finish."

Dr. Blackwell's smile faltered for a moment, but he quickly regained his composure. "Of course, your concerns are valid, and I assure you, our methods adhere to the highest ethical standards."

"Just the same, the auditing team is not up for discussion. I have to be certain that my good name is protected."

His nostrils flared and his aura shifted darker.

This bitch. If I didn't need the capital to fast-track this project, I would cut her out and show her the door right now.

Then, without warning, Zoya felt a twinge of understanding creeping up her spine, and her intuition whispered in her mind. It was a possible solution to her deepest dilemma.

You might want to coddle this obnoxious bastard after all. Perhaps Dr. Blackwell could be a worthy sacrifice to Lilith. Talk about a win-win situation! This vile man could be condemned to hell and eternal servitude, along with all of his fertilized specimens. True, they are not technically children, yet, but the Dark Goddess surely will savor the irony of damning this religious hypocritical nut bag to the fires of eternal damnation.

Zoya grinned at him and turned on the charm. "Sorry to be so cautious. I'm sure you have all the necessary protocols in place since you're a legend in the fertility industry." She paused for a long moment, chewing her bottom lip, as he reveled in her praise. "I believe we can come to some sort of agreement to keep my board of directors happy and help you further your mission," she lied, her voice a practiced pandering tone she'd developed talking to the world's most self-important men. "It's critical, life-affirming work you are doing here, and with the full support of my resources, we can change more lives."

Dr. Blackwell's smile widened, revealing a hint of triumph. "I couldn't agree more, Ms. Castanova! Together, we can help more women achieve their dreams of motherhood. Your generosity will enable us to create more miracle babies who will change the world."

Zoya's lips curved into the first genuine smile she'd worn since the tour began. Her thirst for revenge cried out for retribution, and the possibility Dr. Blackwell could become a worthy sacrifice and set Sally's soul free filled her with joy. She tugged off her glove and stood to signal the end of the meeting, bracing for the jolt that contact with his skin would bring.

He smiled like the cat who ate the canary and got to his feet.

Nice job, Sky Daddy. You had her eating out of the palm of your hand.

Zoya had to stifle the urge to gag, witnessing him patting himself on the back and using the vile nickname to refer to himself. Sky Daddy? It was revolting. She couldn't wait to bring him to his knees.

Their palms met, his cooler than hers, and she took a stuttered step as a message filled her subconscious.

Seventeen. She calculated the date in her mind. December 26th. Perfect. Delighted with the knowledge of his imminent demise, Zoya was giddy at the prospect of making the trade. Seventeen more days until Sally's soul would be set free.

TWENTY-FIVE

Lorelei was supposed to be resting. She adored her parents but carved out a few hours every day for herself, where she wasn't subjected to the strain of their constant observation. Stage-five kidney disease meant whispered pow-wows between her parents and them tiptoeing around her on eggshells. It felt like an intrusive existence most days, as her parents constantly scanned her environment for threats or physical changes. She yearned for her independence to be reinstated; it wasn't natural to live with your parents at thirty, and she felt guilty that they'd put their lives on hold to care for her.

Alone in her room was the only time of day when she could fully relax. It's when she could drop the mask she put on to relieve their fears. The sicker she became, the harder it was to maintain the façade she'd built so they wouldn't worry.

In her lap, her phone dinged a notification, silencing

her thoughts. When she tapped on it, she was thrilled to see the email she'd been waiting for. She rolled herself over to her desk and wiggled her fingers over the pad on her laptop to wake up her computer. Then she opened a browser and the email from Ancestrify. She hastily read a few lines, eager to get into the meat and potatoes of it quickly:

"Your results have been posted to our secure website. Log on and discover more about your ancestral and medical history today."

With a giddy thrill in her belly, she clicked on the link, created a login, and impatiently drummed her fingers on the desk while she waited for the page to load. Finally, the window opened, and she read through the miscellaneous information compiled in a summarized report. It contained many mundane and weird biological facts about herself. She found out her ear wax was most likely to be the dry variety and that her urine would not emit a foul odor if she ate asparagus.

"Wow. This is riveting," she deadpanned as she scrolled to the next screen. At the top of it was a tab that read "DNA RELATIVES." This was the information she couldn't wait to share with her father. Lorelei dove in and clicked on the tab, and it opened in a new window. At the top of the screen, her full name was posted. She clicked the button to download the entire report as a PDF and sent two copies to the printer.

Father 50.1% shared DNA
Full Siblings: 0
Half-Siblings: 4

"What in the heck?" she whispered as her eyes continued to scroll down the page. "Dad didn't take the test already, did he?" she questioned as she mumbled to herself.

There was a matrix composed of single lines and an entry for each of her half-siblings that had voluntarily completed the DNA test at Ancestrify and were already in the database. She scrolled down the page, seeing cells of the shocking discoveries organized in a table.

Half-Brother 23.7% shared DNA
Half-Sister 24.2% shared DNA
Half-Brother 24.9% shared DNA
Half-Brother 23.8% shared DNA

"What is happening?" she asked out loud and studied the screen in front of her. Still in a state of surreal disbelief, Lorelei leaned closer to try to absorb the information. Each entry featured a small magnifying glass icon. Clicking it allowed her to share her contact information with the anonymous person listed. It was a one-way exchange, placing the decision to respond entirely in their hands. If they chose to reach out, the next move would be theirs.

She hesitated, her finger hovering over the back button as unease prickled at her skin. The thought of opening Pandora's box made her pull back. Then she froze. Stunned, she sat motionless in her wheelchair, eyes glued to the screen, unable to process the revelation staring back at her.

"How is this even possible? There has to be some sort of mistake."

Having been an only child her whole life, the concept that four half-sisters and brothers existed was mind-blowing, and she struggled to wrap her head around the truth in front of her eyes.

"I have half-siblings?" she questioned. "This can't be right."

Maybe they mixed up her results with another person's or the barcode got affixed to the wrong results panel. She clicked through all the other reports, scanning pages for any abnormality that would prove a mistake had been made. Seeing a positive diagnosis of kidney disease from her medical results, it was harder to deny there had been a mix-up.

Her thoughts spun in her mind on a full tilt-a-whirl. Four half-siblings that she didn't even know existed. What did that even mean? Slowly, realization dawned on her, and it took her breath away. It was like she'd been sucker punched and the truth sent her reeling.

To her knowledge, her father hadn't taken the test. If these results were accurate, the man who'd raised and doted on her for Lorelei's entire life was not the man she thought he was. The idea set off a flutter of panic she couldn't contain, and she needed answers.

"Mom!" she shouted, and within seconds, Liz was

flying through the door to her bedroom with her father close on her heels.

"What is it?" Liz asked. "Are you hurting? Do we need to call Dr. Pamulapti?"

"Yes… no." She didn't know how to answer. Lorelei pointed one shaking finger toward the computer monitor.

Confused, Liz pulled on her reading glasses that perpetually dangled from a beaded chain around her neck and leaned in to read the small type on the screen. After several long seconds, she gasped in horror and covered her mouth with her hands.

"What in the Sam Hell is going on with you two?" Charlie asked as he walked over to the monitor and leaned in to read the report.

"What is this?"

"It's my DNA relatives' report from Ancestrify. Did you take the test?"

"What? No?"

"Then who is listed here?" She pointed at the line that said Father. "Dad?" Lorelei asked. His lips were still moving as he read the words under his breath. His face flushed pink, and a red rash started to crawl up the sides of his neck as he continued to read. Seeing him in distress, a whimper escaped Lorelei's lips. "Is it true?"

"What? It can't be," he cried and staggered back in shock. He collapsed at the foot of her bed and buried his face in his hands. In shock, Liz fell down next to him onto Lorelei's bed. Her forehead wrinkled and her eyes darted wildly around the room as her mind worked feverishly, trying to put all the pieces together.

"One of you better start talking," Lorelei threatened. She was desperate for answers and burst into tears. "I'm sorry. I didn't mean it. I'm just so confused." She shook her head in an attempt to clear it and tried to calm the panic attack that was pressing in and sucking all the air out of her lungs. She grounded herself by focusing on the orange-peel texture of the leather armrests on her wheelchair. "I took the Ancestrify test as a Christmas gift for you, Dad," Lorelei said as tears welled at her lashes. "I wanted to help you create a virtual family tree and was hoping we could uncover the history of some of our ancestors together. I never thought we'd get blindsided like this."

Liz reached one arm toward Charlie, who was shaking. In a small voice, she began, "We had some trouble conceiving, and since I was thirty-seven and running out of time, we worked with a fertility clinic." She blinked hard several times and then continued, "It doesn't make any sense. I'm floored."

Charlie's eyebrows arched in shock. "How could this happen?"

"The sperm they inseminated me with was supposed to have been your father's," Liz clarified. "We were both adamant we wanted a biological child." She was lost in the past, scrambling for information. "Remember, they sent you into one of those little rooms with a stack of *Penthouse* magazines?"

Lorelei held up one hand. "TMI, Mom."

"No. I only say that because I vividly remember we provided the sample the same day as our intrauterine insemination," Liz explained.

"Did you know?" Charlie asked Liz. The question spun Liz in a dizzying circle.

"What?" Liz was shocked. "Of course not! I would have never consented to it, ever! I wanted *our* child or none at all." She gripped her stomach. "God, I feel sick," she cried, wrapping her arms around her belly, and ran into the adjoining bathroom where retching sounds could be heard seconds later. When Liz stumbled back into the bedroom, her face was white as a sheet, and a light sheen of sweat covered her brow.

Charlie's eyes were wild, shooting across the room as he navigated the shocking truth that had been discovered. "But *I'm* your father," he whispered. "I don't know who I am if that is taken from me."

Liz reached out to pull Charlie toward her, and he hugged her for dear life, burying his head into her stomach and holding on to her like she was his only port in the storm. "He had no right."

"Why didn't you tell me the truth of my conception?"

"We thought about it. But we didn't think it was important to share the nitty-gritty details, and honestly, I was embarrassed," Liz admitted. "How was I supposed to tell you that you were conceived in a doctor's office? We wanted a child, our own *biological* child, and Dr. Blackwell promised us we would have one."

"But I'm *not* your biological child," Lorelei answered. "I don't know *who* I am anymore."

"You're our beloved daughter and the child we begged to conceive," Liz answered. Trembling with emotion, she cried, "I feel violated. To know that another man's semen was used to conceive you. I just feel sick."

"Blackwell made a mistake," Charlie muttered. "We need answers. We deserve to know who your biological father is."

"I can try to message the DNA relatives listed in the report and see if any of them want to correspond. Maybe they have the answers we're looking for. Maybe my biological father will respond." Lorelei paused then, realizing how much it would hurt her father, and added, "I'm sorry, Dad. I have to know."

Charlie crumpled at the request. "Someone or something is always threatening to take you away from me."

Lorelei opened her arms and reached out to her father. He knelt by her chair and hugged her around her waist, his head in her lap. Lorelei stroked the ring of hair at the nape of his neck and tried to soothe his fears as he cried. She'd never witnessed this level of devastation coming from him, and her heart was breaking.

"You will always be my father in every way that matters. Regardless of what I find out, *you* will be the one who taught me how to dance, how to fish off the pier, and how to drive a stick shift. *You* put in the real day-to-day effort, and no stupid DNA test can ever change that."

Liz crept closer and whispered, "I'm so sorry, honey."

"It's not your fault," Lorelei said. "We are all victims here. You put your trust in Dr. Blackwell because you wanted to be parents. You cannot be blamed for what transpired."

"He's going to answer to me," Charlie said, wiping his palms over his beleaguered face. "We're going to Blackwell Reproductive Health tomorrow and getting to the bottom of this."

"I'm sorry, Daddy." Lorelei felt distraught over the pain she saw on his face.

He bent down to kiss her cheek. "It's not your fault, sweetheart." Then he stood and strode out of the room.

Liz stood. "Is it okay if I go talk to your father? I'm worried about him. Can I have one of your printouts?"

"Of course. Go. He needs you now." She handed over the thick sheath of paper that had changed her entire life in mere minutes. Lorelei was discombobulated, floating in the strange truth she was now forced to accept.

Who am I? She'd always thought it was the easiest question to answer in the world. Lorelei thought she knew without a doubt *who* she was because she knew *whose* she was. To have her connection to her father severed and to know there was another man she'd never met walking around in the world who was biologically her father was earth-shattering. With one report, her sense of identity had crumbled into a heap at her feet. It was another weakness she would be forced to accept, and she was angry.

Once the door was closed, Lorelei's body shook with sobs. A fresh well of guilt reared up. Not only were her parents forced to take care of her due to her illness, but now she would be asking her father to continue when he wasn't even her father at all.

Twenty-Six

The next morning, Lorelei rolled into the kitchen where her somber parents were gathered with their red-rimmed eyes sipping on coffee. Their whispering silenced when they saw her roll into the room.

"Looks like you guys slept as well as I did last night."

"It was a rough one," Charlie affirmed, getting up to pull Lorelei's favorite mug from the strainer and filling it with coffee before bringing it and the carton of cream to the table. It was an everyday act of love that she'd taken for granted, but on that morning, it made her heart clench.

He bent down to brush his lips on her cheek. "Those results from yesterday change nothing." He cupped her chin in his fingers and tipped her head up. "You are mine, no matter what any DNA test says."

Lorelei flashed him a pained smile and turned her head away to brush tears from her cheeks.

After a breakfast of scrambled eggs and toast, they drove silently to Blackwell Reproductive Health. Each was lost in their own sea of emotions and what this visit would mean to their family. Charlie pulled the car into the handicapped parking space and stared at the building. "He seems to have done quite well for himself over the years," he remarked ruefully. "I wonder how many families he's destroyed and traumatized. When this news gets out, he won't be able to afford a pot to piss in."

Liz reached over to squeeze Charlie's arm. Lorelei wasn't used to hearing her happy-go-lucky father speaking with such bitterness. She unbuckled her seatbelt and waited while Liz popped the trunk and unfolded the wheelchair. Charlie gathered his daughter in his arms and set her down gingerly on the seat like he had hundreds of times before. This time, Lorelei brushed her lips across his cheek and whispered, "I love you, Dad." The words helped him square his shoulders, and within minutes, they were inside the building and standing in front of the frumpy receptionist. She had the quintessential gatekeeper look, with a professional-level resting bitch face and an asymmetrical Karen-esque bob.

"Do you have an appointment?"

"No. But we are not leaving until we see Dr. Blackwell."

"I'm sorry. He's in such high demand that his waiting list is a year out."

"He's going to want to make an exception."

"I doubt that." She turned away, and Charlie leaned in closer.

"We are the Sandersons, and unless you want me to inform every woman sitting in your waiting room right now that Dr. Blackwell committed fertility fraud, I suggest you find a way to squeeze us into his busy schedule," Charlie demanded. The usually passive and gentle man was trembling with unbridled fury.

"Those are wild accusations, and I must ask you to keep your voice down so you don't distress our patients."

"We will not be silenced." Liz stepped in, supporting her husband. "I suggest you convince him to see us right now, or things are going to get loud around here."

The receptionist's eyes widened. She jumped up and raced around her desk, hissing, "Follow me. I'll show you to his office right away."

Charlie pushed Lorelei down the long hallway and settled her in front of the solid walnut desk in the middle of the room. Liz's mouth was dry as she glanced around Dr. Blackwell's sunny office. It was a far cry from the one she'd sat in with Charlie thirty years ago.

On a shelf, a crystal award gleamed. Liz stood to take a closer look at it. She pulled out her reading glasses and bent closer to make out the inscription.

Lifetime Achievement Award for Advances in

Fertility from The Society of American Reproductive Health.

Clenching her jaw, she shoved the glasses back into her handbag. She picked up the award in her two hands. It was weighty and constructed of Waterford crystal. She set it back down, muttering, "A Lifetime Achievement Award? He makes me sick." Taking her seat once again, they waited. As the minutes ticked by, the thin air crackled with tension, each of their hearts heavy with the weight of betrayal. There was a subtle shift as the collective anger in the room started to rise.

Finally, Dr. Blackwell strode through the door and promptly closed it behind him.

Disgusted, Charlie shook his head, a sneer of contempt destroying his usually sunny features.

"It's good to see you again, Mr. And Mrs. Sanderson."

"Is it?" Charlie dared to ask, the doctor's pleasantries falling on deaf ears. "Cut the crap, Blackwell! We have a bone to pick with you. Some upsetting new information has come to light."

"Oh?" Dr. Blackwell leaned in and adopted a practiced expression of concern on his face, feigning innocence.

Tears streamed down Liz's face as she clutched her husband's hand. Her voice trembled with pain as she spoke through choked sobs. "Lorelei completed a DNA kit from Ancestrify, and we discovered that she has four half-siblings! But most distressing is the fact that Charlie is not Lorelei's biological father."

"Maybe you could explain to us simpletons how that is even possible when we came to you to help us conceive a *biological* child," Charlie interjected.

"We trusted you, and you violated us in the most intimate way possible."

"What do you mean?" Dr. Blackwell replied, still clinging to innocence. In shock, Liz watched his Adam's apple make the journey up and down.

"Don't play dumb with us!" Charlie shouted, leaning forward, enraged.

Lorelei spoke up. She pulled a sheath of papers out of her purse and waved it in the air. "Based on this report, you impregnated my mother with the wrong semen. If Charlie Sanderson is not my biological father, then who is?"

Liz burst into tears.

Dr. Blackwell flinched before attempting to regain control of the situation. His voice dripped with false empathy as he desperately tried to rationalize his despicable behavior. "I understand that this paternal revelation has shaken you, but you must understand that my intentions were never malicious. I believed my methods would provide you with the best chance of conceiving. You wanted a child, and I gave you one."

"We deserve to know the truth," Liz shouted.

Dr. Blackwells's composure wavered for a moment as he clenched his fists into tight balls, his knuckles turning white. He struggled to maintain his sense of superiority, and his body language betrayed his mounting desperation. He took a step forward, invading their personal space, his eyes blazing with a mix of hubris and dread.

"Who is Lorelei's father?" Charlie demanded as he stood and leaned closer.

"Very well. If you must know," he acquiesced, then dropped a bombshell. "Statistically, the sample that yields the best success rates in this clinic is my own."

Liz burst into tears at the admission, and Charlie staggered back to his chair in shock as Lorelei gasped and stared at the doctor's facial features, noticing for the first time they had the same nose.

"You don't understand the pressures I face," he continued, his voice dripping with disdain. "The expectations, the demands of my patients and colleagues. I've had to take matters into my own hands to ensure success."

Charlie found his feet again, his face contorted with a mixture of anger and anguish, and lashed out at the doctor. His voice, filled with righteous fury, shook the room. "You dare try to justify this? To use your own sperm without our knowledge or consent? It's vile."

"I am a pioneer in this field, and my methods have yielded exceptional results." His eyes darted between Lorelei and her parents. "While my methods were a bit unorthodox, I truly believed they were necessary to give you the miracle baby you so desired. Please understand that I only had the best intentions."

Charlie interrupted with a sharp tone. "Best

intentions? How can you justify such a heinous act? It is an unforgivable breach of ethics."

Liz, her face etched with pain and fury, could feel her body trembling with rage. She leaned forward, desperate to understand. "How could you?"

Dr. Blackwell's face flushed with anger, his carefully constructed professional mask crumbling under their accusations. He attempted to regain control, though his voice wavered with desperation. "You do not know what I've sacrificed for my work. The miracles I've brought into this world! Exposing me would be a grave injustice, not only to me but to all the families I've helped. Not to mention, it would destroy my own family."

"Destroy *your* family?" Charlie laughed in contempt. "Just like you destroyed mine?"

Liz sobbed as grief and violation cut deep into her heart. Finally, with her voice strained with heartache, she stood up, her body trembling, and faced the doctor. "You lied to us. We came to you seeking help, and instead, you violated our trust in the most unimaginable way. The pain and emptiness we feel cannot be forgiven by any success you claim to have achieved."

Dr. Blackwell, cornered and desperate, clenched his jaw, his eyes darting around the room as if searching for an escape route. His arrogance faltered, replaced by a palpable sense of fear. Sweat dripped down his forehead as the wheels turned in his head.

Liz locked eyes with Dr. Blackwell and leaned

forward, her voice steady but filled with rage. "How many other families have you defrauded?"

Dr. Blackwell's face grew paler as beads of sweat formed above his lip. He could sense the walls closing in around him, the threat of exposure hanging heavily in the air. He needed to convince them to keep his secret at all costs.

"Please, understand," he pleaded, his voice trembling. "Exposing this would destroy everything I have worked for. My reputation, my life's work… it would all be ruined. I am willing to compensate you financially to ensure that this remains between us."

Charlie's eyes narrowed, his voice seething with determination. "Money can't undo what you've done! Your actions have irreparably damaged our family, and you must be held accountable."

Lorelei, her voice quivering with devastation, added, "You played God with our lives. We will not rest until we make sure the world knows what you are."

Dr. Blackwell's desperation grew as he realized his attempts at negotiation were failing. Panic filled his eyes, and he struggled to understand the ramifications of this truth coming to light. "You can't ruin me," he muttered, his voice a mere whisper. "I won't let you destroy my legacy."

Lorelei, her resolve unwavering, locked eyes with Dr. Blackwell. She spoke with a voice laced with determination. "Your reign of manipulation ends here. We will expose you for the monster you are. The truth will prevail."

Scrambling, he asked for time. "Can you at least give me forty-eight hours before you alert the authorities? I need time to speak to my wife and children."

"We aren't going to give *you* anything," Charlie spat out. "But we will honor the request out of respect for your wife and children who are also innocent victims in this disaster. You have forty-eight hours, Blackwell, that's all." They stood and pushed Lorelei back down the hall, leaving Dr. Blackwell alone in the room. He sank into a chair, his once-confident posture crumbling under the truth. Silence hung heavily around him.

His mind raced, desperately seeking a way out, a way to salvage what remained of his reputation and legacy. As he sat there, reality began to sink in, overwhelming him with a deep sense of regret and despair.

He ran a trembling hand through his silver hair. With a heavy sigh, his voice filled with a mix of self-pity and desperation, Dr. Blackwell muttered to himself, "You've given me no choice."

His gaze fixated on a framed photograph of his family taken two years ago. The weight of his failure settled heavily on his shoulders, a suffocating burden that seemed impossible to bear. His hands shook as he reached for a glass of water on the table, trying to steady his nerves, then instead reached for the scotch and poured himself a double.

Thoughts raced through his mind, the consequences of his actions playing out in a never-ending loop. With his fist clenched, Dr. Blackwell slammed it onto the table, as frustration and anger bubbled to the surface. He would not allow his legacy to be tarnished and for the medical community to label him as a pariah.

He picked up the phone at his desk and pressed the receptionist's extension.

"Please cancel all my appointments today. I have fallen ill."

"But the waiting room is full, and the Morrisons flew in from…"

He cut her off. "Just do as you're told. Who are you to question my authority?"

She backpedaled. "You're right, I'm sorry. If you're ill, it's better not to expose anyone." She apologized and hung up.

Dr. Blackwell picked up the crystal tumbler and made one final phone call. It was time to exercise the nuclear option. A man with a gruff voice answered on the first ring. "This is Genesis. I need to report the mission has been compromised. The broken arrow cannot be salvaged."

"Does the arrow require a clean-up crew?"

"Yes."

"State the address."

"I don't have a current one." He then said, "Sanderson, Elizabeth and Charles. Daughter, Lorelei."

"King James will be in contact with you. Blessed is the man whose quiver is full."

"Blessed indeed."

Dr. Blackwell hung up the phone and allowed

himself a second glass of scotch. He ignored the other phone calls, texts, and emails and sat in his office, waiting for the rest of the staff to leave. Hours later, when he was slightly tipsy, he scanned his card and let himself into the laboratory. He brushed away any remaining concern regarding the Sanderson family, knowing they'd been reduced to an annoying wasp who would soon be exterminated. He'd already wasted so much precious time, and he had important work to do—God's work.

Dr. Blackwell long believed he was an instrument of the Lord, who had blessed him with the power to bring new lives into the world and expand the ranks of the faithful. He had been anointed with the divine duty to ensure the growth of the Abundant Quiver Movement. Their core principle was based on the notion that every child was a heavenly gift and that contraception directly defied God's will. Over the past two decades, with the resources available through his network of successful fertility practices, he dedicated significant efforts to the cause. He meticulously screened and selected candidates who aligned with his religious beliefs, convinced that his actions were justified as long as they served the greater purpose of the Abundant Quiver movement. Then he genetically selected and implanted male embryos into their mother's wombs. The irony that a baby girl would be his downfall was not lost on him.

"Strengthen my resolve, O Lord, as we create more soldiers for your army. Amen," he prayed as he brought the bible to his lips to kiss it, then rose and washed his hands again before donning a pair of rubber gloves.

"Sleep well, my sons. In a few days, you have work to do," he whispered to the embryos growing inside the warm incubator. With pride, he counted the dishes. Eleven more disciples had been conceived by his expertise. The healthiest males among them would be selected and implanted into his most devout patients during the next few days.

The Sanderson Family was simply collateral damage in the Abundant Quiver Movement's spiritual war. Dr. Blackwell knew that his genetic legacy would thrive, that his dark lineage would endure long after his departure from this mortal realm and guarantee his immortality. After years of steadfast dedication, he had transcended his mortal existence and stepped fully into his role at the right hand of the Lord. No longer having to look up in awe at God the Father, instead, he was his full partner, in lockstep with him, and creating a powerful army that would use its vast human resources to step into politics and other positions of power in the United States. It was the only way they could take their power back from those hell-bent on the destruction of mankind. It was a grandiose mission that the Lord had indoctrinated him with, and he would not fail. God always gave his toughest battles to his strongest soldiers.

TWENTY-SEVEN

The next day, just before closing time, Katie was working through her list of tasks at Kandied Karma while Yuli counted down the drawer in the back of the shop. Katie wrung out a damp cloth and wiped down the chairs and tables. It had been a non-stop ten hours on her feet all day long.

"I'm beat!" she complained to Arlo, who, in solidarity, circled, then plopped down with a heavy sigh behind the counter as if he were just as exhausted.

"We need to train you to run the cash register," Katie said.

"Although that sounds like a great idea, it will just add fuel to the fire around here. You think the flash mob video increased traffic at the store? Think how long the lines would be if Aura Cove's famous talking dog was running the register."

Katie laughed. "Aura Cove's *self-proclaimed* famous talking dog," she corrected Arlo, who huffed and closed his eyes, bored already. "Okay. You might have a point."

With Christmas only two days away, the shop was bustling with last-minute shoppers. Katie had been run ragged the week before, when orders that needed to be shipped were the priority. She thought business would slow down after the burst of new customers from the viral video subsided, but it felt like Kandied Karma was busier than ever.

The bell on the door jingled as a despondent Liz came through it. Happy to see a friendly face at the end of a long shift, Katie shot Liz a megawatt smile that dissolved quickly when she noticed the woman seemed troubled.

"I'm sorry to show up here unannounced so close to closing time, but I am..." Distracted, her words dwindled away. She was wringing her hands, and Katie sensed Liz was on the verge of a breakdown. Katie rushed to the front door to lock it and turned to the distraught woman.

"Let me grab you a cup of coffee and we'll sit down and chat. Why don't you grab a seat?" She pointed to the table closest to the glass case. Katie turned to the espresso machine, and a few minutes later, brought a tray with two cups and an assortment of truffles out to where Liz was seated.

With a shaking hand, Liz brought the tiny cup from the saucer to her lips and took a small sip. "Thank you." Her gaze darted to the plate-glass window, and she let out an overwhelmed cry. Covering her face with her hands, she sobbed.

Concerned, Katie slid her chair closer and wrapped an arm around the shaking woman's shoulders. "I don't even know where to begin," Liz admitted. "These last couple of days have been an absolute nightmare."

"Is it Lorelei?"

"No…yes. I mean…" Liz exhaled a hot breath and blurted, "It's a long story, but to sum it up, Lorelei took the Ancestrify DNA test as a Christmas gift for Charlie, and when she got the results, we discovered he is not her biological father." Liz burst into tears again.

The bombshell hit Katie head-on. She gasped, "What?"

Liz bent down to her feet where her handbag rested on the floor, removed a thick printed report from her purse, and handed it over to Katie. She flipped through it as Liz continued to explain, "And… it turns out she has four half-siblings." She dissolved into another pile of tears. "Charlie is understandably devastated."

Seeing the proof in black and white, Katie was in shock. She set the report down on the table. Arlo trotted over to where Katie and Liz were seated and pressed his head into Liz's hand resting in her lap. She absentmindedly stroked his soft fur while Katie exclaimed, "Oh my God, Liz. I can't imagine what you are going through right now. That must have been a painful discovery." She added, "What did you do?"

"We confronted that evil man," Liz answered. "Do

you know he had the audacity to ask us to keep this report a secret? When we refused, he tried to bribe us for our silence to keep his legacy intact." Liz shivered, remembering. "That man's selfishness knows no bounds!" She shook her head in contempt and plucked a chocolate off the tray, pulled off the accordion liner, and bit into it. "Yum." She closed her eyes for a moment and savored it.

Katie leaned in to confide, "I'm sharing this with you in confidence, but Lauren had an egg retrieval procedure done recently at Blackwell Reproductive Health."

"Oh my God," Liz cried. "You cannot, under any circumstances, let her move forward with the fertilization."

"Agreed," Katie said. "He needs to be stopped. We need to report him to the medical board." She paused, trying to come up with the right legal term. "I think it is called fertility fraud."

"It is, but it happened so long ago. Wouldn't the statute of limitations be up?"

"I don't know, but I can put you in touch with someone who might. Davina Thorne is an excellent family law attorney who can help with your case or refer you to someone who can answer your questions."

She exhaled a heavy sigh. "We're barely scraping by as it is. I'd never tell Charlie this, but for the briefest second, it crossed my mind to take the bribe."

"No one would judge you for thinking that way."

"We don't have the resources to hold him accountable *and* survive a lengthy court battle since the ongoing medical bills for Lorelei's care have depleted our assets. Who knows how many other women he's violated? If Lorelei's test at Ancestrify uncovered four confirmed biological half-siblings, how many more are out there that haven't been tested?"

"It's mind-boggling," Katie empathized.

"The idea that Dr. Blackwell pleasured himself and then returned to complete the insemination procedure in an aroused state makes me nauseous." She recoiled with a shiver. "Not to mention, Charlie having to degrade himself to produce a sample that would never be used in the first place!"

Katie's mouth twisted up into a grimace. Her flashes from Lauren's consultation raced through her mind. All of them became crystal clear now that she'd heard Liz's story. "Your feelings are completely valid. I'm truly sorry your family is going through this, especially with everything else you've been facing."

Liz choked out a sob. "Yesterday was a total nightmare. It feels like he destroyed our family. Charlie is grieving, and I don't know how to help him."

"Do you believe in Karma?" Katie asked.

"I don't know if I do anymore," she admitted, her eyes swimming with fresh tears. "It feels like we're being punished, and all we've ever tried to do is be decent people and raise our daughter."

"That's a completely reasonable reaction," Katie validated. "Can I offer you a new thought?"

"Of course," Liz answered.

"In every painful event, there is a seed of something

good." Katie tried to explain, "Maybe the silver lining in this whole messed up situation is that there are now more blood relatives who could be potential donor matches for Lorelei."

Liz gasped as her hand flew to her mouth. "We've been so blindsided by this, the thought didn't even occur to me! Do you think a stranger would willingly give a vital organ to someone they've never even met?"

"I honestly don't know," Katie answered. "It's a big ask, but I believe in the innate goodness of people. It's worth a try. You have all been victims of his fraud and deceit, but what if the bigger purpose was to bring you all together to give Lorelei a second chance?"

Liz got up and hugged Katie. "I have to go!" When their skin touched, Katie saw a flash. Red numbers on a screen blinking. An emergency room and a heart monitor flatlining.

"Wait!" Katie said, trying to interpret the flashes in a logical way that wouldn't sound like she was a complete lunatic, but Liz was already out the door and bee-lining to her parked van. On the table, the offensive report lingered. Katie gathered it up and walked back to the kitchen where Yuli was wiping down the counters. Seeing the panic on Katie's face, Yuli quickly returned the cloth to the outgoing laundry pile and took a step closer.

"What is it, Katia?"

"Liz just came by, and I got another flash." Her mind was spinning. "I think Lorelei is going to die."

TWENTY-EIGHT

The clock chimed, and Arlo walked over to the mat and waited by the patio door. Katie's house was darkened and empty since she was out having drinks with Frankie, and Beckett had picked up Marisa for the evening.

Right on time, Zoya stood in front of the door, snapped her fingers, and a golden trail of sparks illuminated her face as the lock and alarm system disengaged. She quickly slid the door open and stepped inside Katia's home, eager to avoid being seen by her nosy next-door neighbor, Oz. Arlo let out distressed yips until she let him outside, Zoya followed him, concealing herself in shadows and darkness.

When he was done relieving himself, Arlo raced over and sat on his haunches. Zoya snapped her fingers twice, and he spoke. Normally, these reports were mundane, and she only half paid attention. "It's been a roller coaster around here. Katie just learned the family

Karma assigned her to rebalance were victims of fertility fraud. The doctor inseminated her with his own semen!"

Prickles of intuition walked up Zoya's spine. She forced a calm expression on her face and asked, "Who was the fertility doctor?"

"Blackwater?" he tried. "Blackwave?"

But as Arlo struggled to come up with it, she blurted out, "Black*well*?"

"Yes!" Arlo said. "How did you know?"

She pinched her lips tight, knowing Arlo's total allegiance was to Katia, while he worked off his sentence with her. She couldn't risk him reporting her interest back to Katia and ruining her plans.

"That's a no-brainer. He's one of the leading fertility experts on the east coast."

"Not for very much longer," Arlo muttered under his breath and lay down to deliver a series of leisurely licks to his paw.

"What do you mean?"

"Katie told Liz they should report him to the medical board and press charges for fertility fraud. But Liz and Charlie agreed to give the doctor forty-eight hours to tell his family before they go to the police with the proof in the Ancestrify report."

"Where is this report?"

"On the kitchen countertop." Zoya's eyes widened and her gaze narrowed on Arlo.

"Wait here," she instructed and then quickly climbed the steps and slipped into Katia's home to find the report. She picked up the papers and brought them back down to where Arlo sat awaiting her return, anxiously licking himself. In the moonlight, she quickly flipped through the report, digesting the results instantly, confirming every thought she'd received from Dr. Blackwell during her tour.

His paw now soaked, he stopped licking. "Fun fact. It's the same fertility practice where Lauren's eggs were harvested a few weeks ago."

"Is that right?" The last little tidbit got Zoya's full attention. Those eggs could be the beginning of her end. If they were fertilized, implanted, and carried to term, the next supernatural generation would be born, and Zoya would be forced to move on to the afterlife and serve the eternal coven. Stuck in the cosmos, surrounded by the women of past generations for eternity, and enslaved by servitude was not part of her master plan.

She rolled the report into a tube and bopped Arlo on the head with it. Arlo had to swallow the angry growl deep in his throat that welled up from the obnoxious act. He was shocked when the next words out of her mouth were, "You've pleased me."

Praise from Zoya was rare. Arlo got to his feet and, seeing this was the opportunity he'd been waiting for, asked, "Am I still on track to earn my freedom on Katie's next birthday?"

"All signs point to yes," she confirmed, throwing him a trite Magic 8 ball answer as she climbed the stairs. Arlo's tags jingled as he followed closely behind.

She pulled open the door, and he darted inside. Then Zoya turned on her heel and made a hasty exit to the car, where Higgins awaited her return.

With this new discovery, all the pieces of the puzzle revealed themselves. Zoya sped to the hangar, eager to get back to the compound to devise her plan. With only three days remaining of Dr. Blackwell's life, the week between Christmas and New Year's would virtually shut down the fertility clinic and give her the opportunity she'd been waiting for. All the stars were aligning, and she tingled in anticipation.

TWENTY-NINE

On Christmas Eve, mulled wine simmered on the stove at Liz and Charlie's home, infusing the air with the scents of cinnamon, cloves, and citrus. Liz pulled out a ladle to stir the pot before scooping the liquid into three mugs and setting them on a tray. She pulled a bag of popcorn from the microwave and poured it into a bowl, then while it was still warm, sprinkled it with kettle corn seasoning. She hoisted up the tray and walked into their modest living room where the rest of her small family gathered and set the tray on the coffee table.

Charlie was preoccupied, staring out the large picture window at the street. "Do you recognize that car?" He jerked his head toward a dark sedan where a shadowy figure sat hunched in the driver's seat.

"No," Liz said as she joined him and squinted at the nondescript vehicle. "Seems a little odd for someone to be sitting inside a car on Christmas Eve," she mused.

"It's definitely got my Spidey-senses tingling," he murmured. "Do you think it's Blackwell?"

"He wouldn't," Liz said, her words shaky, and when they left her lips, she was having a hard time believing them herself.

Charlie shrugged his shoulders, still staring down the figure in the darkened car. "When you push a man like Dr. Blackwell up against the wall, I'm pretty sure he's capable of anything."

Liz shivered, trying to dispel the nervous energy that gathered. She didn't disagree.

"Let's watch the movie," Lorelei requested from her spot next to the sofa, eager to change the subject. "Dr. Blackwell has already taken so much from us. Let's not allow him to take our Christmas Eve, too."

"You're right, dear." Liz turned back to find the remote and pressed play on their annual Christmas Eve movie lineup. First was the vintage black and white *It's a Wonderful Life* followed by *Elf*. Watching movies together on Christmas eve was a tradition they'd started when Lorelei was three and still wearing footie pajamas. Liz passed the warm mugs of the mulled wine to Charlie and Lorelei, and she noticed Lorelei flinch when she sipped.

"Are you in pain?"

"I'm sorry, Mom. I don't know if I can drink this. My stomach is cramping." She rubbed her distended belly and shifted in her wheelchair.

"How about some water?" Liz offered and ran off to the kitchen to grab a glass.

"Thank you." Lorelei took a sip, and they settled in to watch the movie. When it was over, Lorelei yawned, "I'm beat." Picking up on the signal, Charlie stood and stretched, then rolled Lorelei to her bedroom and lifted her into bed.

"Love you, kiddo," Charlie said, looking down at her with a smile, his eyes crinkling in the corners as he brushed her hair from her face. "You feel warm," he said, then flattened his palm against her forehead to gauge her temperature.

"You worry too much. I'm okay, Dad." Lorelei flipped over and pulled up her comforter, and within minutes, she was dozing. Charlie walked back out to the living room, where Liz was sitting on the sofa in the dark.

"She's warm," he told Liz, taking a seat next to her. "And we didn't even get to *Elf.*"

"I was afraid of that. She's deteriorating," Liz acknowledged with a heavy sigh. "Remember when our biggest headache on Christmas Eve was if we had enough time to assemble the toys before she woke up?"

"Those were the days, and we didn't even know it." Charlie whispered, "God, I wish we could go back."

"Me too," Liz said. "Christmas was magic when Lorelei was little."

"It was," Charlie agreed. "It's been a long while since we had any magic in our lives."

"Maybe it's time to make our own magic. I can't stop thinking about what Katie said yesterday about silver linings and that maybe one of these half-siblings we've discovered would be the ideal donor. I know Lorelei's been trying to open a line of communication with them since they were discovered."

"I was thinking the same thing, but was afraid it was being too selfish." He paused, then added, "I also don't think we should move forward without Lorelei's permission. This nightmare has been a violation for all of us, and I don't want to add to those feelings. Let's discuss it with Lorelei in the morning."

Liz reached out to stroke his arm. "You're a good man, Charlie Brown," she said with a wink.

"You haven't called me that for years."

A sad smile crossed her lined face. "We've had to walk an impossible road, you and I."

"We have."

"And it hasn't gotten any easier, but without a doubt, I'd always want to walk it with you." He stood and pulled her up for a hug, planting a kiss on her forehead.

"Let's go to bed." They gathered up their empty mugs and the popcorn bowl and, after depositing them in the dishwasher, shut off the lights in the kitchen. Charlie began his nightly safety inspection and walked over to the window again. He twisted the blinds shut, noticing the car he'd seen hours before was still there. He walked around their ranch home, checking the windows and doors and locking them, then settled in his bed with his wife and fell asleep.

Four hours later, Liz was startled awake from a deep sleep. "Mom!" Lorelei's panicked shout echoed down the hall, and Liz popped up and raced to her bedroom. "I can't see! Everything is blurry," she cried, then doubled over as a sharp pain tore through her abdomen. She clutched her side, gasping for breath. "Something is wrong."

"Charlie!" Liz screamed, and a disheveled Charlie appeared in the doorway. "We need to get her to a hospital." Lorelei was moaning and crying out. Charlie leaped into action and executed a firefighter's carry, gathering his frail daughter into his arms and rushing out the front door to their van. Liz folded up the wheelchair and, within minutes, they whipped by the car parked in the street that had been their biggest worry only hours ago.

Charlie raced down the highway, taking a route so familiar at this point, the car could have driven itself. He pulled into the valet parking in front of the emergency entrance, and Liz popped open the trunk and unfolded the wheelchair. Charlie scooped up a moaning Lorelei, depositing her in the chair, while Liz grabbed the handles and rushed her through the automatic revolving door and he parked the car. "We need a doctor. Our daughter has PKD. She's lost her vision and the belly pain is elevated." Lorelei was whimpering in the chair, her body constricted in agony. A nurse rolled her into an examination room, and Liz followed closely behind. Charlie joined them a few minutes later.

"It hurts," Lorelei cried, tears coursing down her face.

"Can you give her anything for the pain?" Liz

begged, feeling helpless watching her daughter tremble, her face white.

"We will," the blonde nurse said. "I promise."

Over the next two hours, Lorelei was poked and prodded, and her condition was assessed. Liz answered all their questions, confirming the lengthy medical history that already existed in the computer system from their frequent visits for checkups and dialysis.

She was whisked away to the ICU where doctors worked fervently to stabilize her condition. The diagnosis, a massive renal hemorrhage, came like a hammer blow and confirmed her parents' deepest fears. The fragile blood vessels in her damaged kidneys had ruptured, leading to severe bleeding. It had taken several transfusions and intravenous fluids to stop the bleeding. Her blood pressure had plummeted so dangerously low they had almost lost her.

Liz and Charlie spent an hour in the chapel on their knees, begging for their daughter's life. Unable to bring themselves to pray for a tragedy that would bring a life-saving kidney to their daughter. It was simply too cruel to pray for the Christmas Eve devastation of another family. She was stabilized, and that was enough for now. They sat with her, with no place else to go, surrounded by the constant beeping of machines and the hushed conversations of the smaller staff of doctors and nurses while Lorelei fought to survive. She drifted in and out of consciousness, as Liz and Charlie took turns holding her hand and talking to her, their faces etched with worry and anguish.

The nursing staff allowed them to linger well past regular visiting hours, but eventually sent them home to take a nap and shower.

"You can come back in the morning at eight and stay all day," the nurse told them. "Don't worry, we've got her."

"Okay," Liz whispered. "We'll be back at eight. I can't bear the thought of our child alone in the hospital on Christmas."

They both brushed a kiss to Lorelei's pale forehead and left hand-in-hand, swiping tears from their eyes.

The drive was silent on the ride home.

"At least that car is gone," Charlie confirmed as he pulled into the driveway a few minutes later and, still dazed from exhaustion and worry, they stumbled to their bedroom to sleep for an hour. Then, after showers and coffee, they started the drive back to the hospital.

Christmas dawn was a gorgeous, sunny morning. A soft breeze tickled the palm trees that lined their drive back to the hospital. A notification dinged on Liz's phone in her purse, and she bent down to pull it out of her bag.

> ***Katie:*** *Merry Christmas! If you are available, we'd love to have you join us at noon for our Christmas feast.*
> ***Liz:*** *Wish we could! We had a setback with Lorelei. She's in the ICU.*
> ***Katie:*** *Oh no! So sorry to hear that! How about Yuli and I bring it to you?*

Liz: No. It's too much fuss. Enjoy the time with your family!
Katie: I'm not taking no for an answer. Plan on seeing us around 2.

"Katie wants to bring us Christmas dinner at the hospital," she told Charlie, who was navigating down the deserted streets as she tucked the phone away.

"She's good people," Charlie said as he eased into the empty parking lot at the hospital. They entered through the revolving doors, noticing it was quieter than usual, operating with a skeleton crew holiday staff. Even the coffee shop was shuttered. Liz punched the button for the third floor and gave their names to the lone nurse holding down the nurse's station. A few minutes later, they were shown to Lorelei's room, where she lay on the bed sleeping.

Beep. Beep. Beep.

The monotonous rhythm of the heart monitor echoed around the sterile white walls. Tubes snaked their way in and out of an unconscious Lorelei, who lay motionless on the bed. Liz sat down in the chair next to her and sandwiched her daughter's cool hand between her own warmer ones, willing her to summon the strength to fight. She rubbed the pads of her thumbs gently across Lorelei's hand, where her dry skin felt like sandpaper due to dehydration.

An instrumental track of "Silent Night" played on the Muzak that was piped out of the sound system in the hospital room, and her door was decorated with tinsel and a construction paper cut-out Christmas tree. It was a futile attempt to inspire Christmas spirit in the cheerless room. A long hour passed as they took turns holding their daughter's hand, waiting for her to wake up. Liz stood to stretch her legs and wandered down the hallway to watch a volunteer Santa make his rounds in the pediatric ICU down the hall.

At noon, Dr. Pamulaputi conducted a video consultation and delivered another devastating blow. Lorelei's kidneys had lost almost all functionality, and despite undergoing frequent dialysis treatments, her condition was steadily worsening. She'd been moved to the top of the transplant list due to the deterioration of her medical condition, and without a kidney, she would continue to weaken and eventually die.

Liz brushed away the hair from her daughter's forehead as she slept fitfully. She was afraid to wake her up because her hours were filled with pain. Even in slumber, her pinched forehead and restlessness gave her agony away. The pain was unrelenting, and Lorelei was exhausted from fighting the daily battle against it.

"We need to consider the very real possibility that we will have to let her go," Liz whispered as she brushed her tears away. In their marriage, Liz had always been the more realistic, pragmatic one.

"No!" Charlie said.

"She's in so much pain. What kind of life is this? It breaks my heart to see her suffering, and it's been going on far too long."

"I refuse to give up," Charlie admitted, and silence hung heavy between them.

For the next hour, Lorelei's parents clung to each other, praying for a miracle as she drifted between consciousness and sleep.

In desperation, Charlie pulled Lorelei's laptop out of his bag. He stared down at it for a long time before opening it, pushing away the violation of trust he was committing.

"I thought we were going to wait to get her permission?" Liz asked as she watched Charlie fight an internal battle whether or not to invade their daughter's privacy.

"We don't have a choice. She has to be around in order to get mad at me," Charlie offered in explanation.

"Okay, if you think it will help, do it."

"I don't know if it will, but it's worth a shot."

He navigated to her browser history and was grateful she was still logged in to her messages on the Ancestrify website.

"We have names!" he exclaimed in astonishment as he clicked through the messages. "They all want to meet her!"

"Really?" Liz dared to let herself hope. "That's fantastic news!"

"I have an idea." He immediately got to work, grateful to have a task to accomplish that might help the dire situation.

Between cups of bitter vending machine coffee, Charlie dedicated the next few hours to creating a private social media group called "Lorelei's Christmas Miracle." He wrote a detailed plea for help, uploaded photos and videos of his family, and invited her four half-siblings from the Ancestrify results.

When he stood to stretch, Lorelei's eyes fluttered open, and she offered her parents a weak smile. "Merry Christmas."

Tears spilled down Liz's cheeks, and she brushed them away. "It is now," she added and brought her daughter's pale hand to her lips.

Seeing the exhaustion on her parents' faces broke Lorelei's heart. "You guys look terrible," she teased, and the corners of her mouth curved up in a slight grin. "Can you raise me up?"

Liz pulled out the remote, and the mechanical bed whirred into an upright position. She re-tucked the blankets around Lorelei and settled the meal tray in front of her. Lorelei pulled the foil off of a container of lime Jello and spooned it to her mouth. She glanced over at her father, who still had her computer on his lap. "What is my laptop doing here?"

"I need to show you both something," he said as he pulled the screen open and turned it toward Lorelei and Liz.

On the screen was a secret Facebook group. She saw a photo of her family on it. "What is this?" she asked. "I'm confused."

"Well, I have to make a confession. I opened your messages in Ancestrify, and all four of your half-siblings want to meet you! So, I took a few liberties and created a social media group. Then I posted some photos and videos about our family and told them all about you. Three accepted the invite already, and I've been chatting with them while we've been waiting for you to wake up." Lorelei scrolled through the messages, touched by the response. "Two have offered to be typed and tested as potential donor matches for you."

Lorelei's hand flew to her mouth in shock. "What? Really?" She was afraid to hope they could give her the keys to leave behind the painful life she was currently living.

"Really," Charlie said. "Turns out our little girl is pretty darn likable." He grinned and scrolled down the page where Lorelei noticed he had posted the flash mob viral video.

"You didn't," she gasped.

"I did. Are you mad? Don't blame your mother, honey. This was a decision I made."

"No, Dad. I'm not mad at you. I'm only mad at this misery I'm in." Lorelei closed her eyes as the pain in her belly intensified. She focused on her breathing, inhaling through her nose and gritting her teeth together to power through it.

The nurse breezed in and checked her vitals and then administered a fresh IV cocktail of pain medication and electrolytes. "It should kick in shortly and you'll be more comfortable."

"Thank you," Lorelei mumbled as she prepared to drift off again.

Charlie bent down, wrapped his arm around her

head, and whispered into her ear, "You rest, sweetheart. I've got you. I am certain one of these half-siblings is a perfect match."

"The chances are pretty slim, but I hope you're right," Lorelei whimpered. "I don't know how much longer I can live like this."

Lorelei dozed again, and Liz turned to Charlie. "What are we going to do about Dr. Blackwell?"

"I've been filling in the others about what transpired. Eventually, we are going to need to go to the police and press charges. The only difference now is that instead of one family making allegations, there could be four."

"Do any of them want to meet him?"

"They are understandably furious. I think, after the dust settles, they will want justice for the havoc he's reeked in their lives," Charlie answered softly, letting Lorelei sleep. He wanted her to save her strength to fight more important battles. "I want to help facilitate the conversation. Each family he has wronged deserves to have their moment to confront that monster."

He added, "I think we should focus on getting Lorelei healthy again, and then we can worry about what to do about Dr. Blackwell." He looked down at his daughter's sleeping form. "Lorelei deserves to stand with her half-brothers and sister and bring him to justice."

Liz nodded. There were only so many minutes in any day she could devote to retribution.

"I've been doing a lot of research, and it turns out

fertility fraud is a lot more common than most people think. Lots of doctors played fast and loose with fertility ethics thirty years ago. They never saw home DNA profiling coming, and that future technology would eventually expose their lies. Too many morally gray doctors used their own sperm to impregnate their patients to artificially inflate their success rates."

This information left Liz speechless, but she eventually gathered the courage to ask the question that had been on her mind since they received the report. "Why?"

"I'll never understand it either, darling," Charlie whispered. "But Katie might be right. The ultimate silver lining is a willing donor who can give Lorelei her life back. I would endure this nightmare again for that opportunity."

THIRTY

"Merry Christmas, Mama!" Beckett called, waltzing through Katie's front door carrying a bouquet of white roses wrapped in red tissue paper.

"Thank you, sweetheart!" Katie exclaimed as she reached out for the bouquet. "Oh! Flowers? For me? You shouldn't have!"

"I didn't," he admitted sheepishly. "They're for…"

"Marisa?" Katie guessed with a laugh, letting go of the tissue paper-wrapped bundle as she stood on her tiptoes to brush a kiss across his cheek. "She's sitting by the pool." He departed quickly, and Katie turned back to see Lauren walking up the steps with her pink-manicured fingertips wrapped around Tom's bicep. On his other side, an older woman had a canvas grocery bag hanging from one shoulder and was cradling an apple pie in her hands.

"It's nice to see you again, Tom!" Katie smiled.

"As requested, I brought my two favorite women to Christmas dinner." His voice was warm and inviting.

"Merry Christmas, Mom." Lauren disengaged herself from him and hugged Katie.

"I know you hate it when I make a big deal out of things like this," Katie whispered in her ear. "But I've got a good feeling about this one."

"Stop." Lauren pulled back with a smile, then leaned back in to whisper in her ear, "But I do, too." Katie grinned as she turned toward Tom and his mother.

"Thank you for having us."

"This is my mom, Roxanne," Tom introduced.

"It's wonderful to have you here! I'm Katie." She opened her hands to take the pie. "Let me help lighten your load." When their skin touched, she felt a tingle and saw a flash of bright white light. Confused, Katie shook it off.

"Thank you! But please call me Rox," she said, handing the pie off to Katie while making direct eye contact. There was a bold confidence in her gaze most women lacked. She exuded strength and capability, and her hair was shorn close to her head and smooth. Simply dressed in corduroy and a cardigan, her face was plain and devoid of any makeup. Thick black lashes framed her brilliant blue eyes, and when a smile broke out across her features, it was like the sun popping out from behind a cloud. "It smells so good in here, doesn't it, Tommy? We've died and gone to heaven!" Katie always loved it when mothers called their adult children by their childhood nickname, and it instantly endeared her to Rox.

"Thank you. I can't take all the credit. As you can see, I've had a lot of help." Katie hiked a thumb behind her, indicating where the rest of her family was engaged in last-minute tasks to complete dinner preparations under Yuli's tutelage.

"I'm a terrible cook," Rox admitted as she leaned closer. "I have subjected this poor kid to more than his share of inedible experimental meals over the years."

Tom pulled a face. "Mom, I love you, but calling them meals is a stretch. At least on holidays, you gave it a rest, and we splurged on those Hungry Man TV dinners with the apple cobbler." He grinned at the memory.

"It was either that or MREs!" Roxanne opened her wide mouth, and a brash laugh escaped that startled Katie. It was a loud, stilted sound that resembled a machine gun. Seeing Katie's eyes widen to the size of dinner plates, she confided, "I know, the laugh, it's ridiculous. My sarge gave me the nickname Ricochet because of it." She grinned and shrugged her shoulders and then threw her head back and laughed again. This time, she mimed shooting an assault rifle, and Katie couldn't stop herself from dissolving into a pile of giggles. Across the room, all the heads cocked toward Rox in amusement, and she noticed Frankie's eyebrows arch so high they almost touched the ceiling.

Getting herself back under control, Katie cleared her

throat and told her sincerely, "Thank you for your service."

"She's a West Point grad," Tom offered, clearly so proud of his mother's accomplishments, he'd forgotten he's already shared this detail.

"Stop boring the woman, Tommy!" Rox teased with a disarming grin.

"Wow! West Point is impressive!" Katie said, acting as if it was the first time she'd heard. "Most men would name-drop the heck out of it. You should, too!"

"It's not my way." Rox deflected the praise, and it only made Katie like her more.

"I retired from the Army about ten years ago, but soon learned retirement wasn't for me," she admitted. "I like to stay busy. You know, idle hands, devil's workshop and all."

Tom piped up again, eager to sing her praises. "She serves on the board of directors for the Adapt4Heroes Foundation, and three years ago, she was appointed CEO. It's true, the woman is an absolute disaster in the kitchen, but when it comes to helping disabled veterans wounded in service return to homes that are equipped to handle their special needs, she's unstoppable."

"I just know how to play the game," Rox said, brushing off his praise.

"You're going to have to tell me more about the work you do at the foundation sometime," Katie offered.

"Roger that. For the record, you do not need to

worry. I did not bake this pie. The fine people at Publix did," she said with a wink.

"You're in for a treat today because all the women in my family are great cooks!" Katie boasted as she led them into the house and set the pie on the countertop where Kristina grabbed a knife from a drawer and began to slice it.

The noise level increased as more of Katie's friends and family gathered and spilled out into her beautifully decorated home. She'd put up three Christmas trees. She filled one with the ornaments the kids had made when they were in elementary school. It included hand-drawn snowmen, several clothespin reindeer missing a goggly-eye or two, and popsicle stick snowflakes with brilliant colored beads glued to each end haphazardly glued together. The second was her yellow tree; it was new this year, and filled with ornaments in her favorite color artfully placed an equal distance from the others. It was a far cry from the Christmas trees they'd had when the kids were little where all the ornaments were gathered at the bottom, squished together in a festive clump. She'd spend nights when they were asleep, relocating the worst offenders while sipping wine. The final tree was artfully constructed of fresh white poinsettias. It was an addition she'd splurged on at Boutique de Fleur, the new florist who'd just opened her store two doors down from Kandied Karma. Katie loved supporting the fledgling women-owned small businesses that popped up in the town square, instead of giving her money to big box stores in nearby St. Pete's Beach.

Through the ceiling-mounted speakers, Katie's old-fashioned Christmas playlist provided a nostalgic ambiance to the gathering. Nat King Cole's smooth voice gave way to the controversially offensive carol "Baby, It's Cold Outside".

At the sink, Callie groaned, "Mom, can we play something a little less disturbing? The lyrics are bordering on condoning date rape."

"Sweet Jesus, it's a classic."

"Yeah, classically controlling and misogynistic!"

"Okay, I give up. Alexa, skip this song." She spent the next few minutes circling the clusters of people, offering to refill drinks, overseeing the plating of the food, and locating serving utensils.

Lauren was at the sink washing a head of romaine lettuce while Yuli wrestled the enormous prime rib from the oven and covered it in foil to let it rest before slicing. Frankie was standing with her arm casually wrapped around Harry, canoodling near the liquor cabinet, chatting with Kristina and David. Katie grinned from ear to ear, seeing everyone gathered at her home. She tucked a thick white curl behind her ear. Just that morning, she realized she was down to one last black patch. Soon, her entire head would be brilliant white, and she didn't hate it at all.

After dinner, Katie herded everyone out to the great room. "I know we said no presents, but I couldn't help myself. Instead of picking out useless junk that will just turn into clutter in your houses, inside each of these envelopes is an experience hand-picked for you." She handed an envelope with a gift certificate to a nail salon to Marisa.

"I've loved having you here, and when you get settled in your new place next month, you better not forget me."

"Oh, I never will," Marisa vowed, and the smile on her face was genuine. She was looking forward to starting over in a new apartment. Since Rocco was still missing from the divorce proceedings, with the help of Davina, a judge was ruling soon and she would be able to move forward. It would take some time to completely heal, but Katie could see glimmers of a new version of the woman emerging from the ashes, and she was grateful she'd been a part of her journey.

Next, she handed an envelope to Beckett, who was sharing the oversized ottoman with his sisters. "You're going to Kayak with the manatees with your sisters and me."

A huge grin overtook his features, and he stood to hug her. "I've always wanted to try that."

Callie let out a squeal and even Lauren grinned as she handed them their gift certificates.

She took another step. "Yuli, Mom, and Dad, I scheduled an appointment with a medium. Her name is Talulah LaRue."

Kristina cut in immediately, "No way! We've been huge fans of her YouTube channel for years."

"Wait, you watch YouTube?" Katie asked. "How do I not know this?"

"There are a lot of things you don't know about us!

We're out there living our best lives," Kristina teased, winking at her. "I'm just happy we can still surprise you!"

"I've asked her to try to connect with Grandpa," she said to Kristina.

"Really? Dad?" Kristina's eyes welled up with tears. "Gosh, I miss him so much." It had been almost thirty years since his heart attack.

"Mediums are shysters and charlatans profiting from the grief of others," a skeptical Yuli muttered.

"Give her a chance, Mom. She's the real deal. I get goosebumps every time I watch one of her videos. We'll need to provide a couple of personal objects for the reading," Kristina explained, already intimately familiar with Talulah LaRue's process. "This is a once-in-a-lifetime opportunity to connect with Dad, and we have to make the most of it. What a gift! Thanks, honey!" Kristina threw her arms around Katie and hugged her tight.

Then Katie stepped toward Frankie and Harry, handing them the last envelope in her hand. "This contains a secret adventure date for the two of you."

"What is it?"

"You might want to wait…" Katie cautioned, but it was too late. In typical Frankie fashion, she ripped into the envelope with wild abandon and yanked out the heavy card stock. Her lips moved as she read it silently to herself, then blurted loudly, "A tantric workshop? Oh, bestie, you know me so well!"

She slapped Harry on the chest with the back of her

hand. "I've heard Sting can go for hours, and after this workshop, my Harry Willey will, too!"

All of Katie's kids groaned in unison.

Katie noticed the tips of Harry's ears turn crimson and his reaction made her grin. That poor, poor man.

"What?" Frankie said. "Sex between two people who love each other is the most natural act in the world."

Beckett clasped his hands over his ears. "No, no, no! This isn't happening."

"She's never been great at reading a room," Katie whispered to Harry who was turning beet red by the second.

"Agreed. She sure puts the frank in Frankie," he said unapologetically and pulled her tighter to him. He gazed at her with such adoration, Katie's heart nearly burst with joy for her friend.

"And we are going to give you the gift of a clean kitchen," Kristina said while she wrangled her grandchildren together. "Come on, kids. I know you know how to properly wash and dry the dishes." Frankie and Harry said their goodbyes, and while everyone else was busy, Katie pulled Yuli into the study.

"Lorelei was rushed to the ICU. I offered to bring them Christmas dinner today because I doubt the cafeteria is even open," Katie said, then lowered her voice. "Can you do anything to help?"

Yuli nodded. "I can give her more time."

"Good, that might give them a chance to find a

donor." Then Katie apologized, "Sorry to spring the reading on you with Talulah."

"I don't want to see them get their hopes up and have the reading be a fake. You know your mom can be too trusting and gullible."

"She can, but I know she misses him terribly."

"I do, too," she agreed. "After all these years, I thought I'd gotten used to living without Otto, but all it takes is one mention of his name, and all the feelings come rushing back."

"Speaking of feelings rushing back, the lunar event is only six weeks away."

"Zoya has offered the compound, which is the place that makes the most sense, but to be honest, it also brings up a lot of feelings for me," Yuli admitted.

"I bet." Katie reached out to squeeze her shoulder.

"The private plane will come for us," Yuli said. "The *Fioletovy Mahiya* is on a Monday. It's kismet, I guess, since Mondays are ruled by the moon and divine feminine energy. Though I doubt Zoya's feminine energy is very divine."

"Maybe try to go with an open mind and see what happens?"

"Your positivity is one of your sweetest qualities, though in this situation, very naïve," Yuli answered. "It will be interesting to be on the compound again. I wonder if it will feel the same."

"What do you mean?"

"There's a magnetic, peaceful quality I've only ever felt there."

"Imagine how peaceful it will be when we all reunite and let bygones be bygones?"

Yuli cackled. "Again with the jokes. You must warn me before you do that or I may piddle."

Katie chuckled and checked her watch. "I told Liz we'd come by at two. Let's make three plates and head over to the hospital. I'm sure they'd love to have a home-cooked meal and see a couple familiar faces." Thirty minutes later, they said their goodbyes and got into Katie's Beetle to head over to bring some Christmas cheer to the Sandersons, who were stuck at the hospital.

THIRTY-ONE

At the medical center, the elevator dinged and Katie and Yuli stepped out of it, holding takeout containers and a huge golden box of truffles. Liz was waiting for them and offered a wan smile.

"Merry Christmas!" Katie gushed as she followed Liz down the hall and into a family gathering room.

"Thank you for coming! We would be reduced to cobbling together dinner from the vending machine today if you hadn't shown up."

"How's Lorelei?" Katie asked, focused on Liz as Yuli pulled the containers of food out and set up plates and silverware.

"She's stable right now, but overall, her condition is deteriorating." Liz's voice trembled. "She needs a donor as soon as possible."

"I'm so sorry."

"Thank you," Liz said. "By the way, I shared your

seed of something good philosophy with Charlie, and he created a social media group and invited all four of Lorelei's half-siblings to it." Her voice cracked. "Two of them have already offered to be tested to see if they can be a living donor."

"Wow! That's incredible news," Katie exclaimed.

"It is," Liz agreed. "I'm trying not to get my hopes too high, but this could be the miracle we've been praying for."

"I hope it is. You deserve some good Karma. How about we sit with Lorelei while you and Charlie eat dinner?" Katie offered. "I know it's supposed to be immediate family only, but maybe they will make an exception on Christmas."

"That's a wonderful idea. I would hate for her to wake up and be alone."

"Should we ask the nurse?"

"Actually, I've learned it's better to ask for forgiveness than permission when dealing with hospital officials," Liz said. She thought for a moment, then said, "I have a plan. I'll go distract the nurse, and you two slip in to see Lorelei and send Charlie out. She's in room three."

Yuli's footsteps were silent on the vinyl floors as they dodged the nurses' station and waited for their chance to dart into Lorelei's room. In the distance, they could hear Liz chatting up the nurse and inviting her into the family gathering room to sample one of the chocolates. After the door closed behind her, Katie and Yuli sped toward room three and quickly entered.

Charlie was staring bleary-eyed at a computer screen next to a sleeping Lorelei. "Hi, Charlie," Katie addressed him. "We set Christmas dinner up for you down the hall. Liz said we could sit with Lorelei while you're eating."

He stood and stretched. "You are lifesavers." He motioned to the remote lying next to Lorelei. "The call button for the nurse is right here, but if she wakes up, please come get us."

"Of course."

He left the room, and they turned to the younger woman sleeping in the bed.

"Guard the door," Yuli ordered as she stood next to the bed and released the guardrail to lower it. Then she leaned over Lorelei, chanting and swirling her hands in circles over her body. On the bed, Lorelei's skin took on a golden sheen. Sparks flew from Yuli's palms as she continued to sweep in figure-eight motions over Lorelei's body, using Reiki movements. Yuli's eyes glowed with warm golden light as waves of warm colors washed over Lorelei's body. Within minutes, her forehead relaxed and the pinched look softened. Then her heart rate slowed on the monitor, and she began to breathe more deeply as if she was in a deep state of meditation with Yuli.

Katie watched in awe as Yuli continued to work on the woman. Sweeping her palms over and around her broken body, a shower of golden sparks traced up and down her limbs and converged to the center of her abdomen. The temperature in the room spiked, and

Katie felt a hot flash wash over her. Sweat prickled at her hairline and raced down her shoulder blades. Then Yuli extended both of her palms and swept up to the ceiling repeatedly in a series of rapid movements. On the bed, Lorelei's body began to levitate an inch off the mattress as the ball of golden light engulfed her entire body. Katie had never seen a more spectacular sight. Yuli's chanting grew louder, and then with one final burst of golden sparks, Lorelei slumped back down to the bed and Yuli staggered to a chair, exhausted by her efforts.

Katie watched Lorelei's eyes flutter, then open, and her cheeks flushed with color.

"Katie?" Lorelei smiled. "I was dreaming about Kandied Karma." Her eyes swept the room, landing on Yuli, who was hunched over and weakened in the chair. "Yuli was there, too! She was singing to me. It was the most beautiful, enchanting lullaby, and then she wrapped me in her arms and hugged me so tight."

"Yuli does give the best hugs," Katie admitted. "They are my favorite, too. How are you feeling? Should I get the nurse?"

"I'm starved!" Lorelei admitted. "You didn't happen to bring any truffles with you, did you?"

"We did!" Katie was thrilled to hear her appetite was restored. "Let me get your parents. They've been worried about you. I'll have them bring in the food and candies we brought." She hiked one thumb toward the door. "We're going to have to sneak out of here, anyway. It's supposed to be immediate family only."

"You sure feel like family to us," Lorelei said. Katie reached out to squeeze her arm and received a flash. Lorelei was laughing, surrounded by a sea of people who resembled her. She was spinning round and round on a wooden dance floor.

"You're going to get your miracle," Katie said as she turned to help Yuli to her feet. "I just know it."

"Thank you. Gosh, I hope so."

Katie led Yuli out of the hospital room and back down the hallway. Once they cleared the door, their pace slowed and Yuli leaned on Katie for support. She guided her to the chairs lining the hallway outside the family gathering room. "I'll be right back. You rest." Yuli nodded and leaned her head against the wall, closing her eyes.

"Lorelei's awake and asking for truffles," Katie said, popping her head into the gathering room.

"She is?" Charlie quickly wiped his mouth and got to his feet, still chewing. Liz jumped up and re-packed the bag of food Katie brought in, handing it off to Charlie. "Whatever our sweetheart wants, she gets today." He left the room to head back to Lorelei while Liz stayed behind to say goodbye.

"I don't know how to thank you." She opened her arms, and Katie hugged her tight, bracing for the moment of skin-on-skin contact. She closed her eyes and received the message. A much younger Liz and Charlie were at the park with a little girl in glasses and pigtails climbing the stairs that led to the slide. Grinning from ear to ear, Charlie swept her into his arms at the bottom of the slide, delivering ticklish kisses to her neck, and then set her back down on the ground where Lorelei raced to the stairs to repeat the process.

Relieved the vision of the coffin no longer remained, Katie and Yuli leaned on each other as they navigated the empty hallway on the way to the elevators.

"You did it," Katie whispered. "You gave her more time. Lorelei is going to have a long life free from constant doctor's appointments and dialysis. It's a Christmas miracle."

"It is," Yuli agreed. "It never gets old, and I will never take the ability for granted." She turned to Katie and yawned. "I'm quite tired, Katia. Can you take me home?"

"Of course."

"Conspiring with Karma sure is exhausting, but ain't it grand?" Yuli's sweet smile softened the lines on her face. Her steps were slower as Katie led her to the car, and by the time Katie pulled up at her house, she'd completely dozed off.

THIRTY-TWO

The week between Christmas and New Year's Day was a throw-away week of time for the ordins, when the world came to a screeching halt. Zoya counted on the fact that the clinic would be closed and they would push all routine appointments to the new year while ordins stayed at home in their stretchy pants and ate themselves sick.

The day after Christmas, Zoya's driver, Higgins, sped toward the clinic while Zoya ran through her plan one last time. Tingling with excitement, her legs were restless. She crossed them and swung one black boot back and forth as they sped closer to the clinic in total darkness.

She'd demanded an early morning conference with Dr. Blackwell to hand deliver the first installment of the Foundation's donation, knowing he would be too greedy to refuse her. With a wicked grin, Zoya pulled out a bottle of champagne she'd brought along for the event and a decanter of bitter nettle and wolfsbane, an ancient recipe she'd infused into orange juice. Violet sparkles swirled in the orange liquid, hinting at their divine purpose as it sloshed from the car's movement. She clasped the decanter in both hands and closed her eyes. Then she deeply inhaled, centering her mind to connect with her intuition to charge the liquid to full potency. It began to glow and showered her with light, as she tucked it back inside her bag for safekeeping.

When the car slowed to a stop, Zoya pulled her navy cloak up around her shoulders and donned black glasses to conceal her face. She circled her palms, gathering energy, and then snapped her fingers. Instantly, the security cameras that ringed the perimeter of the grounds went offline, and the feed filled with static.

She smoothed the front of her cloak and stepped out of the car, glancing up at the waxing gibbous moon illuminating the sky, feeling the gathering energy in her center. With renewed zeal, Zoya proceeded up the curved sidewalk and knocked gently on the employee entrance door. Humming with glee, she waited, and a few moments later, it was opened by an amiable Dr. Blackwell. Freshly showered, his hair was combed back from his face and held in place with gel. He held the door open for her, and she breezed past him, getting a whiff of Irish Spring, a cheap scent that made her nose wrinkle. "Thank you for seeing me at such an early hour! I find the reason I get more accomplished than most people is I get up and start my day while most of the world is still sleeping."

"You're a woman after my own heart!" he gushed.

"I figure, we can sleep when we're dead." She added a cheerful, good-natured chortle, biting back the desire to add, "And for you, Dr. Blackwell, that will be later this evening!" She licked her lips in anticipation. Bringing a pompous man like Blackwell to his knees was always a delicious victory, and she couldn't wait to savor it. She followed his wing-tipped shoes that led her down the darkened hallway into his office, which was dimly lit by a few scattered lamps. She opened her bag and extracted the bottle of champagne and the bitter nettle and wolfsbane elixir and set them on his desk.

"I'd like you to indulge me. It's become a tradition to allow myself the luxury of one cocktail to celebrate the close of important business deals."

"It's a little early for me to imbibe." He frowned, trying to wiggle out of it.

"It's tradition. I insist," she declared as she uncorked the bottle, ignoring his objection. "I'll go easy on the champagne for you, but it's bad luck to refuse a toast," Zoya added with a winning smile as she mixed the concoction in front of him.

Fine. One drink and I'll have the first installment. If the Abundant Quiver Movement only knew the lengths I was forced to go to further our mission.

Hearing him give in, she offered him the crystal flute and raised hers. "First, we must toast." She grinned and said, "To a genuine meeting of the minds and to all the miracles that will be born from our brain child at

The Castanova *Blackwell* Center for Reproductive Miracles."

At the surprise inclusion of his name, Dr. Blackwell puffed up like a peacock as a smug smile curved his thin lips.

What was it about men always wanting to mark their territory? Thinking they would achieve immortality by attaching their name to architecture. Fools.

"Now, that is something to celebrate, indeed." He smiled triumphantly and reached out to chime his glass against hers, then took a sip. "Ooh. That's sour," he exclaimed, making a smacking noise with his mouth.

"Bottoms up and then we can get down to business." Zoya eyed him over the top of her flute as she sipped.

Swallow the vile liquid and be done with it.

His internal pep talk narrated his next action. He lifted the glass back to his lips and drained it in several long gulps before handing it over to her.

"Very well. I see you don't like to dilly-dally." She pulled out the check from where it was tucked into her handbag and handed it over to him. "Two million dollars," she said. "It is the first of three installments that will be awarded as we meet construction benchmarks and pass inspections."

His eyes glittered with greed as he reached out to grasp the check in his hands. "Please have a seat." He offered her the chair opposite his desk magnanimously, and she took it. Her eyes were glued to him for any sign of the elixir beginning to work. Across the wide expanse of his desk, she saw Dr. Blackwell awkwardly fall down into his chair, and Zoya glanced at the gold watch inlaid with rubies that ringed her wrist. His first symptom was right on schedule. After ingesting the bitter nettle and wolfsbane elixir, basic motor skills quickly became compromised.

He looked down at the check on his desk, and it took several failed attempts before he could grasp it between his thumb and forefinger. Zoya's eyes glittered with glee, seeing his fine motor skills being severely affected. Dr. Blackwell was fixated on the check that rested between his hands. Confusion slowly snaked its way across his features, and Zoya watched him struggle to put words together.

"The signature," he said, noticing the check was unsigned.

"Oh, dear. My apologies," she said as he clumsily slid it over to her. "Do you have a pen?"

He opened the desk drawer, and after two attempts, pulled out a pen and reached out to hand it to her, but it dropped several inches short of her outstretched palm. The pen clattered to the desk and rolled toward Zoya. She couldn't conceal her excitement as she watched him struggle to put simple words together. It was as if every word he desired to speak was just out of his reach and took every bit of concentration he could muster to form a coherent sentence.

"I don't..." Dr. Blackwell slurred. "I'm not... feeling well. Cramps." He barely got the words out before he doubled over and then slumped back into his chair. The right side of his face slackened, and his eyes darted around the room, panicked.

"There, there," Zoya cooed as she stood and inched toward Dr. Blackwell like a black widow who'd ensnared a grasshopper in her web. She always savored the moment of recognition, and seeing the light of truth flashing in his eyes, it was obvious he'd just experienced it. "Although it might feel like the symptoms of a stroke, I can assure you it is not."

His eyes flashed to hers and darkened.

"The bitter nettle and wolfsbane elixir was infused with a paralytic. Right now, your heart rate is slowing and your body is shutting down all extraneous processes to focus on survival."

Fear welled in his eyes.

Lord, Save me from this wicked...

His internal dialogue slowed to a stop. "What a pity I won't be able to hear your thoughts while you're under the influence! I'm sure you'd have plenty to say if you could speak!"

Zoya was delighted and dusted off her hands. "And now that you cannot put more than two words together, this visit will be much more tolerable for me." Zoya threw her head back and roared with laughter. The doctor emitted a low growl from deep in his throat.

"Never fear, darling! You'll be awake and coherent the entire time and in the perfect incapacitated state to carry out the rest of my plan."

She held the check in front of him and tore it in half

and then again before scooping the remains into her handbag.

He mumbled incoherently as she pulled her gloves off and brushed her hands together. "Now that the dirty work is out of the way, we have things to do." He muttered and mumbled, his body quivering. "Darling, you are going to want to conserve that energy because I have big plans for you!"

She pulled out the sheath of paperwork she'd helped herself to from Katia's kitchen counter. "After our initial meeting, I did a little research on you and the Abundant Quiver Movement and discovered you've been a very bad boy! Impregnating women with your own sperm? Shame on you! You know, at first, I was appalled. I mean, what God-fearing man would violate a woman's sacred trust like that?"

Dr. Blackwell started to drool.

"You've got a little something…" She waved her hand around her face, then cackled with laughter. "Oh, that's right, you have lost all control of your bodily functions." She leaned forward and tapped his shoulder. "Don't be ashamed. It happens to the best of us."

"Now, you might have been able to strongarm the Sandersons and that poor sick daughter of theirs, but you can't fool me. I knew you were evil the moment I laid eyes on you. You violated countless women without their consent for decades, and the only appropriate punishment for a man like that is to burn in everlasting hell. What I wouldn't give for your pious brothers in the Abundant Quiver Movement to be in this room to witness our journey today! Oh, the irony… it's delicious," she declared with wild abandon as she flung herself back in her chair.

"Enough words, my friend! We are people of action!" She stood and pounced, circling the doctor in his chair. "It's time to get cracking." She patted him down, then pulled the key card from the pocket of his lab coat. "I'm going to need to borrow this for a moment." She walked behind his desk, shoved the moaning man still reclined on the rolling chair out the door, and then pushed the incapacitated doctor down the hall.

"We're going to have so much fun together, you and I!" She stopped his chair next to the security keypad and slid the card through to gain access. She pushed the doctor through the door and into the center of the room. "Thank you for giving me the VIP treatment! An all-access pass!"

He mumbled. His eyes darted around the room, glancing up at the security cameras in the corner.

"Don't worry, darling! I took care of those, too!" She threw her head back and cackled with joy. Glancing around the room, her eyes settled on a stainless steel rolling cart. She grabbed it and walked over to the wall of incubators, where she retrieved over thirty petri dishes in different stages of fertilization. She pulled them out of their warm cocoon and stacked them in storage boxes on top of each other. Zoya heard a chorus of boys' voices as she loaded them into a box.

Wahoo!!! It's our birthday!!! Wheeeeee!

Then she walked over to the cryogenic storage area on the west wall of the sterile laboratory. Twenty storage tanks ringed the room, and she knew one of them contained Lauren's harvested eggs bathing in a sea of liquid nitrogen. She walked over to the elaborate alarm system and pressed the palms of both of her hands to the front of it, focusing her strength. Rage tingled from her core and then out to her limbs and raced up the metal sides and around the unit as it began to glow with bright purple light. It shuddered and then shorted out, and the lights on the display in the front went dark.

Faintly, she heard a series of text notifications coming from the phone in his pocket. She pulled the iPhone out and crushed it under her boot. Then she walked over to an open locker, pulled out a face shield, goggles, and gloves, and put them on. Zoya raced around the room in her protective gear as she opened every tank. There were repeated whoosh sounds as vacuum seals disengaged, and the ventilation system automatically turned on when the nitrogen level in the room peaked. With the tanks all opened, she set the furnace as high as it would go and disposed of her protective gear. By the time the first employee would arrive to open the clinic almost a week later, none of the samples stored there would be viable.

"Children are overrated anyway," Zoya claimed, not even feeling a glimmer of guilt for destroying the dreams of the infertile couples who stored their genetic material at the clinic. The only way to be certain

Lauren's eggs were unsalvageable was to destroy them all.

Zoya tapped out a text to summon Higgins. When he appeared, she barked directions out quickly. "Get him in the car. We only have a few hours to get back to the compound and summon Lilith before the effects of the paralytic wear off."

She returned to his office and turned all the lights on, taking time to spread the pages of the report from Ancestrify over the top of his desk. A jingle distracted her, and she opened the drawer to pull out a key rattling in a plastic organizer in the back of his desk. Testing it, she was curious when it turned in the lock of a filing cabinet. Metal at the bottom of the file shuddered, and she reached in to pull it up to reveal a thick stack of file folders hidden in the false bottom. Inside those folders was the most damning evidence of all—detailed accounts and medical records of the families he'd inseminated with his own semen that, at first glance, looked to number over one hundred. Filled with righteous justification, Zoya left them all out in plain sight. She didn't have time to peruse all the records but knew the ordin police officers would.

"I have a feeling this is just the tip of the iceberg," Zoya remarked to herself, looking at the havoc he'd wreaked on full display. She strode over to the whiteboard and wrote in huge red letters, Dr. Damian Blackwell, guilty of fertility fraud. "Now the world will know what he has done."

Disgusted by the actions of the vile doctor, she

hoisted up the crystal Lifetime Achievement Award and heaved it over her head and to the ground, where it shattered into a million pieces. The shards crunched under her boots as she walked out of the clinic and to her town car.

An hour later, back at the compound, she summoned Terrance and, with the help of Higgins, dragged the disheveled doctor into her meditation chamber where they dropped him with a thud to the ground. He lay there like a lump, eventually stirring. His limbs were heavy, but he swung his torso to roll over. It was an awkward exercise since his entire body was still sluggish and noodle-like. Vocally, Dr. Blackwell was protesting with grunts and moans, and Zoya could discern a few scattered syllables from the noises he was making.

"Take… me… home."

Zoya shook her head no and said, "You're made for more, darling! You are the key to setting my beloved free." He continued to protest, and she ignored the rest of the sounds he made as she raced around the altar, lighting black candles and burning incense. She knelt in front of it and cupped her hands together to wash the smoke over her as she chanted in a deep register. The candles flickered and then the flames doubled in size as she moaned. She bent forward at the waist, prostrating herself to the altar, then swept back up and whipped her hair back as her eyes glowed a bright violet.

"Demon mother, it is your faithful daughter who wishes to lay an offering at your feet. I summon you now." The candles flickered again, and then a burst of flames encircled the front of the altar, warming Zoya's face from the light. A flaming portal opened and Zoya remained on her knees in front of it.

"Yes, daughter?" Lilith's voice was sensual and hypnotic as she stood bound to a St. Andrew's Cross, where Sally was dragging a feather up and down her naked torso slowly. A spiral of jealousy started to unfurl in her belly as she witnessed the intimate act.

"I have brought you a worthy sacrifice," Zoya declared, pushing away twinges of jealousy that reared up in waves. She pointed at Dr. Blackwell, who was inching away from the portal of flames, dragging his body by his floppy forearms and legs that refused to engage. "I'd like to make a trade for Salvatore's spirit."

"Who is this, and why is he a worthy sacrifice?"

"This is Dr. Damian Blackwell. He's been violating women for decades. Impregnating them with his seed to create an army of Christian fundamentalists who will crush the freedoms of women in this country under their boot of control. I have also brought along his future children. The embryos and zygotes he was planning on implanting into the wombs of unsuspecting women."

"Untie me!" Lilith barked the order to Salvatore, who rushed to cut her free. Interested in the offering, she stepped closer to the portal and leaned out of it. Her face enlarged and filled the meditation space, and she was close enough to touch the doctor. He let out a terrified yelp before the ammonia scent of urine assaulted their nostrils.

"He's fathered over one hundred children he was planning on indoctrinating into service, impregnating women in families who upheld the values of the Abundant Quiver Movement. This unscrupulous doctor reduced his female patients to mere barn animals whose only purpose was to carry his abominations to term."

Lilith reached through and poked the man, whose eyes were bugging out of his head. He tried to roll away from the portal of flames, but she rolled him back, like a cat playing with a mouse. Dr. Blackwell tucked his hands into fists and curled into the fetal position, crying and quivering in fear.

Lilith's lips quirked up, and she returned her gaze to Zoya. "You have pleased me, dear daughter. This *is* a worthy trade." She turned to Salvatore and swept him into her arms for a long, lingering hug. Her eyes remained glued to Zoya's as her fingers ran up and down his back.

She pulled back and cupped his face in her hands. "I *am* going to miss you, dear one. You have been my favorite, but I am a woman of my word. I hereby decree your servitude is complete. You have earned your freedom to transition to the next place with the full support of your mistress."

Lilith reached through the portal and pulled a protesting Dr. Blackwell to his feet and then yanked him through it where he landed hard on the rocky terrain of her throne room. Zoya observed the interaction and tingled with satisfaction.

"Return me at once!" Dr. Blackwell demanded, getting his voice back as flames licked the rocky walls behind him.

"Hush!" Lilith declared. "Do you know who you are speaking to?"

"A harlot!" He knelt and began to pray, "Lord, I beech you. I am your humble servant on my knees, begging for your swift and righteous punishment for this Jezebel."

Her rage shook the room and everything in it. Her fury was like an earthquake, rattling and vibrating with power. "Get the seed!" she demanded to a compliant Rocco, who quickly reached out to gather up the boxes of Petri dishes and tugged them back through the portal.

"I'm not Jezebel. I'm Lilith, you dolt!" Winged flames sprouted from her back and created a flash of heat that seared Zoya's cheeks. Lilith picked up the dishes one by one and smashed them on the rocks surrounding the doctor. With each crash, shards of glass scattered around him. Seeing his life's work destroyed made the doctor roar with anger. From each dish that was shattered, a wisp of a being floated up like a firefly and disintegrated into the air with a hiss.

Lilith threw her head back and roared a throaty laugh. "God, I'm going to have fun with this one." She sauntered behind the kneeling man and raked her fingers through his hair, then yanked his head back, exposing his throat. "A man like you believes women exist to serve him." She let go, took one step back, and then kicked him between the shoulder blades. He used his hands to break his fall, screaming when the glass cut through his palms. "Stay down until I give you permission to rise," she growled at him, her violet eyes flashing. He followed her directions, remaining frozen on all fours, bleeding and trembling in terror.

Lilith whipped around to face Salvatore one last time. Cupping his roguish face in her hands, she kissed him, then took his hand and guided him out of the portal of flames and onto the floor of Zoya's meditation space. "Goodbye, my love. I'll give you a moment to say your farewells before your transition begins."

The portal of fire began to shriek and hiss, and then slowly shrank before disappearing, leaving the meditation space blissfully silent and lit by soft candlelight.

Stunned, a shaky Zoya gasped for breath, her heart still hammering from the intensity of the interaction with Lilith.

"Doll-face," Sally whispered. He reached down with one hand and pulled Zoya gently to her feet. "You did it. You set me free."

Zoya wrapped her arms around his glowing form. She felt the familiar tug on her heartstrings. Being in his arms felt like coming home. "I promised I would," she affirmed and closed her eyes, desperate to make the moment last forever.

"I never doubted you for a single second," he

mouthed into her hair, and she felt the sandpapery brush of his stubble on her cheek.

"You are the only man I ever loved," she whispered back. "When you were taken from me, I wanted to die, too."

"You've known great suffering in your long life," he acknowledged. "And I am deeply sorry I added to it." He pulled back, and she felt his fingers brush away a lock of her hair. "You're still the most beautiful woman I've ever laid eyes on."

"And you're just as handsome as I remember," Zoya replied, grasping his wrist as the pads of his thumbs caressed her cheeks. She closed her eyes, reveling in the sensation, knowing it would be the last time she'd ever feel it. She felt the shiver of butterflies tickle through her core, and a tear broke free and cascaded down her cheek.

"You've set my soul free, and I'd like to return the favor," he said. Confused, she opened her eyes and searched his for meaning. "Your thirst for revenge and control is keeping you stuck. Set yourself free and repair the rift in your family."

"You too?" she asked, feeling ganged up on. "How do you even know?"

"There is a lot of time in hell, and watching your life unfold has been my favorite pastime." He covered her heart with his hand. "I never left you. I'm right here. I have always been."

A glowing orb of light detached from his head and floated away before popping like a bubble.

"No!" Zoya cried. "I need more time."

"That's the problem, doll-face. We always think we have more time." Another bubble broke free from his pinky finger and floated away. He was deteriorating before her very eyes.

"Heal the hurt and connect with the women who love you. Promise me you will."

A hot tear rolled down her face, and Sally reached up to brush it away. "I promise," she whispered. With mere minutes left of his existence, she focused all her attention on him. "Are you afraid?"

"Of the next place?" he asked, then laughed. "I just survived the bowels of hell. In comparison, the next one should be a cake walk."

"I want to go with you," Zoya whispered, her eyes begging as they locked on his.

"It doesn't work that way, sweetheart. You were always destined to serve the eternal coven. I am a simple ordin and will be connected to the flow of the universe, awaiting my next assignment and reincarnation."

"What if I rebuked the coven and asked to be reassigned to the reincarnation of the ordins?"

"That would be insane." Sally's forehead wrinkled. "You'd be sacrificing it all. Your family, your birthright, your legacy. Everything you spent several lifetimes building."

"It would be worth it for a chance for our souls to connect again," she pleaded as bright light outlined his shoulders and broke away like bubbles floating up and disappearing.

"I cannot allow you to do that." He swept her up in what was left of his arms and whispered in her ear, "I will always love you, Zoya Castanova. Loving you was my greatest adventure. Heal the hurt, give yourself the gift…" His voice dropped off, and Sally's body fragmented then, drifting up in bubbles that popped as they hit the ceiling in the meditation space. Zoya fell to her knees and sobbed. It was the end to the grandest love affair of her life. She'd gotten what she wanted. His soul was free and his spirit was released into the other dimension, so why did it hurt so much?

THIRTY-THREE

Six days later, Katie was getting ready at home for her workday at Kandied Karma. In the background, the television was on and her favorite anchor, Melanie Stevens, appeared on the screen during the local news portion of the morning show. Katie was standing in front of the TV, running a comb through her hair, when an image of Blackwell Reproductive Health filled the screen and stopped her cold. The comb clattered to the ground as she reached for the remote to turn up the volume.

"Good morning, Tampa Bay." Melanie's throaty professional newscaster voice continued, "Police are searching for a world-renowned fertility specialist, Dr. Damain Blackwell. He is a person of interest in an ongoing investigation, and police need your help locating him." After a brief pause, she went on, her voice steady but heavy with the weight of the accusation. "He stands accused of fertility fraud.

According to authorities, instead of using the sperm his patients requested, he allegedly inseminated them using his own." Melanie's voice quivered with emotion as she recounted the events, and a stunned Katie dropped to the end of her bed in shock. Her eyes stayed glued to the broadcast.

"Officials have indicated there is substantial evidence to prove he is the biological father of almost one hundred children throughout his network of fertility clinics in the United States."

Katie gasped at the sheer magnitude of his depravity.

"But the horrors don't end there. Over the recent holiday weekend, the tanks of liquid nitrogen used to store all the clinic's specimens were compromised, and upon inspection, the emergency alarms were found to be disengaged."

Her voice trembled with anger and frustration as she continued, "This catastrophic failure resulted in the loss of all stored genetic material, leaving countless families who were already struggling with fertility issues without any hope of conceiving a child of their own. Officials have confirmed it was a total loss."

Melanie paused for a moment, taking a deep breath to compose herself. She looked directly into the camera, her brown eyes glossy with empathy, but her expression was stoic. "The grief and pain these families are experiencing is unimaginable. Channel 7 has learned the tanks had been malfunctioning for months and required manual monitoring. Dr. Blackwell's office staff confirmed that the missing doctor was the only person tasked with this important duty. It appears when Dr. Blackwell is found, he will have a lot of explaining to do. This series of shocking events comes just months after he was awarded the Lifetime Achievement Award by the Society of American Reproductive Health."

She looked down at the notes in front of her, and then right back into the lens. "On a personal note, eleven percent of women in America are affected by infertility, and I am among them. Dr. Blackwell came highly recommended, and after fully vetting him, I chose Blackwell Reproductive Health to help my husband and I conceive. I am one of Dr. Blackwell's victims, and I stand with you." Her voice cracked. "I want to extend my deepest sympathy to all the families affected by this tragedy."

Melanie leaned forward, her eyes narrowing with focused determination. "We, as a society, must demand accountability and justice for the families who have been so deeply betrayed. We cannot stand idly by while those in positions of trust violate the sanctity of their professions and prey on vulnerable people yearning for a child. We will continue to update you as this story develops. This is Melanie Stevens, Channel 7 news."

As she concluded her report, Katie's phone rang at her hip.

"Mom?" Lauren's voice was panicked. "Were you watching the morning news?"

"Yes," Katie confirmed, the word heavy on her heart. "I'm so sorry, honey."

"I'm in shock. I can't believe it."

Katie wanted to comfort Lauren but struggled to find the right words. She was still reeling from the broadcast and the ramifications it held.

Lauren continued, her voice shaky with emotion, "I guess I should feel lucky that it happened so early in the process. Can you imagine if I'd been inseminated with his sperm? God. It gives me the willies."

"Me too," Katie agreed. "Try not to think about it, sweetheart. Things have a way of working out the way they should."

"People love to say everything happens for a reason, but what about all those families who were deceived and lied to? What about those couples who lost their last chance to have a biological child? It's deplorable. Police need to arrest that monster and throw away the key."

"They do. I'm sure they will when he's located."

"I don't know if I could put myself through the procedure again," Lauren admitted. "Especially now with Tom in the picture."

"Did you tell him?"

"No. I'm hiding in the bathroom. I can't stop crying. It's a stupid reaction, right?"

"Of course not," Katie empathized. "You suffered a loss."

"Not as devastating as some of those other families did." Lauren shuddered on the other end of the phone. "They are the real victims."

"Agreed." Katie's voice dropped to a whisper. "You

have to tell Tom. Especially if it is affecting you so deeply."

"I will." Lauren then added sheepishly, "He deserves to know. Especially since I think he might be the one."

Katie chuckled. "I wondered when you'd finally admit it when you were not under the effects of anesthesia."

"What are you talking about?"

"You were pretty chatty when I drove you home after the procedure."

"I was?" Horrified, Lauren let out a nervous chuckle. "Thank God you were the one to drive me home. If I'd let that one slip to Tom, he'd have ghosted me by now."

"He's not like that," Katie said.

"How do you know?"

"I've always had great intuition."

Her voice wavered. "I love you, Mom."

"I love you, too," Katie said. "And, honey? You *are* going to be one heck of a mother one day."

"Promise?" Her voice broke.

"Absolutely."

THIRTY-FOUR

A few weeks later, the Sanderson family's biggest dream came true. One of Lorelei's newly discovered half-siblings was a perfect tissue match, and it was transplant day.

Soft fluorescent lights illuminated the pale green walls of the sterile hospital room. Inside, tension buzzed with a mixture of excitement and fear. Beeping monitors seemed to echo the anxious rhythm in the hearts of Lorelei's parents as they passed the last few minutes before she would be wheeled into surgery. All the final instructions had been given, and Lorelei and her donor, a half-sister named Rachel, passed all the preliminary tests with flying colors. Any minute now, the nurses would appear and they would both be whisked into surgery. Lorelei lay on the crisp, white hospital bed, her face calm but her heart pounding with nerves. Liz and Charlie lingered at her bedside, their love and concern evident in their teary eyes.

"Those better be happy tears," Lorelei scolded them.

"They are," Charlie promised as he reached out and pressed his lips to Lorelei's hand. "You've been a fighter. I'm so proud of how you battled through the pain, but I *am* looking forward to seeing you get your second chance today."

"Me too. But if I'm being honest, I'm scared." She admitted, teary-eyed, her voice trembling with vulnerability.

"I know, sweetheart. But remember, we're right here with you every step of the way. We'll get through this together."

A soft knock on the door interrupted their moment. Dr. Sanjay, a seasoned transplant surgeon, entered with a reassuring smile. "Good morning, everyone." His voice instilled confidence. He leaned closer to Lorelei and asked, "Are you ready to get your life back today?"

Lorelei nodded eagerly as the doctor offered words of encouragement to put them all at ease. "You're in excellent hands. My transplant team is one of the best in the country, and your donor is as close to a perfect match as I've ever seen."

"That's fantastic news." Liz stood as the nurses worked around them, disengaging the rails on the bed and readying Lorelei to be rolled down the hall to surgery.

Liz bent down to give her daughter a kiss on the forehead. "We love you, honey. Relax and believe your miracle is on its way. No one is more deserving than you are, sweetheart."

Charlie gave her hand one last squeeze, and then he and Liz wrapped their arms around each other and watched helplessly as their only child was wheeled away.

"We'll get you settled in the surgical waiting room, and when she's in recovery, we'll bring you back to see her," a soft-spoken nurse instructed. "Follow me, please."

Liz clung to Charlie, who guided his wife out of the room and down the hall. For the next six hours, they tried to pass the time. Their eyes drifted to the closed-circuit television, where identifying patient numbers were posted and updated periodically throughout the day. Pacing and drinking pitifully weak coffee, they refused to leave for a second to even grab a snack. They were desperate to watch her status change through every step of the procedure on the screen.

Finally, her status changed to recovery, and Dr. Sanjay came out and pulled his surgical cap off his head. He walked over to Liz and Charlie, who jumped up from their chairs, eager for a status report.

"It was textbook. We removed both damaged kidneys laparoscopically and replaced them with a donor kidney. Both Lorelei and the donor are doing well. We're monitoring them right now as they wake up from anesthesia, but I'm confident you'll be able to see your daughter soon."

"Thank you!" Liz cried with relief. Charlie was so choked up he couldn't put a sentence together. Dr. Sanjay reached out to squeeze his shoulder.

"Her pain from the procedure will gradually subside, but it will be nothing compared to what she's already been through."

"We can't thank you enough." Charlie finally gathered his wits enough to speak.

"It's been a long journey to get here for all of you, but now you can celebrate her new beginning."

An hour later, they were escorted into a semi-private hospital room. Lorelei was on one side of it, and as Liz and Charlie walked by, they caught a glimpse of another patient lying in a hospital bed. Quietly, they navigated to the chairs near Lorelei's bed. Liz bent down to brush her hair from her daughter's cheek, and Lorelei's eyes fluttered open.

"Hey," she said with the tiniest of smiles.

"Hey, you." Charlie threaded his fingers through his daughter's, carefully avoiding the IV. "You made it. How's the pain?"

"Surprisingly, under control right now. I'm a little woozy, but the nurses said everything looks great. They're bringing Rach and me some Jell-o soon. Right, Rach?"

From behind the curtain, Rachel's voice was soft, her tone teasing. "I went to Florida to give my secret sister a kidney, and all I got was some lime Jell-O. I'm going to get that printed on a t-shirt."

Lorelei chuckled. "Stop making me laugh. It hurts."

"Why are you hiding behind the curtain? Open it up and let me see how my kidney is treating you."

Grinning at their easy shorthand with each other, Liz

stood and yanked the curtain down the track to open up the room. "How are you feeling, Rachel?" Liz poured fresh ice water into the cup near her and brought it to Rachel's lips.

After a long sip, she offered a wan smile. "I'm pretty sure it's the good drugs talking right now, but I have to say I'm feeling much better than I thought I would." She glanced over at Lorelei. "She had the hard part."

"Can you raise me up?" Lorelei asked. Charlie bent to operate the remote control, and the bed whirred as it transformed into an elevated position. "How's my new kidney looking?"

"Not too shabby," Rachel admitted. "We've got to get you back into fighting shape because, when they find that bastard, Dr. Blackwell, we're going to give him the one-two punch. He's never going to know what hit him."

"I always wanted an older sister," Lorelei offered as Liz filled a cup to the brim with water and then lifted it to her lips to sip.

"After all this, I better be your favorite," Rachel joked, and they all laughed. For the first time in forever, Lorelei saw the pain in her mother and father's eyes lift, and she felt a spring of hope well up in her heart.

THIRTY-FIVE

A month later, the bell jingled, and Katie's eyes darted to the door to see Lorelei and Liz walk through it. A huge smile broke out on her face. "No chair?" Katie squealed as she rushed over to envelop Liz in a warm hug. Liz was grinning from ear to ear, and the heaviness that plagued her was gone. Katie's hand brushed across her arm, and although she braced for a flash, she saw nothing. The absence of it confirmed her assignment from Karma was complete.

Katie stepped closer to Lorelei and cupped the young woman's face in her hands. "You are glowing, my dear! The very epitome of health."

"I feel incredible!" she said. "There are still check-ups and we're managing side effects of the anti-rejection drugs, but it's a breeze compared to cyst bleeds and dialysis." Her face clouded slightly, and she said, "Since there are no guarantees, I made the conscious decision to enjoy my healthy days and go out and live my life to the fullest."

"That mindset is crucial and will serve you well. Good on you!" Katie exclaimed.

"I worry this one spends too much time waiting for the other shoe to drop." Lorelei grinned, hiking a thumb over at Liz, who looked sheepish.

"I'm working on it," Liz declared. "It's a process."

"You're absolutely right," Katie empathized. "Now, what can I box up for you to take home to Charlie to celebrate?"

Lorelei made her selections that Katie placed with a gloved hand into a golden box, taking extra time to curl the ribbon into bows. At the register, Liz tried to offer her a credit card to make the purchase, but she gently nudged the woman's hand away.

"Nope. A promise is a promise." Katie grinned. "Every check-up equals free truffles."

"But she'll have them her entire life."

"Exactly." Katie grinned. "Looks like you're going to have to add a few more lines to that bucket list," she told Lorelei, whose smile lit up her face when she bit into a chocolate-covered orange slice.

"I didn't tell you about this yet, Mom, but the sibs and I are thinking about going on a cruise together later this year."

"The sibs?" Katie asked, confused.

Lorelei explained, "The craziest part of this is now I have half-siblings all over the world. Every month, I log into Ancestrify and there is at least one more! If this keeps up, the entire ship will be filled with us."

Liz grimaced.

"How are *you* handling it?"

"When we first found out, I thought I wouldn't be able to enjoy my life until he was held accountable. I wanted to see him pay for destroying our family."

"I can understand why you feel that way."

"But it was eating me up inside. Our family could only be destroyed if we gave him that power, and Charlie and I decided not to. Charlie is Lorelei's father in every way that matters. Dr. Blackwell does not get to take that title away from him."

"Yes!" Katie cheered in agreement, punching one fist up in victory.

"He vanished, and as days turned into weeks with no sign of him, we had to acknowledge he might never be held accountable for his crimes. Even if law enforcement apprehended him, the wheels of justice turn slowly. It would have meant a long, drawn-out lawsuit and years of litigation, not to mention the financial impact of a lengthy trial. I don't want the rest of my life to be consumed by retribution. We've already lost so much time as a family fighting Lorelei's PKD."

"You have." Katie nodded, touched by Liz's ability to see what was important. "What a beautiful way to look at it."

"Honestly, it was enough for me to see the clinic shut down. Don't get me wrong, I hate that so many other families were left devastated and hopeless, but to know that another family will not be taken advantage of and blindsided by his agenda is a gift."

Katie nodded her head in consensus. "I'm sure there is a hot little place in hell reserved for a man of Dr. Blackwell's caliber," she surmised. "Karma will come for him."

"Yes, it will." Liz's resolve strengthened. "Now we want to turn the page and focus on enjoying our family."

THIRTY-SIX

A few days later, in the late afternoon before the *Fioletovy Mahiya,* Katie sat in the aircraft gripping Yuli's hand as it departed down the runway headed to the Castanova Compound. The interior of Zoya's private plane was enveloped in ivory-colored leather. It was a luxurious way to travel that Katie had never experienced before.

"Legroom for days," Katie murmured as she brushed one hand over the supple leather. She breathed in and could swear there was a lavender scent in the air. "Even the air smells expensive in here." In the cabin, Arlo hopped up on her lap and yawned twice then began to tremble.

"Are you afraid of flying?" Katie asked as she pulled him closer to her and gently tugged on his ears, an act that usually soothed him.

"No, the first time I spent more than a few minutes with Zoya, I ended up condemned to her servitude in this dog body." He shivered and snuggled closer. "Trauma always finds a home, in the body *and* the mind."

"Ah." Katie understood. "Zoya seems to have that effect on everyone," she said, nodding her head toward Yuli, who was lost in thought. A grim expression took up residence on her face. Yuli's lips were clamped tight, and she was silent during the plane ride. Tension grew as they approached their destination, causing Yuli to instinctively curl her shoulders forward to shield her heart.

"You're so quiet." Katie made the observation, and Yuli finally turned toward her granddaughter.

"I'm sorry." She covered Katie's hand with her own. "I'm stuck in the past."

"Are you excited to see your mother again?"

"Of course," Yuli admitted. "I've been dreaming of this moment my entire life. There were so many nights I cried myself to sleep, begging to be reunited with her, but in my dream, Zoya was never part of it."

"She's a necessary evil then?" Katie offered, and Yuli offered her a sad smile.

"Correct on both accounts," Yuli said, looking out the window. "We're almost there. Can you feel the energy shift? It's electric, like a storm gathering power."

Katie nodded. There was a pull she couldn't deny the closer the aircraft got to the compound. "I'm apprehensive, too."

Yuli nodded and then began to explain, "When the triad is united with the eternal coven during the

Fioletovy Mahiya, we are going to be filled with higher powers. We will be connected to our lineage, and all our female ancestors who came before us will be in attendance. I've never experienced being tapped in and connected at a level like this. I wish I could tell you what to expect."

"Then it will be a new experience for both of us."

They jolted forward in their seats as the plane touched down and taxied down the landing strip, coming to a stop moments later. The flight attendant pulled their carry-on bags out of the storage bins, rolled them over to the door with a smile, and then opened the hatch. She handed the bags to Higgins, who loaded them on the back of a golf cart.

Yuli exited the aircraft first, and Katie followed closely behind as the sun dipped lower in the sky. Puffy white clouds were strewn across it, filtering the last of the sun's rays. Around the edges, a peach tint outlined the clouds, making them look like colorful cotton candy.

They climbed onto the golf cart and were driven down a gravel path to the main house. The cart curved around lush pathways filled with palm trees and tropical foliage and swayed in the breeze. Colorful parrots and birds of paradise filled the branches with bright pops of color.

When they rounded the corner and Katie got her first glimpse of the estate, her jaw dropped. "Whoa! The pictures don't do it justice."

The main house rose three stories high and was wrapped with verandas on every level. Fuchsia bougainvillea climbed up the sides of the smooth, white stucco structure, and the heady scent of gardenias and lavender luxuriated in the air. Katie closed her eyes and breathed it in. "She's living in a five-star resort."

Yuli smiled. "It's a beautiful home, and someday it will be yours." It was a bold statement of fact that Katie had a hard time wrapping her head around.

Higgins stopped the cart in front of the house on a pad of cobblestones. There, a staff of four strong women and a small group of dogs stood at the ready.

Arlo sniffed the air and then hopped down off the golf cart and over to the group of dogs, pushing his delicate nose into the middle of the pack, first nose to nose, then he circled around to their back ends.

The hairs on the back of Katie's neck rose, and she glanced around. "It feels like we're being watched."

"Make no mistake, on the compound, Zoya's eyes are everywhere." Yuli scanned the area, then she muttered under her breath. "Looks like the drama queen is holding court on the veranda." She pointed up at Zoya, who was staring down at them.

On edge, Katie followed the woman carrying her luggage into the grand home. Impeccably clean, the marble shone in the twilight hour. Katie was given an opulent bedroom with an enormous four-poster bed in the center. The maid started to unpack her suitcase, organizing her clothing in the armoire.

"You don't have to..." Katie said, feeling uncomfortable watching the woman perform tasks she was completely capable of doing herself.

"Zoya will join you in the dining room at eight for dinner," the stoic woman announced. "Is there anything else I can do to make you feel more at home?"

"No, thank you."

She pulled the door shut behind her, and Katie ran and jumped up on the bed, flopping her arms and legs out and sinking into the softness of the memory foam. Relaxing for a long moment, she looked up at the ornate plaster ceiling covered in a hand-painted fresco. The longer she stared at it, the more mesmerizing it became. There was a soft knock at the door, and she climbed off the bed and crossed the room to open it to see Yuli waiting on the other side. She was dressed in a long, flowing, purple cloak and held a gift-wrapped black jewelry box in her hands.

"I've never seen you wear that cloak before."

"There's one for you in the wardrobe," Yuli said as she crossed the room to open it. Inside, an identical cloak rested. Katie rubbed one hand down the front of it and found the fabric was smooth and cool to the touch. She unzipped and tugged it over her body, and it fell like a curtain down her back and legs to the floor. The cloak was a flattering fit-and-flare shape that hugged her curves.

"It even has pockets!" Katie squealed with excitement. She always thought pockets were the seventh wonder of the world. With glee, she stuffed her hands inside and withdrew a beautifully gift-wrapped box. "And presents, too!" she sang out with a grin. Without hesitation, she tore the wrapping off and pried open the box. There, resting on black velvet, was a jeweled amethyst amulet. When she touched it, the center stone began to glow. Gingerly, she pulled it out and secured it around her neck. When it found its resting place at the base of her throat, she felt a rush of adrenaline. The stone hummed and vibrated, sending fissures of pleasure on a circuit running through her body.

"Put yours on!" Katie enthused. Yuli opened the case and looked down at it suspiciously.

"It feels like she's manipulating us with trinkets and baubles that I couldn't care less about. Zoya has always been materialistic."

"Just try it on. I want to know if you feel the same sensation I do."

"Okay," Yuli finally relented and let Katie secure it to her neck. Yuli's glowed when it rested at the hollow of her throat, and then, together, they began to glow even brighter.

"It's like they are connected," Katie mused.

"That's because they are," Zoya confirmed from the doorway, making Katie jump. Katie turned to face her, walking the edge of terror and curiosity. Zoya was dressed in the same cloak, but it fit her body differently, showing off her voluptuous figure. Where Yuli's draped in a soft, roomy flow, hers accentuated every curve of her body. The three amulets powered even brighter as Zoya strode closer. Katie took a protective step toward Yuli, sandwiching herself in between the two powerful women who were sizing each other up.

"I've prepared our sacred circle near the sea for the ritual this evening," Zoya explained. "Now that we're properly attired, I think it best to make our way to the dining room to fortify ourselves for the journey tonight." She turned on her heel and led the way down the curved marble staircase.

Katie quickened her steps to follow her, and Yuli eventually brought up the rear. Not wanting to be left behind, Arlo raced forward until he was hot on Katie's heels as they wound down the staircase into the grand hall toward the scent of roasted meat. The formal dining room featured a long wooden table dressed with the finest linens and a mass of long tapered candles of varying lengths in cut crystal holders. Dark green wax trailed down the sticks, and the soft glow illuminated the elaborate place settings. A wall of tall windows bathed the room in the first shafts of cool moonlight as a lavender moon began to rise over the sea.

Zoya took her place at the head of the table. A chocolate lab rose on his back legs and tugged the chair out with his teeth. Zoya smoothed her cloak and perched on it as he nudged it closer to the table with his head.

"Thank you, Terrance," she said. "Please instruct the chef that we are ready for the first course."

"As you wish," he barked once and then nosed his way through the swinging door that connected the dining room to the kitchen.

Katie cleared her throat and tried to make small talk. "The estate is beautiful. I've seen photos in the tabloids, but they do not do it justice."

"Quit drooling, dear. Soon enough, it will all be yours."

Her offensive tone shocked Katie silent. She gulped, and Yuli took the opportunity to cut in. "Did you settle your debt with Lilith?"

Zoya's eyes leveled on hers, and her jaw twitched. "Going right for the jugular, are we, Yuli?" Her eyes flashed with anger as she balled up the cloth napkin on her lap and threw it down on the table.

"We deserve to know if you've written a check our family can't cash."

"I have handled it."

"Excuse me for not taking you at your word, but I'm going to need more details," Yuli demanded and stood in defiance, a sneer distorting her features. Her eyes narrowed and locked on Zoya's.

Zoya leaped to her feet and leaned in, both her palms spread out on the table as they stared each other down. Under the table, Arlo whined. Katie reached to pat his head to reassure him when he muttered, "This will not end well." Between the two older women, sparks flew, and a wave of electric energy crackled between them that made the air tingle with trepidation.

"If you must know, I made a trade."

"What kind of trade?"

"A soul for a soul," Zoya spat at her. "A crooked fertility doctor."

"Wait…" Katie pushed her chair out and found her feet. "Are you talking about Dr. Blackwell?"

"Yes, thanks to me, the cretin is now burning in the

fires of hell for an eternity. You're welcome," she said, balling up her hands and placing them on her hips.

"My daughter's eggs were being stored at that facility!" Katie cut in. "Not to mention, you destroyed the hopes and dreams of thousands of infertile couples."

Zoya waved off the criticism like an annoying bee buzzing around her head incessantly. "It was collateral damage." Her tone was callous and dismissive.

"You're lying," Yuli accused. "You destroyed those eggs on purpose because they threatened your reign as the supreme being in our mortal bloodline." Yuli shook her head, disgusted with Zoya. "You will never change."

"She wouldn't," Katie gasped in shock as she fell back into her chair, still stunned by the revelation. She'd wanted to believe it was just a mechanical malfunction. To know it was a deliberate action was mind-blowing.

"She *would*," Yuli answered. "And she *did*."

Distraught, Katie pressed her hands to her face. The amulet at her throat burned in response to the anger that clawed at her insides and made her thoughts spiral. As if on cue, the chef and two servers came through the door with their hands filled with pristine white plates. Their interruption deflated the tense energy in the room. The chef stood next to Zoya, awkwardly waiting to be acknowledged. When she didn't tear her gaze away, he cleared his throat, a sound that effectively ended Zoya and Yuli's staring contest. Zoya clapped her hands twice and turned to the chef with an engaging grin. "Very good. Let's begin. I'm famished!"

"Your first course is butter-poached prawns with a

mango relish." Synchronized, they set the first course plate in front of each woman at the table. Katie stared down at the elaborate place setting in front of her, wondering which fork was the most appropriate, while her mind whirred with the new information.

Zoya delicately cut the prawn into quarters with a knife and fork and then dipped it into the bright orange and green relish before popping a bite into her mouth.

"Did it ever occur to you that I might be protecting our bloodline?" she asked Yuli, who refused to make eye contact, her anger palpable. "What would have happened if Dr. Blackwell hadn't been stopped, and he fertilized Lauren's eggs with his own seed? What kind of plague would his DNA have brought to our legacy?"

"I guess we'll never know the truth," Yuli admitted.

"Why do you second-guess every move I make?" Zoya asked. "I disposed of Jefferson, didn't I, and Katia benefitted greatly from my involvement."

Both Katie and Yuli's heads snapped up at the outrageous brag.

"What did you do?" Yuli asked.

"I executed the Perfect Pear spell."

"What's that?" Katie asked.

"It's blood magic. A very dark pairing that gives a witch control of an ordin for a limited amount of time," Yuli explained.

Confused, Katie leaned back in her chair. "But he apologized and took responsibility for the first time in our marriage. Are you telling me it wasn't genuine, and he was under your control the entire time?"

Zoya huffed in frustration. "I watched that man use and abuse you for decades, Katia. He had it coming." She popped another bite into her mouth, her appetite ravenous and unaffected by the evening's confessions. Katie swallowed hard and pushed away her plate sickened by the truth.

"While I don't agree with your methods, we have common ground where Jefferson was concerned," Yuli stated.

Zoya offered her a curt nod and then continued her confession. "And he'll never use another woman again. I saw to it personally."

"What does that mean?" Katie asked.

Zoya stabbed her fork into another piece of the prawn, then blurted, "I gave him a micro penis." She waved her slim pinky finger in the air. "It's about yay big now, smaller than a cocktail sausage." With a self-satisfied smirk, she popped the last bite of shrimp into her mouth.

The wine Katie was sipping shot out of her nose, and she started to choke on it. It took several hard pounds to her chest with a closed fist before she could croak out, "I wondered what was different about him! I couldn't put my finger on it."

"And thanks to me, neither can he!" Zoya burst into peals of laughter. She pinched the tips of her fingers together and mimed the tiniest hand job in the history of hand jobs, moving mere millimeters up and down.

The over-the-top hand gesture broke the tension.

Katie clutched her stomach, chuckling at Zoya's pantomime. "Stop. You're going to make me pee."

"Do more Kegels, dear," Zoya offered. "That man was a cheating pig and needed to be taught a lesson, and I was just the woman for the job."

Katie snorted and then started to giggle. Next to her, Yuli fought the amusement that yearned to break out across her features. Glee crept up on her anyway, and she sniggered then broke down into serious guffaws. Hearing Yuli laugh, Katie gripped her stomach and laughed until she cried. "And here I thought he was remorseful and a changed man. God, I'm so gullible!" She erupted into uncontrollable cackles, and her cheeks ached from laughter.

The chef and servers appeared again and set fresh plates in front of each of the women. They lifted the cloches in unison, announcing, "The second course is pan-seared leg of lamb with mint jelly and a trio of grass-fed beef medallions."

Katie picked up her fork and knife and cut through the buttery beef in front of her. When she bit into it, she groaned with pleasure.

"It's halfway decent," Yuli mumbled. "Food has always been one of our bloodline's weaknesses."

"It's an act of pleasure," Zoya admitted as she sipped from the goblet in front of her. "Food is hedonistic at its core. It's very sensual."

Yuli rolled her eyes. "Everything with you is a pursuit of pleasure. Food, men, all of it."

"Everything with you is *duty*," Zoya retorted. "But I ask you, darling, which one of us is having more fun?"

"It's not about fun; it's a divine calling." Yuli was annoyed. "It's a sacred responsibility that has been put on our bloodline's shoulders."

Zoya shrugged. "Can't they coexist? Or are they mutually exclusive?" She banged her fist on the table and Katie jumped. "I may have unorthodox methods, but I always get the job done."

The tingling sound of a tuning fork resonated through the air, and Katie cringed and pressed her hands to her ears.

"Don't worry, dear, you'll get used to it," Zoya explained. At each of their throats, the amulets brightened. "We're being summoned. It is time."

THIRTY-SEVEN

The salty breeze carried the tang of the sea as it swept across their faces while Zoya navigated the golf cart down the gravel path from the main house to the edge of the ocean. The night sky was exceptionally clear, an ebony canvas speckled with stars, but their eyes were drawn to the glorious full moon rising above the vast ocean. As it ascended, the moon's lavender cast transformed the dark waters with a mesmerizing purple sheen that seemed to stretch out to infinity.

Filled with trepidation, Katie focused on the sound of gentle waves lapping against the shore to soothe her fears. She felt a harmony seep into her heart, connecting her with the cosmos as she got lost in the symphony of the sea. From the distant cries of seagulls to the faint splashes from sea creatures leaping out of the water only to splash back in it, she felt a synergy with the ocean and let it rock her gently into a state of flow.

In the darkness, their amulets gleamed, creating shadowy effects on their faces. As they neared the coastline, lavender moonlight painted the ocean with an ethereal glow and bioluminescent organisms lit up the water like fairy lights, leaving trails of shimmering jewel tones as they floated in the water. Every cresting wave seemed to dance with light, adding an otherworldly touch to the already captivating scene.

"This is the real magic. It's so beautiful," Katie whispered to Yuli, reaching out to squeeze her hand.

"You're right, it is," Yuli whispered back, just as enchanted. A few minutes later, Zoya slowed the golf cart to a stop near a large circle of torches that lit up the dark night. The flames crackled and burned inside their glass hurricane lamps.

"Leave your shoes here," Zoya instructed.

Katie was confused.

"We must connect to the earth to gather the power of the triad," Zoya explained as she unlaced her boots and then abandoned the golf cart. As she picked her way closer to the lanterns, Katie and Yuli followed closely behind. Twenty feet away from the edge of the surf, the glowing lamps formed a tight circle around a thick ring of salt her staff had readied an hour earlier. Zoya slid between the tightly packed torches with ease. Katie got stuck.

"Uh oh! Looks like there's a little too much junk in my trunk," Katie joked with a self-deprecating grin. She was surprised when Zoya came to her aid and pulled two of them out, giving Katie, then Yuli, easier access to reach the center of the circle. Then she shoved the torches back into the sand to close it.

Once inside, Katie waited for instructions, hovering close to Yuli, dispelling her awkward energy by dragging her toe in the sand.

"We need to form a circle and face each other," Zoya began, getting right down to business. "Press your palms out on either side." Yuli and Katie spaced themselves out and opened their palms, and when they connected, tiny purple sparks shot from hand to hand, brightening up the night. Katie jerked back reflexively and let out a nervous chuckle. The sensation was like a build-up of static electricity being released and had startled her.

Zoya eyed her impatiently. "Again," she demanded, and Katie felt her cheeks flush with embarrassment. She glanced over at Yuli for reassurance, and when Yuli gave her a nod, she raised her palms once more to connect to the other women. Now knowing what to expect, she weathered the small discharges of electricity more easily.

Sparks built up power until they were lightning bolts racing from palm to palm to palm. High in the sky, the moon began to glow with even more intensity, and the amulets at their throats brightened in unison. Katie felt the hairs on the back of her neck rise, her hair becoming statically charged as she witnessed Zoya's do the same across from her. Her eyes were burning, and in fear, they darted over to Zoya and Yuli, whose eyes were glowing bright violet.

The lightning racing from their palms tracked faster and was soon screaming around them in a circle.

"Chant with me now," Zoya shouted over the crackling of the electricity. "Sisters, Mothers, Grandmothers of the Eternal Coven. We are here on the night you decreed. Make your presence known and walk amongst us once more." Katie strained to hear her vocal incantations and tried to mimic them with her voice. Next to her, Yuli's voice swelled with hers, picking up power as they beseeched the universe to lift the veil between the living and the dead.

Katie's hands felt magnetized, and her body lurched forward in conjunction with Yuli and Zoya's, knotting their hands together. When the circle was complete, they felt the first tremor. A wave of power jostled them in a circular motion, spinning them faster and faster until they were dizzy and thrown to the ground. With a loud clap of thunder, the torches surrounding them flickered, then burned more brightly. Dazed from the fall, Katie opened her eyes to see the circle was now filled with over twenty women. Yuli was the first to get to her feet, and she scanned the group, eagerly searching for Nadia.

"Mother!" Katie heard her exclaim, her voice cracking. Just a few feet away, Katie watched her barrel into Nadia and cling to her for dear life. Nadia's eyes were closed, drinking her daughter in with a huge smile on her face. Zoya hung back, waiting. Katie watched her impatience grow as Yuli and Nadia were completely engrossed in the other, unable to break the connection.

Olena stood only as high as Katie's ribs. She pulled

out her pipe and lit it with a match, sucking in the flame until it smoldered, smelling like vanilla and cloves. She crossed the sand, making her way closer as she puffed on the pipe. Katie didn't know what to do with herself. The female ancestors of her family surrounded her and filled her with curiosity, but she felt a shyness overtake her.

"Well, aren't you an awkward one?" Olena said with a wicked grin when she landed in front of Katie.

"I'm new at this," Katie offered in explanation. "I'm still adjusting to the truth."

"It does kind of tear your head off, doesn't it?" Olena remarked, taking a long inhale from the pipe. "You went inside the boxes?"

"Yes," Katie confirmed. "I tried to talk to Yuli, but there is so much hurt there. Decades of it. I don't know if we can overcome it in one night."

"Look at you, doubting our abilities already!" Olena acted wounded at the suggestion. "You greatly underestimate the combined power of the women standing in the sacred circle with you right now."

"I hope you're right."

"I usually am."

Finally, Yuli let go of her mother and returned to Katie's side, giving Zoya a chance to welcome her daughter.

"She's so beautiful," Yuli remarked, watching her mother take Zoya in her arms and hug her tight.

"She is," Katie agreed.

"What a gift. Tonight. To see her and touch her again."

"I'm glad you see it that way," Olena said, "because we have real work to do." She waved an arm behind her. "The eternal coven wants to begin deliberations." She snapped her fingers, and three black thrones appeared side by side. Across from the black thrones, stadium seating appeared for the rest of the women. Katie watched them file into rows and then sit down silently. Each one wore an aubergine cloak that matched hers, though it fit every woman differently, bringing her most beautiful assets to light. At each of their throats, a purple amulet glowed in a heartbeat pattern that synced with Katie's. She felt the pool of strength and brilliance gathering and joining together. It made every cell in her body tingle with anticipation and possibility.

Olena walked over to a special chair in the front of the sea of women. She picked up a smooth black stone with a hole in the center and struck it on the wood of a table in front of her, calling the meeting to order. Reluctantly, Zoya disengaged from Nadia and sat down. Yuli chose the farthest seat opposite, leaving Katie in the middle.

"Tonight, we are given a chance to make amends with the souls of those we have wronged or have been wronged by in our previous life. It is a chance to come to terms with our mistakes and reflect on the lessons we were given to learn. None of us are without blame," Olena said in a steady voice. "It is the order of the eternal coven to use this opportunity to its fullest and reunite the mortal members of the coven—Zoya, Yuli, and Katia. In order for our power to strengthen, we must learn how to forgive and live in harmony with humility and grace.

"Zoya Castanova, please stand." Olena pulled out a pair of glasses and perched them on her nose then looked down at an ancient book. "You've increased the wealth of our ancestors and created a secure legacy, and the coven thanks you for your service."

A smug grin broke out across Zoya's features as she flushed pink with their praise and wallowed in her own accomplishments.

"But," Olena interrupted her wallowing and watched as a confused expression darted across Zoya's features.

"But what?" Zoya dared to ask.

Her hostility set off a sea of whispers from the coven.

"SILENCE!" Olena shouted, and in the seconds that followed, you could hear a pin drop.

"Zoya, your arrogance is costly, and your complete focus on your own selfish goals must stop. You have exhibited a pattern of self-serving behavior, summoning black magic for your own personal gain. As your sisters, we must hold you accountable for your actions. Let us view the footage." Olena pulled a box from the folds of her cloak, set it on top of the table in front of her, and cranked the tiny lever on the side. She flipped up the top panel, and a scene projected above them on the sky like an old-fashioned movie.

In the footage, a much younger Zoya was stuffing

clothing into a trunk while a toddler (who had to be Yuli) teetered around on thick, unsteady legs like she'd just learned to walk. At Katie's right, Yuli leaned forward, concentrating on the footage of herself at such a young age.

"You can't shack up with a known criminal." Olena pulled dresses out of the trunk as fast as Zoya was shoving them in. "What about Yuli? Let us keep her here."

"In a brothel?"

"No, you're right. The home of a known gangster is a much safer place for a child to grow up." Olena's sarcasm was a mile thick. "Do not do this. The only way it ends is in your total destruction."

Katie glanced over at Zoya, who shivered in the chair watching the scene play out. She hadn't known it at the time, but Olena had seen her future and was trying to save her from it.

"It's my decision. Stay out of it."

The movie stopped, and Olena turned to the coven. "We've built our legacy on the principles of light magic, letting Karma be our guide. Zoya has renounced our ways, time and time again, in favor of darkness. Free will gives every woman the right to choose the path she wants to walk. Good or evil."

Yuli muttered under her breath at Zoya, "It's about time you were called to the carpet for your transgressions."

The next movie streamed into the thick clouds above, and a rumble of thunder set an ominous tone.

Zoya was holding a jeweled dagger, her nostrils flaring, and winced as she slid the blade across her open palm. She squeezed her fist, breathing through the pain as drops of her blood fell onto the soil of an ornamental tree where one pear was nestled in the center branches. The pear brightened and enlarged as it drank her blood offering. Yuli leaned forward in her chair, riveted to the screen, and Katie's jaw dropped as she watched her ex-husband devour the plump pear while Zoya sat at his side waiting for him to finish it. A cunning smile slid across her features, and Zoya's eyes darkened as her lust for revenge hit a fevered pitch.

All at once, the panel of witches rose to their feet, protesting in outrage. "Blood magic! Banish her!" Whispers and mumbles became a roar of angry accusations. "She will destroy us all!"

"Calm yourselves, sisters!" Olena shouted over the melee, banging the rock on the podium until the coven quieted. "Please take your seats. The time is coming when your voices will be heard." The sea of muttering and angry protests dimmed to a hum of disgust directed at Zoya.

"Let's see the next clip." The box shot another video into the gathering clouds above. Zoya was standing over a bed where a frail, elderly man lay. Illness had emaciated him into a shell of the man he'd been the last time Zoya had laid eyes on him.

"My darling daughter, I never thought I'd see you again," he whispered.

Her eyes flashed with rage. "You sent me away

when I was still a child with your business partner's baby in my belly!"

"But look at how you've prospered!" He reached out a shaky hand that Zoya grabbed with her gloved one and crushed in her own. His bones ground together into a powder while terror filled his eyes, and he squealed in pain.

"Prospered?" she spat in his face. "I've prospered in *spite* of you. You do not get to take credit for my successes. When I was stuck in that rodent-riddled cottage in America, I had many long nights to dream about this moment. You have no idea how many ways a woman can fantasize about killing a man, but I do, Father. I know them all." She yanked the pillow out from under his head. "I want the last person you ever lay eyes on to be me. The daughter who despises you." She leaned forward as he trembled on the bed. Inches away from his eyes, she glared at him. "Do you sense the contempt I have for you? Do you feel my hatred and disgust?"

"Please," he pleaded.

"The time for begging me to return to your good graces is long gone, Father." She gripped the pillow in her gloved hands. "Now, I must admit, this is going to hurt you far more than it will hurt me." She glowered with glee as an evil sneer curled her lips. Her eyes darkened into two black holes, then glazed over. "It brings me great joy that the last emotion you will ever feel is fear. Just like I did, Father, when you put me on the boat to America, penniless and alone. Rot in hell."

She savored his wide, fearful eyes and his pathetic whimpering for one long second before she crushed the pillow down on his face with all her might. Leaning her body on his shoulders to keep him immobile, she relished his struggle for survival. Several minutes later, he was completely still, and when she removed the pillow, his eyes were bugged open and his mouth was slack. Zoya tucked the pillow back under his head and bent to kiss his cheek. "Give the devil my warmest regards."

She dusted off her hands and smoothed the front of her dress, taking a second to admire her reflection in the ornate mirror on the other side of the room. Her dark navy, velvet brocade dress hugged her curves and delicately flowed to the ground. It was bustled in the back with black lace detail, and she was a vision in it. Knowing this was the last time she'd ever set foot in her childhood home, she surveyed the room for valuables. Seeing a solid silver comb and jeweled mirror on the end table, she picked them up and stuffed them into her handbag. On the wall, she pulled an exquisite oil painting from a nail. It was barely small enough to fit inside her bag. Then she walked down the stairs and let herself out of the back door of her childhood home for the last time, whistling as she sauntered away.

The women in the coven gasped. Katie was taken aback and shot a look over at Yuli, who didn't seem affected at all by the revelation. Filled with self-righteous anger, Zoya leaped to her feet. "He got what he deserved!" She was shaking with fury. "He banished me and left me to die. He disowned you, his own mother, Olena! I did us all a favor!"

"Enough!" Olena shouted at her, banging the stone on the table to silence the outraged voices of the coven. "Your lust for revenge has hardened your heart."

"Am I to applaud your weakness?" Zoya asked, her eyes flashing in defiance. "I was the only woman strong enough to do what had to be done."

"Sit down!" Olena barked at Zoya, who huffed her displeasure and then followed her order. "You will get a chance to refute the charges after all the evidence has been presented."

The next scene filled the cloud. Katie recognized her patio and heard Arlo's familiar bark. Confused, she glanced back and forth, from Arlo at her side to the clouds.

In the projection in the clouds, Arlo panted and circled her patio, clearly distressed. Zoya emerged from the shadows as Arlo said, "I'm afraid I have some disturbing news."

"Speak, you imbecile!"

Arlo swallowed a growl and continued, "Lauren is freezing her eggs to preserve her fertility. She took Katie to an appointment at Blackwell Reproductive Health a few days ago."

Katie gasped in shock and betrayal. At her feet on the sand, Arlo rose on his hind legs, imploring her with his eyes. "I can explain," he whimpered.

She pushed him down and hissed, "Not now."

Arlo whined and then tucked his tail and took two

steps away. Katie's mind raced as the scene continued. Next, she recognized the fertility clinic from her visit with Lauren.

"Welcome, Ms. Castanova, to Blackwell Reproductive Health," Dr. Blackwell said, sweeping one hand back toward the modern office building behind him.

"I'm willing to do whatever it takes to help you further your mission," Zoya said. Shocked, Katie whipped her head over to Zoya, who was barely watching the footage, picking at her cuticles, seemingly bored. In the cloud, Zoya donned gloves and raced around the room, opening each tank in the cryogenic freezing area. One by one, she released vacuum seals and pulled out the metal cylinder thermal regulators inside, exposing all the specimens to a much warmer room temperature.

"Isn't it true that eggs from the next in our lineage were among those you destroyed?"

Zoya sat up straighter in her chair. "Technically." She offered a defiant shrug.

Olena's eyes narrowed. "You decided to destroy the next generation, altering our future without concern for the coven. You were only looking out for your own interests and were unwilling to be unseated."

Olena shut the box in frustration. "We could be here all night, wasting this precious lunar event holding court on your many transgressions."

Yuli nodded in fully justified agreement.

"Is there anyone who will speak on behalf of Zoya?"

Nadia came forward. "I will."

"Yes, child."

Nadia's long black hair rippled in the sea breeze. She laced her hands together in front of her and spoke with authority. "Zoya Castanova is a product of her circumstances. She was dealt an unnaturally difficult fate, and though she made many mistakes with far-reaching consequences, it is my hope that we can set aside these missteps with a heart for forgiveness. It has taken me decades to open my heart to forgive her myself. Only witnessing my daughter embracing her gifts and using them to the highest order has softened my anger."

In the seat next to Katie, Yuli's amulet glowed even brighter in the presence of her mother's praise. A lonely tear broke free from the corner of her eye, and the moonlight reflected in it as it traced back and forth, skirting the network of lines on Yuli's face.

Olena considered Nadia's plea and then turned to address Zoya. "Your future is at stake. Because of your actions, your transition to the eternal coven is not guaranteed." Behind her, the court of women mumbled in agreement.

Zoya got to her feet, threw her head back, and roared with laughter. "The feeling is mutual. The very idea of being imprisoned for an eternity with these old biddies is a fate far worse than death," she waxed dramatically, her hands on her shapely hips. "Perhaps I can provide an alternative that would serve everyone's interests?"

Curious, Olena offered her permission. "Go on. We're listening."

"Allow my soul to move to the next dimension and give me another chance, a rebirth, so I can learn from the mistakes I've made."

"I'm guessing this has nothing to do with Salvatore's recent transmutation and your desire to reunite with him."

Zoya's lips tightened in a scowl, and she shrugged her shoulders. "What if it does? Does it really matter? You said yourself I never learn. What if I was given another opportunity to prove to the eternal coven that I could?"

"A supernatural ancestor has never been reincarnated," Olena considered, confusion knotting up her forehead. Behind her, the other witches murmured in agreement, their voices overlapping. At their throats, their amulets illuminated and glowed brighter. "It seems your sisters aren't thrilled with the prospect of you spending the rest of eternity with them, either." She pulled out her pipe and lit it, puffing as she thought. "We will convene and decide your fate amongst ourselves. Might you take this as an opportunity to show us what you are capable of when you are properly motivated?" She stood and wandered across the sand to the group of women. They joined hands, and a flash of light obscured them from view before they disappeared from sight.

As the luscious moon reached its zenith, its radiant glow intensified, casting long, mesmerizing reflections in the water. Waves shimmered like liquid diamonds, and each white-crested ripple appeared as if it were adorned with lace embroidery.

"Good riddance," Zoya muttered under her breath.

Nadia walked over to where Yuli, Katie, and Zoya sat. "Come, darlings, our time is limited and will pass quickly." She pulled out a blanket and unfurled it in the breeze. Katie and Yuli stood to help shake it out and bring it down onto the ground. It was a mandala, a perfect circle with a pentagram inside. "Sit. We have much to discuss, and I will spend time with each of you. Mother, I'll begin with you."

———

Nadia led Zoya through the torches and out onto the beach. She reached out to grasp her hand, and Zoya felt herself relax.

"It had to be difficult to watch the footage," Nadia empathized. "You've been through many traumatic events that would have destroyed other women. The path you have been asked to walk has been exceptionally arduous and has changed you. I wonder who you would have become if life had been kinder."

"I guess we'll never know," Zoya admitted. "I played the cards I was dealt."

"Do you really want to forsake the coven and be reborn?"

"The idea of joining the eternal coven doesn't

exactly quiver my liver," Zoya said. "To waste away in the cosmos for an eternity? No, thank you."

"But I'll be there," Nadia murmured. "I always thought we'd have all the time in the world when you crossed the veil."

Zoya looked down at the sand. "It's true, I am a selfish being, but it doesn't change the fact that my love for you is as vast as this ocean we are standing in front of now. I love you like the tide loves the shore—an all-enduring, never-ending love—but I know without a doubt, the eternal coven is not enough for me."

"Sally?" Nadia whispered.

Zoya nodded.

"He's your one weakness," Nadia acknowledged. "You're the strongest woman I know, but he's always been your vulnerability."

"Let me try to explain," Zoya insisted as they continued to stroll down the beach. "He's my twin flame, and without him, I feel incomplete. I've spent several lifetimes trying to fill the void, and I've exhausted all the avenues to do it." She stopped in the sand, and the waves lapped up to her feet. "I'm tired, darling. When my service is over, and if the coven grants me permission to reincarnate, I want to take them up on it."

Nadia exhaled a heavy breath as tears broke free and washed down her face. "I was afraid you were going to say that." She turned toward Zoya and said, "Take my hands."

Zoya turned to her daughter and clasped her hands tightly, then felt the magnetic pull and leaned her forehead against Nadia's. At their throats, the amulets illuminated a sphere of sparkles around them. Warm light washed up Zoya's legs and radiated out to her fingertips. The constant pit in her stomach unclenched, and she felt a wave of unconditional love wash over her. Tears rushed down her cheeks as healing light engulfed them both. There was a sucking sensation as she felt the air being pulled from her lungs. Weakened, without oxygen, she fell to the ground a second later. When she opened her eyes, Nadia was standing over her with a sweet, knowing smile. She offered Zoya her hands and pulled her gently to her feet.

"How do you feel?"

"Lighter?" Zoya said the word like a question. She pressed her hands to her face, delighting in the sensation, and an astonished belly laugh burbled up in her.

"What did you do?" Zoya asked as she reveled in the joy.

"We released your pain," Nadia said. "You'll still have the memories, but they will be dampened and won't hurt as much. Maybe you will reconsider your plan?"

Zoya pulled her daughter close and cupped her face in her hands. "I'm sorry, my love, but I cannot."

"It was worth a try," Nadia offered. "I understand." They continued to stroll down the beach, heading back toward the sacred circle. "It's up to you now, Mother. Your fate rests squarely in your own hands, the way you prefer it. You have a lot of work to do with Yuli and Katia."

"I know," she whispered. They continued to meander down the shore, and Zoya finally gathered the courage to ask for the one thing she valued most.

"I need you to forgive me," Zoya asked. "I need to know that things between us are resolved."

"Of course they are," Nadia professed. "There is only love. I will carry you in my heart always. Your path was never meant to be mine. Although we walked a road for a short time together, you were always meant to continue on without me."

"I love you, my darling. Through all space and time, your soul has imprinted on mine. We are forever connected, whether in the eternal coven or not."

"Then go earn your freedom. Be happy, Mother." Nadia opened her arms, and Zoya clung to her with tears racing down her cheeks.

"I don't want to let you go," Zoya sobbed. "The first time almost killed me."

"But you must," Nadia urged as she clung to her mother. "Pour all the love you yearned to give me over Yuli and Katia. That is how you earn your reincarnation. You are the strongest woman I know, but your greatest strength lies in your vulnerability. Open your heart and you will see." Zoya stiffened at her words. Nadia pulled back, and her warm eyes burrowed into her mother's as she whispered, "Trust me."

"I will," Zoya whispered back. With an anguished yelp, she gathered her daughter into her arms for one more hug, understanding the sanctity of the moment. With immense effort, she forced herself to release Nadia, then stepped inside the circle and fell down on the sand, mentally exhausted.

"Yuli?" Nadia turned to her daughter with a warm smile, and Katie stood to help her grandmother get to her feet. Once outside the circle, Nadia laced an arm through Yuli's, and they strolled away. "Where do I begin?" Nadia asked. "There's so much I've wanted to say."

The waves lapped at their feet as they continued down the shoreline. "I am devastated we didn't get to share the mortal plane for longer than a few minutes, my sweet girl."

Yuli smiled over at her mother, her heart bursting with love. She focused on her words, wanting to commit them forever to her memory.

"I've admired how you turned sadness into strength and built a wonderful life filled with great love and incredible success."

"Thank you, Mama," Yuli whispered.

"You stepped into your highest calling without fear, and it took my breath away. Healing is the greatest gift the coven can bestow on a witch, and you embraced it willingly. I am so proud of you."

They stopped in the sand, and Nadia turned toward Yuli. She brushed away her tears and laced her fingers through Yuli's long white hair, then brushed a kiss across her forehead. She pulled back, still cupping

Yuli's face in her hands, and whispered, "But the person you need to heal most is yourself."

Yuli's eyes widened as her mother's words settled deep in her soul. Nadia continued, "The past hurt prevents you from living whole-hearted. It keeps you stuck on the ground, my love, and I want to see you soar!"

"How?"

"You must forgive your grandmother," Nadia told her seriously. "It's the only way to step into the fullness of who you are."

"I don't know if I can. It hurts so much."

"Take my hands. Let me heal the healer." Yuli slipped her mother's thin hands into her own and rested her forehead on her brow. The amulets surged with power as they connected their breaths. When they synched up, warmth flooded Yuli's heart and tingled through every cell of her body. She trembled under the power and felt the knotted coil of hatred deep in her soul unravel and be gently pulled away by Nadia's unwavering spirit. Their voices rose as they chanted together, and Yuli felt herself rise higher and higher on the wings of their love. A sensation like a rollercoaster rising rocked her body, and when it crested and started to scream down, she fell into the sand.

When she opened her eyes, Nadia pulled her gently to her feet. "How do you feel my, darling?" she asked, and Yuli grinned.

"I feel… free." She laughed out loud, unable to stop the jubilation from spilling out of her.

"Now you can love with your whole heart. The damage has been restored."

"How do I thank you?"

"By continuing to live your life in service to others. You have a beautiful heart and are the best of me." Nadia was silent for a long, lingering moment, letting Yuli absorb the information she shared. Nadia reached out for Yuli's hand, and they watched the waves crest and fall for several long minutes, totally content. Eventually, Nadia turned to her daughter with a sad smile. "We must head back."

"No," Yuli cried softly. "I need more time with you."

"Someday, we will be reunited in the eternal coven, and then we will have all the time in the world, my love."

Yuli nodded sadly as they started back to the circle. She clung to her mother one last time, drinking in the sensation of her unconditional love, gathering enough of it to last the rest of her lifetime. Reluctantly, she let go and crawled back through the torches to the center.

"Katia?" Nadia said, extending one hand.

After settling a worn-out Yuli on the blanket, Katie slid through the torches to join her great-grandmother on the sand. They walked down the beach slowly in companionable silence. Finally, Nadia broke it and said, "I want to thank you for loving Yuli."

"She makes it easy," Katie admitted.

"That she does," Nadia agreed. "She's a remarkable woman. You both are."

Katie was touched by the compliment. "Thank you."

They continued down the shoreline as the foamy sea tickled their toes.

Nadia stopped and turned toward Katie. "Do you think people can change?"

Katie considered her question. "I think everyone is *capable* of change, but few are willing to do the hard work it requires."

Nadia quirked her chin up, considering Katie's thoughtful response. "You are the best of us all."

"No," Katie denied, refusing to accept the compliment. "Yuli is."

"Dear one, each generation is stronger, smarter, more emotionally aware, and higher evolved."

Katie gulped, feeling the weight of the bold statement overwhelming her.

"You will grow into it," Nadia offered, trying to put her fears at ease. "There is nothing to worry about. Tonight, I've been given the opportunity to clear the path for you. I've removed the obstacles so you can focus on stepping into your true gifts and uniting the mortal coven instead of having your attention divided."

"It's just that easy?" Katie questioned, full of doubt. "One moonlit walk on the beach with Zoya and Yuli, and everything is magically better?"

Nadia threw her head back and laughed. "Not exactly. I've softened their resentment. The rest of the work is up to the triad." She laughed again. "And if I know my mother, and I do, you're going to want to buckle up because it's going to be a bumpy ride."

Katie gulped.

"But you'll get there," Nadia whispered. "Believe it."

"I will," Katie agreed, feeling the weight of the responsibility this task required settling on her shoulders. "How can I help?"

"You are the bridge that connects Yuli and Zoya together. Be the bridge."

Nadia laced her arm through Katie's and led her back to the sacred circle. Once inside, there was a thunderclap and a flash of lightning, and the coven reappeared. Olena stumbled back to the chair and banged the stone on the wooden table.

"Zoya Castanova, please stand."

A lighter Zoya rose to stand and waited, shifting on the balls of her feet from side to side.

"The coven has made a unanimous decision on your request. You are on probation until the next generation is created. When the next supernatural baby is born to our lineage, we will reconvene to vote on your fate."

Zoya nodded eagerly. "Thank you for this opportunity."

"I suggest you take this time to prove to the coven that you deserve what you desire. You are asking us to make a great sacrifice, and you must prove to be worthy."

The first glimmers of light on the horizon crept into view. "Our time together is drawing to a close," Olena said. "Sisters, please join hands inside the circle." There was a rumble of activity as they scrambled to find their places. Then, as the sun came up, their voices joined together, chanting and singing as, one by one, they dissolved into bubbles that floated up into the air and away, leaving Katie, Zoya, and Yuli behind. Dawn began to break, and they staggered back to the golf cart and headed back to the compound, exhausted, each of them lost in their own thoughts.

THIRTY-EIGHT

ours later, Katie awakened from a deep sleep, disoriented as she glanced around the room. Seeing the four-poster bed and the light streaming in from the windows, it all came rushing back. She stood and stretched, and Arlo jumped down from the bed and sat at her feet.

"We need to talk," Katie said, sitting on the edge of the bed.

He let out an anguished cry and implored her with his eyes. "I must apologize."

"For?" she asked, clearly baiting him.

"For betraying your trust," Arlo admitted. "Zoya placed me in your home to gather intelligence."

Katie rose and paced the room. "How long have you been reporting to her?"

"Once a week, since you adopted me."

"Holy crap." Katie staggered back to the bed. The

fact was mind-blowing. All these years, she thought she'd rescued him, but instead, he'd been placed in her home as a spy.

"At first, it was easy to carry out my mission, but you imprinted on me. I was torn between needing to keep Zoya happy so I could earn my freedom, and being loyal to you."

Katie's arms were crossed in front of her chest, her expression impossible to read.

"But the more I grew to love you, the more difficult it became." Arlo tucked his tail and refused to make eye contact. "I'm deeply sorry."

Katie exhaled a heavy breath, considering his apology. "I don't know what to say."

"Say you forgive me or I won't be able to bear it," he cried as he wiggled closer and nudged her hand with his wet nose, trying to get back into her good graces.

"I will always forgive you, but I will never forget," she finally said. "I need some time to process everything I've learned."

"That's fair," he admitted. "Just so you know, I don't plan on ever committing such a heinous act again. You will have my complete devotion from this moment forward."

"I better!" She reached down to scratch the patch of fur under his chin, and he wagged his tail happily, ready to put the shame of the incident behind him. He jumped up in her lap, pressed her down on the bed with his paws, and licked her face while she giggled.

"Knock it off. Now, you're overcompensating!"

At the door, she heard paws scratching and crossed the room to open it to Terrance.

"Zoya requests your presence in the dining room in one hour."

"Alrighty," Katie acknowledged and headed directly into the adjoining bathroom. She turned on the overhead rain shower and stood underneath it for half an hour, letting the hot water revive her exhausted being. Throwing on a sundress and some sandals, she whipped the curtains open wide and enjoyed the view of the aqua-colored water and sugary sand below. It was a beautiful property, and she could barely comprehend it would someday all be hers.

Katie repacked her suitcase and rolled it down the hallway and to the stairs, letting the maid take it down to the golf cart that would take them back to the hangar.

Yuli was at the table sipping on peppermint tea, humming to herself. Katie walked over with a smile and leaned down to give her a squeeze.

"How did you sleep?"

"Like a baby."

"Very good. Everyone is awake," Zoya said from the doorway. She pulled out the chair at the far end of the long table to sit down, then pushed it back in as if she changed her mind. Confused, Katie watched her walk closer and pull out the chair closest to her. There was a lingering tremble of trepidation as Zoya neared, but she cast it aside. They were all in unfamiliar territory, and a few nervous jitters were completely expected.

An uncomfortable silence lingered as they sat stiffly for a few moments, sizing each other up, unsure where to start. Katie remembered Nadia's instructions. "Be the bridge."

She offered a hand to each of the women. "After last night, I think we all want things to be different moving forward."

She glanced at Zoya, who awkwardly nodded in agreement. She wasn't used to letting someone else call the shots.

"Yuli?"

"Agreed."

"Good," Katie said. "That's all I know right now. We have a lot of baggage to unpack, but can we save it until we're all a little more rested?"

"YES!" Both Zoya and Yuli chorused together, making Katie laugh.

"See? You're already in sync!"

"Yeah. It's a miracle. All it took was a once-in-a-lifetime lunar event!" Yuli declared and chuckled at the absurd statement. It was filled with enough sarcasm to prove there was still a lot of work to do.

Zoya reached inside her pocket, pulled a silver dog whistle out, and blew on it. A few seconds later, Terrance pushed a bar cart with three tiny shot glasses filled with a black liquid closer to the table.

"Let me guess, poison?" Katie said.

Yuli raised a glass and grinned. "Don't be a baby. We're simply trying to help you develop an immunity."

Zoya's eyebrows arched as she picked up a glass and

handed the other to Katie. "To the eternal coven." They cheered, clinked them together, then fought to swallow the vile liquid.

It seemed the most appropriate way to celebrate the dawn of a new age.

THIRTY-NINE

The next Tuesday, Katie and Yuli were back at Kandied Karma. A friendly face walked through the door with two men, wearing ball caps emblazoned with "US Army Veteran" and the Army insignia embroidered on the front.

"Rox!" Katie said with an engaging smile as she crossed the room to hug the woman.

Her hands brushed against Roxanne's forearm, and she shivered. Pulses of offensively bright light obscured her vision, causing her to squeeze her eyes shut, and revealed a series of flashes. A military ceremony. Roxanne in full military dress uniform, being saluted. A purple heart medal in a velvet-lined case slamming shut.

Without warning, her next Karma rebalance assignment had arrived, and she felt a twinge of purpose flutter inside as she opened her eyes to look into Rox's warm, concerned ones. "Are you alright?" She gripped Katie by the forearms and led her to a chair.

"Just a little lightheaded." Katie blinked several times to clear her vision and offered Rox a warm smile. "That's what I get for skipping breakfast."

Seeing the exchange, Yuli rushed over. Katie glanced over at her, telegraphing with her eyes that their next assignment had already strolled through the doors. Yuli understood immediately and focused her attention on the raucous trio. "Do you have a military discount?" the older man to her right asked as he studied the menu.

"This one. He's so tight, he squeaks when he walks," Rox joked.

"Rox is so cheap, she used to call her son 'my little tax deduction,'" he tossed right back, chuckling at his own joke.

She threw her head back and barked out her trademark abrasive Tommy gun laugh, and the three of them cut up for a solid minute.

"Quit busting my balls, Bert!" she cried out. "It's not smart SOP to mock the one who drives your ugly, one-legged ass to the candy shop."

"No one has bigger balls than Ricochet," the other man named Wayne chimed in, using Rox's nickname.

"I think we can do better than a discount for a few of our highly decorated service members," Katie offered as she stood and walked behind the counter to fill a box with truffles.

When she folded it shut and slid it across the countertop, she felt another tingle. It propelled her to ask, "Can I meet you for lunch next week? I'd love to get to know you better."

Before she could answer, Wayne piped up, "Be prepared. Rox has been known to go from table to table asking, 'Are you going to eat that?'" Katie laughed as his eyes twinkled with mischief, and Rox burst into another round of stilted laughter. Still clowning, Wayne pulled up his pant leg to reveal a prosthetic, continuing to tease her. "She also likes to trot out her hardware to elicit pity meals from civilians from time to time."

Rox rolled her eyes, clearly amused by the ribbing. "Wayne, you better shut it if you want me to share *my* truffles with you." She winked at him and turned back to Katie. "Don't pay attention to those ancient nut bags. I'd love to meet for lunch. Let's exchange numbers and we'll make it happen."

Katie watched the threesome walk out of the shop, still razzing each other. Their snappy, sarcastic banter revealed a deep fondness for each other that Katie instantly picked up on. She wasn't sure what was next, but she knew Roxanne would be a significant woman in her future. Katie's intuition had already revealed Tom and Lauren would eventually marry, and knowing they might share grandchildren one day, she was deeply invested in helping Rox. Whatever the next assignment from Karma turned out to be, Katie was determined to move heaven and earth to help the woman.

Thank you for reading "Lunar Flash: Midlife in Aura Cove." The series is complete and ready for

binge reading! Get the next thrilling installment of this hilarious and heartwarming series! **Flash Point: Midlife in Aura Cove Book 4.**

Order here.

When Roxanne Sullivan, a West Point alumna and retired military officer, visits Katie's beachfront home in Aura Cove, a cryptic message from Karma sets an unthinkable chain of events in motion.

A shocking revelation emerges that threatens to shatter Rox's pristine military career. Accused of a grave offense, she faces the impending loss of everything she holds dear—her freedom, her Purple Heart, and her honor—earned through sacrifices that left her scarred in more ways than one.

Desperate to right this egregious wrong, Rox is in a race against time to prove her innocence and uncover the truth, aided by a trio of powerful witches whose destinies are irrevocably entwined. In this fourth installment of Midlife in Aura Cove, Katie, Yuli, and

Zoya form an unlikely alliance to unravel Karma's enigmatic flashes and deliver the rebalance Rox deserves.

Order Flash Point Here.

Also Available on Amazon, BN Nook, Apple iBooks, Kobo, Google Play and many international booksellers. Or request it from your local library.

Like FREE Books? Enter to Win a Gift Card to My Bookstore https://tealbutterflypress.com/pages/join-our-email-list-and-win

There's a new winner every week!

About the Author

I've always been a risk-taker, so at 44 I decided to write and publish my own books. It has been a roller coaster ride with a punishing learning curve, but if it were easy, everyone would do it. I write under the pen names of Ninya and Blair Bryan.

I love to travel and a trip to Scotland with a complete stranger was the inspiration for my memoir. I also seem to attract crazy experiences and people into my life like a magnet that gives me a never-ending supply of interesting storylines.

If you love a good dirty joke, a cup of coffee so strong you can chew it, and have killed more cats with your curiosity than you can count, I might be your soulmate.

Visit me online www.tealbutterflypress.com

Let's connect in my facebook reader group, **The Kaleidoscope: Teal Butterfly Press' Official Author Fandom**